End
of the Road

Amy M. Bennett

Oak Tree Press Hanford, CA

Oak Tree Press
Publishers Since 1998

For information, address Oak Tree Press, 1820 W. Lacey Boulevard, Suite 220, Hanford, CA 93230.

Oak Tree Press books may be purchased for educational, business, or sales promotional purposes. Contact Publisher for quantity discounts.

First Edition, July 2013

ISBN 978-1-61009-071-1
LCCN 2013933628

To my dad, Gilberto Romero (1919-2009), for teaching me to read and to love books and to believe I could do anything I wanted to do. I did it, Daddy.

To my son, Paul Michael Anthony Bennett, for believing that having a mom who writes murder mysteries makes for a normal childhood.

To my husband and best friend, Paul, for always believing that it was a matter of "when", not "if".

Acknowledgments

Being a writer has always been easy for me. The only thing easier was becoming a reader! Becoming a published author, however, has been a long and sometimes difficult journey. I couldn't have done it without the following people:

The teachers who taught me the proper use of English grammar, spelling, and punctuation, and to appreciate fine literature, as well as encouraging me to write. Most notably are the two Pats—Patricia Quinn (Blessed Sacrament School) and Patricia Hollis (Father Yermo High School)—who, to this day, continue to reside in my memory to correct my errors. I hope I made you both proud.

My amazing sister (in-law), Cynthia Bennett, for being my tough yet loving first reader and editor extraordinaire. I'd like to think you really enjoyed my work and not just the lunches out!

Mike Orenduff—we started with me being your fan and you became my mentor, offered advice, and encouraged me. Having someone "in the biz" believe in you is worth more than a million bottles of Gruet champagne (or Jo Mamma's White!) Thanks for everything!

Billie, Suzi, and Jeana—and all the rest of the awesome folks at Oak Tree Press, who gave this author a shot and didn't want to shoot me for all the questions I asked! A million thanks to you all!

My friends and family—for not laughing or rolling your eyes when I said I wanted to be a writer. And for meaning it when you asked, "How's the book coming along?" I'd need to add another chapter to list all of you, but there aren't enough words in the world to express what you all mean to me.

Jasper Riddle and Lynette Woodward—and all the rest of the gang at Noisy Water Winery, for first introducing me to Jo Mamma's White... and then for letting me be part of the family. Cheers!

Prologue

He pulled off the highway onto the clearly marked, paved side road and shut the engine off, letting the Harley coast past the well-lit sign to Black Horse Campground. He pulled his helmet off to let the spring night breeze cool his sweat-soaked brow, shook his head to clear it of the drone of the highway, and looked down into the hollow between the road and the river.

The campground slept below him, dotted with pools of brightness from the safety lights and the outdoor lights of the pool and the dozen or so RVs parked in the pull-through spots. A dim light glowed from the second floor of the main office building. The owners of the campground no doubt lived on site; hopefully without a dog. Or a night watchman.

He dismounted and secured the helmet to the back of the seat then walked the Harley down the gentle asphalt incline. The road was free of gravel and sand and he managed to wend his way to a vacant tent site, situated halfway between the RV sites and the office building, in relative silence. He set down the kickstand and paused a few moments. Except for the breeze stirring in the pines and the babbling of the nearby river, nothing moved or made a sound. He would have preferred a more secluded site, away from the campground office, but his primary concern at the moment was that his arrival didn't wake any other campers. As long as no one was making a nighttime trip to the bathroom, it was unlikely that he'd be noticed by the other guests. Quickly he set about putting up his tent.

He was done in ten minutes; he'd gotten good and fast at setting up camp in the dark. He unrolled his sleeping bag and apart from removing his boots, chaps and jacket he didn't bother to undress. He checked his watch; it was twenty to two. He allowed a grim smile. At least three or four hours of sleep before he was noticed. Then it would start all over again.

Corrie Black rolled over and swatted the alarm off without opening her eyes. Most mornings she preferred two swats of the snooze button for the classic rock station from the closest "big" city—Roswell—to wake her slowly, but today, Thursday, she needed to be up by four-thirty since Jerry and Jackie Page, her two oldest and most trusted employees, had left for a four-day weekend the night before.

She propped herself up on one elbow and reached for the bedside 3-way lamp, her eyes still shut, and turned it on to the dimmest setting. She opened her eyes and the first thing she saw was the slitted-eye glare from Oliver, her gray-and-black tabby, curled up on the quilt near the foot of the bed. Oliver hated to be awakened this early in the morning and he let out a sound halfway between a growl and a yowl.

"Yeah, I feel the same way," Corrie said, knowing that an attempt to pet Oliver to soothe him would only annoy him more. He let out a protesting "meow" as she pulled her feet out from under him and sat up. Renfro, her father's ancient, half-blind, and mostly deaf black Lab, sat up and yawned, his tail thumping on the wood floor. Corrie gave him a pat. "Go back to sleep, old timer," she murmured. "It's still night time." Renfro gave her hand a lick, flopped obediently down on the floor, and resumed snoring.

Corrie went to the window, which she kept cracked a few inches to let a breeze in during the night, pushed it wide open, and inhaled a deep breath of pine-scented air, fresh and cool from a light spring rain. She looked out over Black Horse Campground and sighed. It was the third week of April and the spring break rush had dwindled to a trickle—not that it had been the torrent she had hoped for. Winter had dragged on into the middle of March, unusual for south-central New Mexico, but after several years of near-drought conditions, no one complained. She tried not to let that worry her, but her father used to gauge how good a summer season they would have by how many springtime clients they'd get.

She headed to the bathroom for a quick shower. Once she was dressed in her customary jeans and Black Horse Campground t-shirt and twisted her waist-length black hair into a single braid down her back, she went downstairs to the campground office and store. She had called the four-room apartment on the second floor of the building "home" for as long as she could remember, but the camp office/store were Corrie's real living quarters. If she wasn't showering or sleeping, Corrie was downstairs in the campground's office.

She inhaled the aroma of freshly brewed piñon coffee, thankful that she had splurged on the deluxe coffee maker with the auto-start feature she had bought for herself the previous Christmas; most mornings, she couldn't imagine how she had ever gotten through the first ten minutes of her day having to wait for the coffee to brew. She had a dual-pot coffee maker for regular and decaf coffee, but she kept *her* coffee maker specifically for the piñon coffee she loved and sold like crazy in the camp store, thanks to having it available for her guests on the courtesy table. She filled her thermal cup, took it to the desk by the front door that doubled as a cashier's station, and flicked on the lights.

The office area occupied a very small amount of space in the store, which sold everything from quarts of milk to quarts of motor oil to local handmade arts and crafts and souvenirs, as well as a few gourmet New Mexico food products, such as the piñon coffee that was Corrie's weakness. Jackie usually manned the store for her and she had made sure to leave everything stocked and organized before leaving on her trip with Jerry. Corrie slipped behind the register and found a carefully numbered list of scheduled guest arrivals for the upcoming weekend.

Jackie's first notation, "Bike Rally Weekend", was underlined three times in red, at the top of the page. Jackie had been the one to push for Corrie to enroll in the chamber of commerce and she kept up on all the local happenings. The annual spring motorcycle rally was held in Ruidoso, twelve miles away, and provided a healthy amount of business for the Black Horse. Jackie had discovered that many motorcyclists preferred campgrounds and she had, despite Corrie's feeble protests, posted a giant ad on the campground's website... another one of Jackie's ideas.

She went into the room off the main store that served as a game room and TV room for the guests. It was furnished with a big screen TV, a couple of couches, several comfortable chairs, and a few tables that could be used as game tables. She settled into what was probably the last Barcalounger in the state and reached for the remote. Oliver's curiosity had overcome his annoyance at his early awakening and he jumped up onto Corrie's lap as she turned on the early morning news.

Nothing exciting or interesting; the usual litany of bad news that seemed to make up the early programs. Corrie sipped her coffee and absently scratched Oliver's ears, barely registering stories of traffic accidents, robberies, and murders... most of them too far away to affect her personally. The mention of El Paso did spark her interest, only because she had a special place in her heart for the city that had been her parents' meeting place. A woman had been found dead in her home, apparently the victim of a house fire ignited by a gas explosion that might, or might not, have been accidental, and the police and fire departments were still investigating. Corrie tuned out the rest.

She sat long enough to catch the weather report and was relieved to hear that the weekend promised sunny days and gentle cool breezes. It was still too early for the pool to be opened, but she knew that if the warm weather continued, she might be able to have Buster get it cleaned and ready for the Mother's Day weekend instead of waiting for Memorial Day like they usually did.

She got up and looked out the window. Morning was breaking over the mountains and she decided it was time to get moving. This afternoon she would—she hoped—start getting the weekend crowd for the motorcycle rally. She was expecting Buster, the maintenance man, in early although she had resigned herself to being happy if he just showed up on time. It would be a couple more weeks before her full summer staff was in place, but she'd never had trouble operating efficiently with her winter skeleton crew. Jackie's note had reminded her that the couple from Winslow, Arizona—the Myers, who were acquaintances of the Pages and whom Jerry and Jackie asked to come down and help Corrie out while they were gone—would be arriving sometime during the morning.

Another exciting day at Black Horse Campground.

Chapter 1

Corrie looked up from the morning paper as the front door opened and Buster slipped in, reaching with lightning-speed to still the bell over the door before it made any noise to alert her that someone had come in. He'd had a lot of practice. She glanced at the clock. Seven-fourteen. She tried—and failed—to restrain her initial sarcastic reaction. "Buster, I can't believe it. You're late. How unusual."

Buster—Oscar Bustamante—gave her a fatuous grin. "Good morning, Miss Black," he said in a barely-audible whisper with a slight bow as his gaze darted around the office. "Beautiful day today, isn't it?"

Corrie sighed and rolled her eyes. "Yes, Buster, good morning, you're still late," she said. "It's way past six-thirty." He gave an apologetic shrug of his shoulders, but remained by the front door. Corrie knew it wasn't to hide the fact that he was late that had prompted him to keep the door bell from ringing. He continued to glance around the office, as if looking for something and Corrie knew what it was. "He's back here behind the counter, asleep," she informed her employee and, as if on cue, Renfro let out a snore that nearly rattled the windows. "If that's the reason you're late, you should know that Renfro wouldn't have the energy to lick you to death until he's had his eighth pot of coffee!" Buster's fear of dogs was legendary, dating back to his early teens when his short-lived career as a paper boy was ended by a German Shepherd that removed a six-inch square of denim from the seat of Buster's pants as he vaulted over the homeowner's fence—the same fence that bore a "Beware! Attack Dog on Duty!" sign that Buster had blithely ignored.

"Is he on a leash?"

"He's in a coma. You're safe."

Buster grinned sheepishly, but looked relieved. "I've already been working," he said, allowing his voice to return to its usual volume and making his way to the courtesy table. "Please Help Yourself!" the hand-lettered cardboard sign cheerfully invited, although Buster didn't need an invitation. He went to the dual-pot coffee maker and helped himself to a cup of regular coffee into which he dumped four packets of sugar. Corrie cringed and silently gave thanks that he hadn't debased her beloved piñon coffee with sugar. "You make this?" he asked, looking over the slices of banana bread and coffee cake under the plastic cover.

"I sliced it," she admitted. She didn't add that she'd only put out half of the baked goodies until after Buster had checked in and departed to take on his duties. "What have you been doing this morning?"

He helped himself to a slice of each, not bothering with a fork, and set his paper plate on the glass counter, still keeping a wary eye on the sleeping dog. "Got the trash picked up," he began. Corrie sighed.

"Buster, you KNOW you're not supposed to do the trash pickups until after eight! What if you woke up the campers? They won't be happy."

"Don't worry," he said, waving off her concern, his mouth full of coffee cake. "I only went to the empty sites."

"Oh, good idea," Corrie said, rolling her eyes. "And just how much trash can there possibly be at the empty sites?"

"You'd be surprised," he said, licking crumbs off his fingers. Sometimes Buster seemed more like a little kid than a man in his mid-thirties. He was tall and husky with a full beard and mustache and looked like central casting's stereotypical maintenance man.

"People don't want to smell their own trash in their campsite and they figure it'll keep flies, raccoons, and skunks away from their sites if they use a trash can that's far away," he informed her with the air of one who knows what he's talking about.

"Hmmm. Wonder what they do when we're full?" Corrie said, draining her cup. Buster shrugged.

"Anyway, I picked up the trash and did a quick check of the men's rooms." Corrie nodded and Buster went on. "And I just wanted to know when the guy in site twenty-three checked in."

Corrie had gone to the coffee pot to refill her cup. She turned and frowned. "Site twenty-three? That's not rented out."

"Yeah? Well, there's a tent on it. Thought maybe we got a reservation that came in after I left."

Corrie shook her head. "The office was open till eight and Jackie was here with me up till that time. Neither she nor Jerry mentioned we had a no-show."

"You want me to go check it out?" Buster said. "Maybe somebody just crashed for the night and planned to sneak out without paying."

"Maybe," Corrie said dubiously. Because of their proximity to the main highway, it wasn't unheard of for the Black Horse to host a guest who took liberties with Corrie's hospitality and didn't bother to check in or pay. There was always a possibility that someone did forget to record a reservation but, given Jackie's conscientious attention to detail and orderliness, it was highly unlikely. Either way, antagonizing or offending a customer was not something she could afford to do. "But he won't get out without us seeing him. What's he driving?"

"Motorcycle. Harley. Really nice one," Buster said enviously.

"Oh!" Corrie shrugged. She filled her cup and returned to her seat behind the counter. "Well, he—or she—is probably here for the rally this weekend and got in late."

"So? They still crashed us." Buster cracked his knuckles, eager for a confrontation. Corrie doubted his customer service skills were up for the challenge.

"They haven't dodged us yet," she pointed out. "Give them a chance to wake up, then we'll see what's going on."

Before Buster could respond, she heard the sound of tires crunching on the graveled parking lot outside the office. She glanced at the clock on the wall. Seven-thirty, right on the dot. As usual. She looked back at the paper on the counter and forced herself to keep her eyes on the article she'd already read twice and not turn and look out the window. Buster craned his neck to look over her shoulder. "Looks like the sheriff," he said.

"Mmm...." Corrie said, as disinterestedly as possible, while her heart hammered in her chest. Surely, she told herself as she did every day, fifteen years was sufficient time to get over anything... or anyone. Even Rick Sutton.

"He comes every morning, doesn't he?" Buster said, as Corrie heard the door on Rick's patrol vehicle, a Chevy Tahoe SUV, shut. She lifted the coffee cup to her lips.

"Yep," she said, still focusing on the paper. Buster was frowning.

"I wonder why," he said, and Corrie heard—she didn't think she was imagining it—Rick's measured steps on the gravel walkway. She glanced up at Buster. She would NOT look at the door, she would NOT look at the door....

"You could ask him," she said, knowing that Buster wouldn't. He had a healthy, fearful respect for the police, especially Rick, who had hauled Buster and his cronies in when they were in their early twenties for reckless driving and public intoxication. Rick had been a mere rookie deputy at the time, and because he had known Buster from the time they were in kindergarten, and knew Buster was being young and stupid and not malicious, he convinced the sheriff at the time to let Buster off with a stern warning that must have made quite an impression. Since then, Buster tried very hard to stay under Rick's radar. He gave Corrie a weak grin.

"Nah. None of my business," he said as the door opened, the bell over it ringing cheerily and eliciting a friendly "woof" from Renfro, who managed to hear the bell over his snores and woke up long enough to make a half-hearted attempt at being a watch dog.

"Good morning, folks!" Rick Sutton came in removing his Stetson and mirrored sunglasses. Only then did Corrie turn and give him what she hoped was a neutral look, even as her stomach did somersaults.

"Morning, Sheriff," she said, her greeting friendly and cool. Buster echoed her greeting.

As usual, Rick looked like he belonged on a recruiting poster for the sheriff's department; his silver-tan uniform was neat and crisp and fit his broad shoulders and trim hips as if he'd been born in it. His light brown hair was trimmed to regulation length, and it seemed to Corrie that it always had been. He rarely smiled, something which had always intrigued her, even back when they were kids. She'd known Rick since they were in preschool together, but in all the years they'd known each other, a slight uplifting of the corner of his mouth was what usually passed for a smile on Rick Sutton.

Not that that made him any less attractive.

Corrie went over to the courtesy table. "The usual?" she asked him.

"Sure. Thanks," he said. He set a large plastic storage container on the counter. "I don't know if you need anything else for this morning, but you could always freeze these if you like."

"What's that?" Buster said, as Corrie came back with Rick's coffee—regular, no sugar, two creamers. Sometimes it annoyed her that she had learned that without asking him, even more than the fact that she'd never sold him on the merits of New Mexico piñon coffee over regular coffee. He gave her his half-smile in thanks and she got over her annoyance and smiled back.

Rick glanced at Buster and frowned. That was something Rick did well. "You're here awful early," he said, which brought a look of panic to Buster's face. He started to stammer an explanation and Corrie spoke up.

"Jerry and Jackie left for Phoenix late last night... their granddaughter's getting married this weekend," she said. "I asked Buster to come in early to help out." Buster looked relieved, although he still had a guilty look on his face, as though Rick might yet find fault with him.

One of Rick's brows lifted. "They kind of left you high and dry on Bike Rally Weekend, didn't they?"

Corrie bristled. It wasn't unusual for her feelings for Rick to go from warm and fuzzy to outright annoyed and irritated. "It's not like they abandoned me without notice. It's their only granddaughter, this wedding has been planned for five years, and weddings are a once-in-a-lifetime event!" She immediately slapped a hand over her lips as Rick stiffened. "I mean...."

"I know," he snapped, which saved her from blurting out any

more embarrassing statements. His dark blue eyes frosted and she wished they weren't trained on her like laser beams. "It's okay. I didn't intend to sound critical. I was just concerned."

In other words, don't try to apologize. She swallowed hard. "Okay," she said. Buster was watching with interest, but she ignored him. "What's in the box?"

Rick's eyes thawed. "Blueberry pecan muffins. Three dozen." He seemed to relax, already having forgiven and forgotten, a quality of his which made Corrie feel both better and worse. "Looks like you already have something out for today."

"Jackie's banana bread and her apple-cinnamon coffee cake," Corrie said. "Would you like some?"

Rick shook his head and sipped his coffee. "I had two muffins before I left home. Quality control check." He gave Corrie a wink and his half-smile and she found herself smiling back.

"Who made them?" Buster asked, and when Corrie made a grand gesture as if directing applause toward Rick, Buster's mouth dropped open. "YOU did?" he said to Rick. "Get out of here!"

"What?" Rick said coolly. "Cops aren't supposed to cook?"

"Cooking, yeah, but this isn't cooking, it's baking," Buster argued. "It's kind of... girly." His eyes widened as Rick's narrowed. Diplomacy had never been one of Buster's outstanding qualities. Corrie stepped in before her maintenance man got his foot any further into his mouth.

"Well, you just remember that tomorrow morning when I put these muffins out," she said, taking the box and heading for the kitchen off the family room. "I wouldn't want you to poison yourself with 'girly' baking." She debated about whether she should inform Buster that many times it was Rick's culinary skills, not hers nor Jackie's, that took the spotlight on the courtesy table and he'd never complained before. She doubted it would make any difference in the amount of his consumption of free baked goods.

Buster backed up away from Rick's glare and swallowed hard. "Yeah, uh, so, Corrie, you want me to go check on that new customer?" he called out to her.

"Is there a problem?" Rick asked Corrie as she came back. She shrugged.

"I don't think so. Someone showed up in the middle of the night and set up camp. Buster wants to check it out, but I'm saying we should give them a chance to wake up and come in first."

"And I'm saying it's best to catch them before they dodge us," Buster argued.

"They didn't have a reservation?" Rick asked. Corrie shook her head. "How'd they get in without you seeing them?"

"It must have been after I went to bed," Corrie said.

"What time was that?"

"Close to one in the morning," she said. Rick shot her a look and almost let a full grin slip out.

"Wednesday night. Shelli was here," he said nodding. "That's kind of late for your usual ladies' night, but I heard about Mark's grandmother."

"Wow. You ever think of maybe becoming a cop or a detective or something?" Corrie said dryly. Not everyone knew about her "ladies' nights" with her best friend, Shelli Davenport. In addition to her full-time job as kindergarten teacher, Shelli held down two part-time jobs, one of them at the Black Horse on the weekends, trying to make ends meet to raise her three kids now that her ex-husband, Mark, had once again slipped off the radar. They usually got together in Corrie's sitting room over a bottle of Jo Mamma's White table wine from Noisy Water Winery in Ruidoso—Shelli's other part-time employer—and a light supper. This time Shelli's visit had gone on longer, her worries over Mark's disappearance compounded by the fact that Mark's family had called to inform her that his beloved grandmother had passed away and, with Mark gone again, she felt she needed to make an appearance, maybe hang around for a day or two after the funeral... which meant leaving Corrie to handle the bike rally weekend even more short-handed than expected.

Corrie went on, "We didn't see or hear a thing and Jerry and Jackie left last night, so no one was in their RV." The Pages' RV sat just inside the entrance, near the main office. For quick weekend trips, they drove their ancient Bronco and left the RV in its usual space. Jerry was a night owl, one of the reasons he preferred to travel by night, and he had ears like a cat. Not much got past him but, with him gone last night, there was no night watchman.

Renfro let out an exceptionally loud snore and Rick gave him a glance. "And your trusty watchdog slept through the whole thing?"

Corrie laughed. "Renfro would sleep through a tornado. He didn't even hear YOU drive up and you parked right outside the door!"

"Yeah, but still, he'd have heard a Harley coming in, wouldn't he?" Buster pressed.

Rick's brows rose. "The guy came in on a Harley and you didn't hear him?" He was in full "cop" mode now, his jaw tight and his eyes stone-hard and cold as granite. Corrie sighed and shot an irritated glance at Buster.

"He—or she—didn't come screaming in like 'The Wild One'," she retorted. "It's quite possible he—or she—walked it in."

"Why would he—or she—do that?" Buster said.

The side door opened, its bell interrupting Corrie before she could answer, and a man walked in. He appeared to be in his mid-thirties and wore faded jeans and a tight-fitting sleeveless black t-shirt. His shoulder-length black hair was slicked back, tied in short ponytail, and his silver-gray eyes contrasted sharply with his bronzed skin. He stood in the doorway, a faint smile on his lips as if he'd heard the entire discussion and found it amusing, and then he spoke.

"Excuse me for interrupting, but I'd like to see about paying for last night and for the next few days."

Corrie shot Buster a triumphant glance. "Certainly. Come on in and have some coffee and we'll take care of your reservation, Mr...."

"Wilder," the man said. "J.D. Wilder. Thank you, ma'am." And he smiled.

Chapter 2

J.D. wondered if he should be concerned by the presence of the law officer in the main office of the campground who had been in conversation with the attractive brunette behind the counter and the husky dark fellow in the navy blue t-shirt with the Black Horse logo on the front. It was obvious they had been talking about him.

He stepped into the room, rubbing the morning stubble on his face. The lawman's jaw tightened and his gaze sharpened; it was a look J.D. often got from "respectable" people. Under normal circumstances, it wouldn't have bothered him a bit; in fact, he would have been amused.

At the moment, however, his circumstances were far from normal.

The woman didn't seem concerned and her smile was warm and friendly. She wore a bright yellow Black Horse Campground t-shirt and had the air of being in charge. J.D. addressed her directly. "Sorry I took advantage of your hospitality," he said. "I had trouble with my bike in El Paso and thought I'd be here a lot earlier yesterday."

The woman's brows rose. "Did you have a reservation?" she asked. The husky guy's eyes narrowed but the lawman's expression remain unchanged. Best to be honest and up front, J.D. thought. Or at least, sound like he was.

"No, ma'am," he said. "Some people I met while I was there recommended the place, said they'd heard good things about it. I told them I was just going to be passing through and I didn't want to go too far out of my way to stay right in town, but they said this was easy to get on and off the highway." He stopped; he was talking too much.

"I see," she said. "Well, we're not full up so you're more than welcome to stay in the site you're in. I just need you to fill out a reservation card."

He nodded and stepped up to the counter. The lawman—sheriff, according to his badge and uniform—never took his eyes off him. J.D. met his gaze for a second or two, then looked at the woman. "Is there a problem, ma'am?" he asked, hoping that neither his apprehension nor his irritation were too obvious.

She was shooting a venomous look at the other two men in the room. "No, not at all. Buster was just going back to work," she said pointedly and the husky guy flushed and made his way out the back door. "And this is our sheriff, Rick Sutton, and he stops by every morning for coffee."

Coffee, huh? J.D. thought as the sheriff's eyes darted toward the lady. The coffee couldn't be THAT good. "I was afraid you thought I was crashing and was going to take off without paying and had called the police," J.D. said, hoping his smile conveyed bemusement.

The woman laughed. "Sorry about that. My name is Corrie Black. I'm the owner of the Black Horse Campground. I'm glad you're here, Mr. Wilder. Is that campsite all right for you?"

"It's fine," he said. He took the reservation form from Corrie's hand and began to fill it out.

The sheriff spoke up at last. "Where you from, Mr. Wilder?" he asked, politeness not masking the suspicion behind the question. J.D. smiled grimly to himself.

"Originally, Dallas," he said. "I've lived in Houston the last three years." He said nothing else, just kept on writing.

"In town for the rally?" The sheriff lacked subtlety, J.D. thought. He looked up.

"Actually, I was just passing through, but I heard about the rally in El Paso so I thought I'd check it out." He was tempted to add, "Is that all right with you?" but he decided that antagonizing an overly-suspicious small-town sheriff was not a smart move and would likely land him in trouble he couldn't afford.

Corrie saved him from further questions. "That site you're on is eighteen dollars a night, but I can move you to a site that has electric and water hookups for about six dollars more. And you get a ten percent discount if you stay seven days or longer," she added. He couldn't tell if she was giving her usual spiel or if she was hunting for information. In any event, she was far more polite and subtle than the sheriff.

"Just four days. Maybe I'll stay longer. We'll see," J.D. said with a shrug. "And I don't need electricity or water."

"All right." She tapped some keys on the computer on the counter and gave him a total. "Would you like to put that on a credit card?" she asked.

"No, ma'am, I'll pay cash," he said, removing his wallet from his back pocket. He wished the sheriff would stop staring at him and he was glad he had removed all but a couple hundred dollars from his wallet.

Corrie handed him his change. "Okay, Mr. Wilder, you're all set. Please help yourself to some coffee and cake over on the courtesy table. The sweets are all homemade and the piñon coffee is highly recommended." She gave him an engaging smile and he couldn't help but smile back, despite the glower he was getting from the sheriff. Corrie went on, "The camp store is open until eight p.m. every evening, the laundry room is open twenty-four hours a day. The bathrooms are closed from eleven a.m. to one p.m. for cleaning; otherwise, feel free to use them at any time. And on the weekends, we have a few things going on here at the campground. Friday nights, we alternate between a fish fry and an enchilada dinner, Saturday morning, we have a pancake breakfast with all the fixings, Saturday nights, we have a pizza party, and Sunday nights, we have a steak cookout. There's a ten-dollar charge for the steak dinner," she added apologetically, "but the other events are by donation. We just ask you let us know if you'll be attending so we have plenty of food."

"Thank you," J.D. said. He doubted he'd be attending any of the social events, but it didn't hurt to be polite. "I guess I'd better go get cleaned up." He started to leave, then thought he should at least get some coffee. No need to look completely anti-social.

He filled a Styrofoam cup with the highly-recommended piñon

coffee and helped himself to a slice of banana bread. He flinched when his stomach growled. He hoped no one had heard it, but it had been well over fifteen hours since he'd eaten. He decided to take a second slice.

The silence in the room made him uneasy. He felt he was being stared at. He turned; Corrie was busy straightening up the counter and avoiding the eyes of the sheriff, who was watching her. So who was watching HIM?

The answer came with a low, rumbling growl from a large gray-and-black tabby curled up on the back of an enormous white-muzzled black dog. The dog was sleeping soundly, but the cat's yellow eyes gleamed like beacons, aimed straight at J.D. He hadn't even realized there was a dog in the room and the dog was equally oblivious to him.

He turned to head out the door, answering Corrie's cheerful "Good-bye!" with a smile. Four days here would probably be too long.

Chapter 3

"Why didn't you just pull your gun on him, if you wanted to scare him so badly?" Corrie snapped as the door clicked shut behind her customer. Rick gave her a cool look.

"If he hasn't done anything wrong, then there's no reason for him to be scared or nervous just because the local sheriff is paying a social call," he said blandly.

Corrie sighed. "Rick, if you'll pardon me for being blunt, you don't exactly have your social party face on right now. You never do," she added. He allowed his usual half-smile.

"You think he's okay?" Rick asked her.

"Don't you?"

He shrugged. "I guess. I'd feel better if Jerry and Jackie were here. And I really wish Shelli hadn't decided she had to go to Mark's grandmother's funeral. I don't like you being here alone." He held up a hand to stop her protest. "And as far as Buster goes, you might as well be alone," he added as he moved toward the courtesy table.

"I have a few other guests besides a couple of year-rounders. The campground isn't completely deserted. Plus, I've got the Myers coming in from Winslow today," Corrie said.

"Do I know them?" Rick asked, filling up his coffee cup. Corrie was surprised. Rick never got a second cup of coffee.

"You've met them. They're friends of the Pages. They were here a year ago at the end of February, when...." She stopped and cleared her throat which suddenly became clogged with tears. Rick nodded, his gaze telling her there was no need to explain; they had come to help out when Billy had taken a turn for the worse. Corrie managed to swallow and then went on. "Jackie asked them to come down and give me a hand while she and Jerry are gone."

"So they're just here for the weekend?" Rick asked, helping himself to a piece of coffee cake. Another surprise.

"What is this, an interrogation?" Corrie asked. "No, as a matter of fact, they're here through the summer. Winslow gets too busy for them, so they'll stay here and give me a hand with running the place in exchange for a campsite. Then they go back to Winslow for the winter and stay at a campground there."

Rick nodded. He absently took a bite of coffee cake and frowned.

"What, don't you like it?" Corrie asked. He looked up.

"Hmm? Oh, no, it's good. I was just wondering...." He paused, took another bite, chewed slowly.

Corrie was ready to throw her pen at him. "What?"

He came back and stood at the counter, took another sip of coffee. "It's about three hours to El Paso," he said.

"Right," Corrie said. What was he getting at?

"What time did you go to bed?"

"Me? I don't know. I got some paperwork caught up after Jackie left at eight-fifteen, then Shelli got here about nine o'clock and we visited for about three hours, then I stayed up to watch the news for a while."

"Here, or upstairs?" Rick persisted.

"Shelli and I get together in my sitting room. When I let her out, I watched the news in the family room." She nodded toward the door. "I don't have a TV upstairs. Why?" she finally asked.

"So it was almost one in the morning when you went to bed?"

"More or less. Why?" She wasn't going to give him any more information until he answered one of her own questions. He set his cup down.

"This guy, J.D. Wilder, had to have gotten here after one a.m. or else you'd have heard him come in. If he really had trouble with his bike in El Paso, wouldn't it make more sense for him to stay THERE? It had to have been after ten o'clock before he left town."

Corrie thought for a moment. "I suppose so," she said at last. "But maybe he's got a good explanation."

"Like?"

"I don't know."

"He's a fugitive from the law?"

"Oh, come on, Rick," she said exasperated. "Just because the guy is no more communicative than you are doesn't make him a criminal!"

Rick shrugged. "It doesn't hurt to be cautious," he said. He looked straight into Corrie's eyes, causing her to blush. His intensity had always flustered her, even when they were younger, but she'd never been able to look away when caught in his gaze. Even though they had been no more than "just" friends for the last fifteen years, the memory of the year prior to that was never far from Corrie's mind, despite everything that had happened since then. "I don't want anything happening to you," Rick went on and she almost let a humongous smile escape before he added, "Your dad would come back to haunt me for sure. I promised Billy I'd keep an eye on things for him."

So THAT was the reason behind his daily visits? A promise on her father's death-bed? She'd be touched if she didn't feel so foolish. She was no more than just some "thing" Rick was keeping an eye on for Billy. She swallowed her outrage. "Dad taught me to look out for myself. I wouldn't worry if I were you," she said curtly.

He gave her a look then nodded. "Well, I'd best be on my way," he said, replacing his hat. She said nothing and he went on, "Enchiladas this week, right?"

Corrie found her voice. "Yeah." That was the best she could do.

"I'll see you tomorrow," Rick said and he headed out the door, leaving Corrie completely confused.

Chapter 4

Red and Dana Myers showed up at one o'clock as Corrie was checking in five reservations and three drop-ins. Dana jumped right in and started helping out while Red quickly parked their restored Airstream and stepped in to escort campers to their sites. It was well after two before they were able to sit down with fresh cups of coffee and say "hello" to each other.

"Glad Jackie called us," Dana said, running a hand through her short, frosted blond hair that belied her almost-sixty years. "Today would have been a nightmare for you! I'm just sorry we didn't get here sooner. I know I said we'd be here at ten o'clock, but we got a late start and I thought you'd have some help this morning."

Red leaned back in his chair and sighed, wiping a handkerchief over his brow. Hustling from one campsite to another, helping the guests with their hook-ups, made the spring afternoon warmth overwhelming for someone of Red's age and weight. His face and arms were the color of his thinning hair and copious freckles. "Dee Dee's off today?"

Corrie grimaced. She'd been so busy she'd forgotten that her part-time help, Dee Dee Simpson, was supposed to have come in at eleven. "She wasn't supposed to be."

"Is she at the sheriff's department today, or the salon?" Dana asked.

Corrie shook her head. Dee Dee held down three jobs, all part-time, and she sold Glamour Girl cosmetics on the side when she wasn't running off to auditions for modeling, singing, or acting jobs of which a cousin in L.A. kept her informed. It wasn't unusual for Dee Dee to take off without letting her employers when she was going, or changing her work schedule without consulting them. It was a mystery to Corrie why she hadn't fired her already. "I can't keep track of her work schedule here, you think I'd know where else she's supposed to be?" Corrie said. She heard the roar of an expensive sports car end with a slight squeal and the sound of tires skidding on gravel. "But I'd be willing to bet that's her right now!"

The front door flew open and Dee Dee charged into the room, a whirlwind of impossibly yellow hair in a skin-tight, black-and-fuschia zebra-striped jumpsuit, talking a mile a minute. "Unbelievable!" she was saying, shaking her head so hard her multiple hoop earrings swung wildly. "I just can't believe it!"

"What, that you forgot you were supposed to be here at eleven?" Corrie asked.

"Oh!" Dee Dee stopped, pursed her fuchsia pink lips and grimaced. "I was, wasn't I? Oh, well...." She shrugged.

Corrie managed to rein in her temper. "What happened this time?" she asked. Somewhere along the way she had become something of a big sister to the capricious young woman and she wondered if Dee Dee had any intention of offering a semblance of apology.

Dee Dee dropped into a chair across from Corrie. "You haven't heard yet?"

Corrie sighed and rolled her eyes. "Evidently not," she said.

Dee Dee glanced at both Red and Dana. Red shook his head. Dana said, "We just got into town about an hour ago."

"It's about Betty Landry," Dee Dee said in what, Corrie assumed, was her idea of a conspiratorial whisper, as she leaned across the table. This time Corrie sat bolt upright and gave her her full attention.

"Betty Landry? What happened to her?" The Landrys—Marvin and Betty—were seventy-something retirees who'd spent the last twenty summers at the Black Horse Campground. They usually arrived the weekend after Mother's Day. Recently, Betty had been plagued with bad health and the Christmas card Corrie received from them in December hinted that she was declining, but Corrie hoped that Dee Dee's announcement wasn't what she was dreading it might be.

Dee Dee's eyes—emerald-green today—widened and her lips trembled. She was in a full-blown "bearer of tragic news" role and only Corrie's fear that maybe Dee Dee wasn't acting kept her from cutting the performance short. Tears gleamed in the corners of Dee Dee's eyes. "She's in a wheelchair," Dee Dee choked and sat back, her hands to her lips and her eyes blinking rapidly.

Corrie and Dana stared at her. Dee Dee seemed unaware that her news was rather anti-climactic. Red spoke up and said what the women were thinking and were too polite to say. "So?"

Dee Dee's eyes turned from glassy to frosty in an instant and she focused her narrowed gaze on Red. "How can you say that?" she gasped. "She's in a *wheelchair*!"

"Dee Dee," Corrie said. "I realize it's a bit of a shock, but didn't you get a card from the Landrys at Christmas telling you she wasn't doing too well?" Betty sent Christmas cards to practically everyone they'd ever met. She told Corrie it was her way of staving off boredom during their non-traveling times.

"Well, yeah, but a wheelchair! How awful!" Dee Dee moaned, her natural drawl replacing her previous funereal tones. Evidently ending up in a wheelchair was, in Dee Dee's estimation, the proverbial fate worse than death and she couldn't understand why everyone wasn't as devastated as she was. Dana spoke up.

"How did you happen to find out about this?" she asked.

Dee Dee's tragic look evaporated. She blinked and gave Dana, then Corrie, a vacant look. "Well... they're here, aren't they?"

"Here?" Corrie echoed. "Here, where?"

"Why, here at the Black Horse. I mean, I assume they're staying here." Dee Dee frowned, wrinkling her nose and shaking her head. "But that's right, you didn't know about Betty being in a wheelchair, so maybe they just haven't checked in yet...."

"Okay, back up, Dee Dee, start over," Corrie interrupted. "Betty Landry is in a wheelchair. You know this... how?"

Dee Dee stared at her. "I saw her and Marvin going into the bank as I was leaving the salon. They've got one of those lifts installed in their RV and I watched Marvin get Betty down and wheel her into the bank."

"You're sure it was the Landrys' RV?" Corrie asked. Dee Dee nodded.

"Of course I'm sure. Not too many Winnebagos that have 'The End of the Road' painted on the back, with 'Marvin and Betty' written right under it!"

Chapter 5

J.D. leaned against the duffel bag that he was using for a back rest and cast a glance at the blue-and-white RV that occupied the site at the end of the gravel road. In the last twenty minutes, he'd seen the curtains move at least fifteen times in such a way that indicated that the occupants were trying to find out as much about him as they could without actually walking over and saying "hello".

So far, the only things they knew about him for certain was that he rode a Harley, he had a dark blue one-man tent, and his favorite reading material was a road atlas.

He tensed when the door opened and a woman in her mid-fifties with hair the color of Hawaiian Punch came down the steps carrying a small black pug. She set the dog down and snapped a leash on its collar, whereupon the dog promptly sat and refused to budge. She tugged on the leash, trying to get the dog to walk along the road in the direction of J.D.'s campsite, but the dog merely yawned and looked in the other direction, toward the dog yard. The woman glanced toward J.D. and then, resigned, allowed the dog to lead her to the dog yard. As her voluminous violet-flowered muumuu blew in the breeze, J.D. made up his mind. He shut the atlas and quickly pulled on his chaps, jacket and helmet. He reached into the duffel bag where he kept his clothes and pulled out a bulky package. He slipped it into one of the saddlebags and mounted his Harley. Time to do a little exploring.

Corrie was rearranging the silver and turquoise jewelry on the glass shelves in the display case, when the bell over the side door jingled. Renfro let out his obligatory "watch dog on duty" woof and went back to sleep. Oliver jumped up on the case and hissed. That let Corrie know it was Rosemary Westlake coming in and that Bon-Bon, her pug, was just outside the door.

After six years, Corrie still didn't know if it was Rosemary or Bon-Bon that Oliver disliked so much. Rosemary and her husband, Donald, were year-rounders. Neither seemed old enough to be a retiree, but Rosemary had alluded to a home-based business as their source of income, without elaborating on the details. They didn't seem to be hurting for money. They owned a Class A forty-foot motor home that hadn't left the site since they first arrived. Their deluxe site rental was always paid on time and they appeared to have satellite TV and internet service. They owned a late-model Lexus sedan that they used for their weekly trips into town and their infrequent weekend trips away from the Black Horse. Twice, Bon-Bon, who had a rather impressive pedigree, had produced a litter of puppies that were sold quickly for an equally impressive amount of money, but surely not enough to support them.

Donald was computer-savvy and did occasional jobs for Corrie, such as setting up the campground's website and helping to iron out occasional glitches in their office program, in exchange for a break on the site rental; besides that, he was a rare sight other than an occasional wave as Corrie walked by while tending to campground business. Rosemary didn't seem to be making any kind of contribution to their finances, other than arranging liaisons for Bon-Bon. The only other thing Corrie felt Rosemary had any aptitude for was snooping.

"Hello, Rosemary, how are you today?" Corrie said, straightening up. Rosemary looked utterly frustrated.

"When did that extraordinary young man on the motorcycle get here?" she demanded.

Corrie's brows rose. Despite the fact that she and Dana had

checked in no fewer than a dozen guests who happened to be young—and not so young—men on motorcycles, she had no doubt to whom Rosemary was referring. "Late last night. Is there a problem?" After all her reassurances to Rick, the last thing she needed was for her mystery guest to be a troublemaker, just as suspected.

"Well," Rosemary said, straightening the neckline of her muumuu, "I'm just not sure...." She pursed her lips. "Did he pay you in advance?" she asked.

"Why do you ask?" Corrie said, her tone, she hoped, leaving no doubt in Rosemary's mind that it was none of her business.

"Well, he just took one look at me and got on his motorcycle and took off!" Rosemary said.

"Wait a minute. He's gone?" Corrie said, coming around the counter. "He packed up and left?"

"Well, er, no, not packed up," Rosemary admitted. "I just meant that... well, I know he saw me coming back from taking Bon-Bon to the dog yard and it seemed to me that he just left in a hurry!"

And if I saw you and Bon-Bon coming toward me while I was trying to have a peaceful, relaxing vacation, I'd run for the hills, too, Corrie thought. "Maybe he had to be somewhere at a certain time. Or maybe he just decided to go for a drive. I'm sure it's nothing personal about you." She fought the urge to cross her fingers behind her back for lying.

"Well, perhaps," Rosemary said, reluctant to concede to Corrie's reasoning. She arched an eyebrow. "He IS rather attractive, isn't he?"

Corrie had begun rearranging the postcards in the spinning rack. Rosemary's words made her drop a whole pack, scattering them on the floor. "Excuse me?" she stammered as she stooped to pick up the cards.

"Ah, so you did notice that about him!" Rosemary said triumphantly.

"A lot of attractive men ride motorcycles and rent campsites," Corrie said, rearranging the postcards without looking up. She didn't want everyone to know just how attractive she had found her mysterious guest. Fortunately, Dee Dee had begged off from work for the rest of the day, claiming that she had some "personal maintenance" to tend to—Corrie assumed that meant some kind of spa treatment—that she'd forgotten she had scheduled.

"Well," Rosemary continued, then repeated the word. "*Well!*" Corrie looked up. Rosemary's attention was riveted out the window. Corrie stood and saw the Landrys' RV pull into the parking lot. "Isn't that Marvin and Betty? What are they doing here? It's only April! They usually come in May, don't they?"

Corrie waited for Rosemary to run out of steam. "Usually," she said.

"Marvin... I mean, Betty never told me they were coming early!" Rosemary's voice had taken on a peculiar shrill note. Corrie gave her a puzzled glance and the older woman's face paled, clashing even more with her Fruit Juicy red hair. "I mean, I thought he—I mean, she, Betty—would have told me, considering how long we've been friends...."

Bon-Bon barked, saving Corrie from answering. Rosemary hurried out the door, stooping to scoop up her pet and waving at the RV as it stopped. Corrie followed her out, anxiety propelling her even more than her desire to see old friends.

To her surprise, it wasn't Marvin Landry, but a younger man, perhaps in his late forties with thinning blond-gray hair, that stepped down from the driver's seat. She stopped, her usual warm greeting freezing on her lips as he gave her a look of contempt and his upper lip curled. "Don't tell me. This the 'towaway zone'? Or can I park here while we get checked in?" He looked her up and down and one brow lifted. "I mean, you *do* work here, don't you?"

A flash of temper surged through Corrie, but she forced herself to respond in a polite, professional manner. "I'm Corrie Black, the owner. The Landrys are old friends of mine. I just heard they were in town."

"Oh, so you're Corrie Black. Heard more about you than I ever needed to hear. Marv and Betty think the world of you, for what that's worth. I don't suppose Marv bothered to call in a reservation?"

"It's not a bother. There's always room here for the Landrys," Corrie said, hooking her thumbs into the belt loops of her jeans to keep from smacking the sneer off the man's face. In addition to the campground, she had also inherited her father's short temper... and, thankfully, her mother's self-control. He snorted.

"That your idea of a compliment? The honor staggers me. We'll take the Presidential suite—excuse me, I mean, site—and damn the expense!" He threw his head back and laughed and Corrie let her father's genes take over.

"Look, jerk!" she snapped. "I don't know who you are or how you're related to the Landrys, but...."

"Corrie."

She spun around and her fury died, her heart twisting, at the sight of the frail, elderly woman seated in a wheelchair. Marvin had lowered Betty's chair using a lift at the back door of the RV and, as he wheeled her toward the office, Betty's back seemed hunched—in pain or sadness, Corrie couldn't tell. But the elderly woman's face lit up and the same sweet smile she'd always had brought a rush of tears to Corrie's eyes. Corrie ignored the blowhard in front of her and rushed over to hug her old friend.

Except for the wheelchair and the look of resignation in Betty's eyes, she looked much the same as always—her gray hair was whiter than it had been the previous summer, but it was tightly permed and every curl was in place. Though Corrie knew it wasn't unusual for elderly people to appear in public wearing comfortable clothes and slippers or house shoes, Betty rigidly stuck to wearing her customary dresses and nylon stockings that had long been her daily uniform, first as a school librarian and then as a postal worker. Her only concession to infirmity in her attire was a pair of sensible, orthopedic shoes.

Corrie had forgotten about Rosemary Westlake. Marvin was valiantly trying to fend off Rosemary's hug of greeting by offering his hand for a shake and finally succumbing when she didn't take the hint. To Corrie's surprise, Rosemary didn't greet Betty, but joined Marvin as he disappeared around the other side of the RV, Bon-Bon's yapping drowning out any words Corrie might have heard.

Betty didn't seem to notice. "Sorry to surprise you like this, dear," she said, her usually clear, well-modulated voice a mere raspy whisper. "Marvin and I decided it wouldn't hurt to start our vacation early this year."

Corrie looked up at Marvin as he came back around from the back of the RV. He was usually a ball of fire, but today his smile was weary and his movements slow. He looked every bit of his seventy-plus years and more. His eyes met Corrie's and he nodded. Corrie felt her stomach lurch. "Don't ever apologize for such a wonderful surprise!"

she said as gaily as she could. She straightened up and saw Rosemary standing at the back of the RV, her lips pursed in concern and confusion—Betty's condition had come as a surprise to her as well. Corrie turned back to Betty. "I'm so glad to see you. And your usual spot is vacant, so...."

Marvin broke in, his voice subdued, not his usual loud, staccato barking. "Corrie, honey, if it's all right, I'd like a different site this year. One closer to the main office, if possible."

Betty seemed about to say something, but apparently changed her mind. She nodded. "If it's not too much trouble, dear," she added, her voice hardly more than a sigh.

"No trouble at all." Corrie led them up the ramp and held the office door for them. "Let's get you all settled." She turned and nearly jumped when the man who had been driving the Landrys' RV straightened up from his position leaning against the driver's side door.

"Oh, Corrie, dear," Betty said, her face coloring. "I almost forgot...."

"Gee, thanks, Ma," the man snorted as he moved toward them. He took note of the surprised expression Corrie couldn't mask and his face darkened.

"Corrie, this is my son, Walter Dodson. I'm sure I've mentioned him before...."

Corrie was positive that Betty hadn't. She managed what she hoped was a sincere response as she walked back down the ramp. "I'm sure you have," she said, cringing mentally as she remembered her first greeting to Betty's son, but forcing a smile and holding out her hand. Walter Dodson's response was to stick his hands in his pockets.

"Let me guess... it's a pleasure to meet me, right?" he growled. Corrie's outstretched hand clenched into a fist and she pulled it back to her side. Walter didn't seem to notice. He looked past Corrie at Betty and Marvin. "Where do you want this thing parked?"

"Walter...." Betty's voice trembled, but Marvin suddenly regained his old spirit.

"I'll park it!" he said, his voice booming out so loud that it made Corrie jump. Betty flinched and grimaced, but said nothing else. Marvin's face and the top of his bald head had turned the color of a ripe tomato and his walrus mustache quivered. "You keep an eye on your mother and I'll see to parking and getting us registered. You've done more than enough already!"

Rosemary Westlake and Bon-Bon had already made a hasty departure and Corrie wished she was as invisible as she felt. She edged toward the door and cleared her throat. "I'll go get the registration ready for you to sign," she said, not addressing anyone in particular. No one responded or even looked her way; Marvin and Walter were glaring at each other and Betty sat staring at her hands, clenched into fists in her lap.

Chapter 6

J.D. cut the engine and glided through the camp entrance. The incline allowed the Harley to roll almost soundlessly past the main office door. He brought the bike to a stop, dismounted and removed his helmet. Corrie's voice almost made him drop it.

"Do you always coast in like that?"

J.D. turned with a start. Corrie sat in a plastic chair outside the side door of the main office, nearly hidden by the low hedge that bordered the walkway. He snatched off his aviator shades, a scowl forming until he saw the snail-tracks of tears on Corrie's cheeks. He reined in his temper and tried to sound casual. "I'm a considerate guy. I thought you'd appreciate me keeping the noise level down in the campground."

"I'll give you that much to explain last night. But right now, I think you're just trying to avoid Rosemary Westlake and Bon-Bon." She gave him a smile and stood up. "And in case you're wondering, yes, she noticed you dodged her earlier."

J.D. shrugged. "Had to go check out the town, pick up a few things." He nodded toward the saddlebags. "No rules against beer on the premises, is there?"

"Not as long as you're of legal age and you aren't having a wild party. And you keep your trash in the proper place."

J.D. nodded. "Something wrong?" he asked. She stiffened.

"No, not at all. Everything's fine."

"You sit outside crying when everything's fine?" he pressed, leaning back against the Harley. She seemed about to argue, but then her shoulders sagged. Although he hardly knew her, it seemed to him that it was completely out of character for her to look so down. "Want to talk about it?" J.D. asked, wondering what had led him to make the offer.

"Oh, it's nothing, really. Just that," she sighed, "facing mortality can be a real bummer, you know?"

Yeah, tell me about it. He raised an eyebrow at her. "Your mortality or someone else's?"

She nodded toward a Winnebago parked in the space across the road from J.D.'s tent site. It hadn't been there before he left. A man who looked to be in his seventies, dressed in the quintessential elderly vacationer's attire of khaki shorts, loud Hawaiian shirt and crew socks with sandals, was puttering around the picnic table, setting up camp and conversing with a frail-looking woman hunched in a wheelchair in the shade. In sharp contrast to the man, she was wearing, not a housedress and slippers as her condition seem to warrant, but a neat old-fashioned print dress with a white sweater over her shoulders and black no-nonsense shoes on her feet. Corrie explained. "The Landrys. Long-time guests of mine, been coming every year since... well, for at least the last twenty years. Betty's health's taken a nosedive and I wasn't prepared to see her in this condition. I've known them since they were in their fifties and much more active, and... I guess, in your mind, everyone is young forever."

"I suppose," J.D. said dubiously. Old age wasn't something he was on familiar terms with. "She real sick?" he asked. Corrie shrugged.

"I'm not sure... I don't even know how long she's been in this condition. I just know last year she was bustling around, helping Marvin set up the site. They usually come around the middle of May and stay till October. This year, they came earlier... just in case, I guess." She broke off as a woman came around the corner from the bathrooms. "Hi, Dana," she said.

The woman smiled and gave both of them a wave. "This must be our mystery tenant," she said. Corrie laughed and J.D. fought the rush of heat to his face. What did he expect? He looked like the proto-typical movie "bad guy" and the way he cruised in early this morning had to have started the grapevine buzzing. He nodded.

"J.D. Wilder, ma'am," he said, taking the hand the woman proffered.

"Dana Myers. My husband, Red, and I have that Airstream parked near the front. We're here to help out for the summer. You in town for the rally, Mr. Wilder?"

"J.D.," he said, not sure if he'd ever get used to being called "mister". "I'll be here through the weekend."

"Well, you'll like it here. Corrie keeps a nice campground." Dana turned to Corrie. "I'm heading over to our place and get dinner started. Want to join us tonight?"

"Sure," Corrie said. "But do you mind if we eat over here, either in the TV room or on the patio? Dee Dee bailed on me and Shelli had some family business come up and had to go out of town. With Jackie gone, I can't leave the place unattended."

"That's fine," Dana said, and she turned back to J.D. "It was nice meeting you," she said and left.

J.D. nodded and watched her walk away. Corrie's voice broke the silence. "Well?"

He looked at her. "Well, what?"

"You seem to be thinking of something," she said and tilted her head to one side. Her dark brown eyes seemed to bore right through him. "What's on your mind?"

"Nothing," he said with a shrug, then added, "You seem to have a very supportive group of friends."

She said nothing for a long time. "I'm very blessed that way," she said at last.

"You're not married? No family?" J.D. hoped she would attribute the fresh rush of color to his face to the warm, late afternoon sun.

She didn't seem to have noticed. "Married, no. Family, yes, but not necessarily blood relations," she said, her smile faint, then she became brisk. "Well, there's work to be done and I'm sure you're eager to get back to your vacation. It was nice talking to you, Mr. Wilder."

Her sudden brush off surprised him, but he decided not to question it. "J.D.," he said, and put his shades back on. "Nice talking to you, too, Corrie." She went inside the office and he sighed as the door shut behind her. *Don't get too close,* he warned himself. He glanced toward his campsite and groaned inwardly when he saw Rosemary and Bon-Bon strolling very slowly along the path toward his campsite.

Oh, well, he thought. *It could be worse.*

Chapter 7

Corrie had the coffee made and the muffins out on the courtesy table when Red and Dana came into the office at seven the next morning. "Corrie, you shouldn't have!" Dana said even as she made a beeline for the treats.

Corrie laughed. "Don't worry, I didn't!" She pushed her cup across the counter when Red gestured and he took it to refill it for her. "And I want to thank you for dinner last night. With Jackie and Jerry gone, I didn't feel like cooking for myself."

Dana waved away her thanks. "I always cook too much for just the two of us," she said. She buttered two blueberry pecan muffins and handed one to her husband. She took a bite of hers and closed her eyes. "Oh, these are wonderful!" she said. "Where did you get them?"

Before Corrie could answer, the front door opened. She turned and nearly spilled her coffee down her shirt. Rick walked in and she couldn't help but stare. He was a half-hour before his usual time, wearing a t-shirt and bike shorts that fit him like a second skin, partly from the perspiration from his daily fifteen-mile ride—which he usually took after work—and partly from his muscled physique. She couldn't remember a day when he'd stopped in in the morning and hadn't been in full uniform.

"Morning," he said, giving her his usual half-smile as he removed his bike helmet. Despite the intensity of his workout—the campground was mostly uphill from the village—his breathing was even, almost relaxed. He pulled off his shades and tucked them into the neck of his t-shirt, raising an eyebrow at her surprised expression.

"Rick?" she sputtered.

"I'm on the late shift today. For the first time in years," he added. He looked over at the Myers. "Hello," he said.

"I remember you!" Dana said. "You're the sheriff, aren't you? Hutton?"

"Sutton. Rick Sutton," Rick said, holding out his hand to shake Dana's and Red's. "You're the Myers, right? How are the muffins?"

"Fabulous!" Dana said. "I was just asking Corrie where she got them."

Corrie had overcome her shock enough to make an attempt to act normal, although her gaze kept darting back to Rick. His less-than-pristine appearance did nothing to diminish his appeal and she knew she wasn't doing a good job at hiding her appreciation. She pointed her pen at him as she answered Dana's question. "Although they're usually delivered in a sheriff's department patrol vehicle," she added, hoping the flush she felt in her cheeks wasn't as obvious as it felt.

"Man after my own heart," Red said. "Anyone who can make sweets is gold in my book." Rick's smile almost grew wider.

"I take it that, unlike Buster, you have no problem with men baking?"

"I don't," Dana said. "I'd give anything if Red could learn to boil water without burning it!" Red shrugged apologetically.

Rick turned back to Corrie. "Any problems this morning?" he asked her in a low voice and Corrie was embarrassed to see Dana give Rick the once-over behind his back and nod approvingly before giving her a wink and urging Red out of the office through the laundry room door.

She was thankful that Rick hadn't noticed. "None whatsoever," she said, almost too crisply. "Were you expecting problems?" He shrugged.

"I feel better now that the Myers are here," he said. "Let's leave it at that."

"Let's," Corrie agreed. She changed the subject. "Did you know that Marvin and Betty Landry are here?"

Rick had helped himself to a cup of coffee and he took a sip before answering. "Dee Dee has made it a point to let everyone she sees know about it."

Corrie's tongue itched to say she was positive Dee Dee made it a *particular* point to tell Rick anything and everything, but she bit it hard. "So you know about Betty's condition."

"Yes." He sighed. "It's sad, but what can you expect? Her health's been declining for years, although Dee Dee said it doesn't seem to have changed Betty's standards of appearance—as gracious and proper as ever. I'm sure Mother will be the same when she gets to that stage of her life."

An unladylike snort escaped Corrie. "As if your mother would ever allow herself to be seen in public in a wheelchair!" she said before she could stop herself. Rick's mother, Cassandra Waverly-Sutton, was one of the wealthiest and most socially-conscious inhabitants of the entire state, far too well-bred to discuss money or position... or leave the house looking less than perfect.

She was also the main reason that Corrie and Rick were friends... and nothing more. Rick's mother was a sore subject for Corrie, which was putting it mildly, and although Corrie knew she couldn't very well ban the topic, she often failed to keep her true feelings from slipping out.

Fortunately—or not—Rick rarely seemed to take offense; in fact, it usually seemed he missed Corrie's badly-concealed barbs. She wasn't sure if he was truly oblivious or just chose to take the high road she so frequently avoided when it came to the subject of his mother. In this instance, he chose to take her remark as a compliment. "That's the truth," he said, a note of pride in his voice and Corrie almost felt ashamed. After all, if she were perfectly honest, the same could be said of Rick. He paused, and then went on in a much softer voice, "Are you okay? I know it's got to be reminding you of Billy and...."

"I'm fine," Corrie said brusquely. Rick knew her too well and it irritated her to no end that he did, a feeling that made no sense to her whatsoever and only increased her irritation. Rick backed off perceptively as she changed the subject. "So what do you think about Betty's son?"

Rick paused in mid-sip and blinked. "Betty's son? What are you talking about?"

Corrie's surprise matched Rick's. "Dee Dee didn't tell you?" She paused, her mind racing. "Well, actually, she didn't mention him when she told us about Betty, come to think of it, so maybe she didn't know about him, as hard as that is to believe... Or maybe she was just too upset to...."

"Corrie!" Rick interrupted as he set his cup down. "What's this about Betty's son? I didn't know she had one." He hated being the only one not in the know. Whether it was because he felt that, as sheriff, it was his duty to know everything that was going on or because he never wanted anyone to have the upper hand for any reason, she didn't know. She was tempted to drag it out, just to annoy him further, but she didn't feel up to dealing with Rick in a bad mood.

"Neither did I... nor anyone else, it seems," Corrie said. "Apparently he's traveling with them. His name is Walter Dodson and it's pretty obvious he doesn't get along with Marvin."

"You called him 'Betty's son'. He's not Marvin's?"

"Betty introduced him as 'her' son, Walter Dodson, not 'our' son, Walter Landry. What else could it mean?"

"How do you know he doesn't get along with Marvin?"

Corrie gave a short laugh. "You should have been here when they arrived. You couldn't miss it and they weren't making an effort to hide it, either. And it's weird, Rick. He didn't seem to want to be on this trip and Marvin didn't seem to be happy that he had come along. I'm thinking his—the son's—joining them was Betty's idea and it wasn't working out the way she hoped."

"What wasn't working out?" Rick asked. Corrie shrugged.

"I don't know... I'm guessing maybe he and Marvin haven't gotten along for years and Betty wanted them to mend fences and be friends before anything... happened to her." She noted the look on Rick's face. "It's not silly, female melodrama, Sheriff, if that's what you're thinking," she snapped, feeling her face redden.

"It's not silly," he said, his soothing tone annoying her more than a sarcastic comeback would. "But if they hadn't gotten along for years, why would Betty think things would suddenly change in an instant?"

Corrie decided this discussion would get nowhere with Rick. "Are you working the late shift all weekend?" she asked.

He shook his head, apparently willing to pretend the change in subject was natural. "Just tonight. One of my rookies had a funeral to attend today—Mark Davenport's cousin, Bobby Fletcher, as a matter of fact—and I told him I'd cover him tonight." Corrie nodded; she'd forgotten that Shelli's ex had a relative who was one of Rick's new deputies. "I've got a dinner break at seven. Think there'll still be some enchiladas left?" That was another thing that drove Corrie mad. Ten years earlier, when the Black Horse began hosting their weekend social meals, Rick had started showing up and helping out, without being asked: flipping pancakes on Saturday mornings, tossing pizzas on Saturday nights—much to the delight of the campers—and on Sundays, for the steak cookouts, he manned the grill. For ten years, despite the fact that they had been "just friends" since their senior year of high school, he'd been an almost constant fixture in her weekends since she had taken a more active role in running the campground and he had graduated from college and the police academy and joined the Bonney County sheriff's department. Rick had rarely missed a weekend social event.

Not even when he and his now-ex-wife, Meghan, had gotten married, eight years earlier.

Corrie had been torn at first; the last thing she wanted to see was Rick's girlfriend, then fiancée, then wife every blessed weekend, but she had gotten some mean satisfaction from seeing that Meghan hated these social gatherings as much as Rick seemed to enjoy them. Towards the end of the relationship, over three years ago, he'd shown up alone, but he never missed. Corrie wasn't sure how she'd felt about that.

On Friday nights, he helped with the cooking if there was a fish fry going on. On enchilada nights, he seemed content to help out with the dishes. He had once said that Corrie's enchiladas didn't need his—or anyone else's—help. She forced a smile to hide the sudden, inexplicable sting of tears. "I'll save you a plate. Red or green?"

"Red," he answered, and set his coffee cup down on the counter. "Business pick up for the weekend?" he asked.

"A little. I've got some bike rally participants scheduled to arrive this afternoon. With any luck, I might have to hang the "No Vacancy" sign on the gate."

Rick nodded. "It'll get better, I'm sure." He strapped his bike helmet on and drained his coffee cup. "Guess I'll—" He broke off as the side door bell jingled and J.D. walked in, wearing baggy gray sweats and a tight black undershirt.

"Good morning," Corrie said, wishing that Rick could drop the suspicious cop aura when he wasn't in uniform. Or when he was IN uniform. "Had a good night?" She was determined to sound as cheerful as possible, as if Rick wasn't standing in the room. The glance and the smile J.D. gave her almost made her wish Rick wasn't in the room and she tried her hardest not to stare. She didn't think abs like that existed except on the covers of romance novels.

"Yes, I did. Morning, Sheriff," J.D. said with a nod toward Rick. "Almost didn't recognize you out of uniform."

Rick merely nodded. He didn't seem to be in as big a hurry to leave as he had been. He leaned against the counter. "I'm on duty this afternoon. Sobriety checks at the county line."

Really? The word almost slipped out of Corrie's mouth and she shot him a glance. Rick rarely worked the checkpoints. Was it because of Mark's cousin being gone, or did it have something to do with the motorcycle rally... and J.D. Wilder in particular? J.D. gave him a tight-lipped grin.

"Well, I guess I'll be seeing you later on," he said. He turned to Corrie. "I was wondering if I could get some change for the laundry."

"Sure," Corrie said, taking the five-dollar bill he held out to her. She waved in the direction of the courtesy table. "Muffins and coffee on the table, if you like." She couldn't NOT make eye contact with him, but the look in his eyes flustered her as much as his appearance had.

"Thank you, ma'am," J.D. said, accepting the change. He jerked his head back toward the door. "I'll go get my wash started then I'll help myself."

"Okay," Corrie said, pulling herself together. "Let me know if you need anything else." As much as she would have liked to, she didn't watch him walk out the door; instead, she watched Rick watch him walk out the door. She sighed. "What?"

"I don't like him," Rick said, surprising Corrie with his bluntness. He fixed his stormy eyes on Corrie. "There's something about him that sets wrong with me. I don't think he's being level with us."

"You've been a cop too long," Corrie said. "If you hadn't known me since I was four, you'd probably think I was some kind of criminal, too." She folded her arms across her chest and leaned against the counter.

"He's a complete stranger. You don't know anything about him," Rick went on.

"So are most of my customers! I don't know anything about them, either," she retorted. "I'd have been out of business eons ago if I had to get to know everyone who rented a site from me personally. You really have to stop this, Rick."

He didn't respond. He pulled on his gloves. "I'll see you a little after seven," he said and went out the door.

Chapter 8

J.D. waited outside the patio door until he heard the sound of the sheriff's bicycle tires on the gravel fade away and he smiled grimly to himself, wondering if Corrie and the sheriff knew how clearly their voices traveled—or if it even mattered to them. So the sheriff didn't like him? The feeling was mutual, although J.D. was loathe to admit why.

But he had a feeling it was the same reason the sheriff didn't care for him.

He turned and nearly collided with a bleached-blonde woman who had just come around the corner from the restrooms. He managed to stifle an impolite word; the last thing he needed was for anyone to see him exhibiting any more suspicious behavior. The woman cocked an eyebrow at him, looked him up and down in a predatory manner and smiled. She was wearing faded jeans and a Harley-Davidson t-shirt and had apparently been a biker almost as long as J.D. had been alive. J.D. gave her a weak grin in return and stepped aside, allowing the lady to continue on her way, and the minute she turned away, he shook his head. He knew bikers who ranged in age from high-school kids to grandparents but his taste in women was set squarely in between the two age groups, with a preference for the younger end of the spectrum. And not necessarily motorcycle riders.

He slipped back into the laundry room, glad to see it was empty although one washer and one dryer were both running. He loaded a washer with what little laundry he had and went into the camp store.

Corrie looked up as the buzzer alerted her that he had entered the store. She stood up, shooing the gray-and-black tabby off her lap. "Did you need something?" she asked.

He stopped by a shelf with a variety of cleaning goods and picked up a tiny box of laundry detergent and a two-pack of dryer sheets. "Just this," he said, bringing the items up to the counter. "And a cup of coffee, once I get my wash going." Corrie smiled.

"Piñon or regular?"

He smiled in spite of himself. "I have to say I appreciate your recommendation... that piñon coffee is quite addictive." She laughed as she rang up his purchase and he took a moment to study her.

An attractive woman, spunky, sure of herself, and... what? There was something about her that appealed to him, something beyond what he could see also appealed to the sheriff. She had silky, midnight-black hair that hung to the middle of her back despite the braid she wore—a strong indicator of Native American genes. But her coffee-colored eyes and olive-toned skin hinted at Hispanic or Latin American heritage. All in all, an intriguing and definitely pleasing combination. What sparked his interest most, however, was the fact that she didn't seem aware of her own beauty. He wondered what her history with Sheriff Rick Sutton was.

Then he decided he really didn't want to know.

He took his purchase into the laundry room, got the machine started, then went back into the camp store. He went to the coffee maker and picked up the pot of piñon coffee. "Need a refill?" he asked her.

"Sure," Corrie said, pushing her cup across the counter. J.D. filled it then took the pot back to the table and filled one for himself.

"Muffin?" he asked her, gesturing to the tray. She grinned ruefully.

"Two's my limit... unfortunately, I've already had three!" And she laughed.

J.D. grinned. He helped himself to a muffin, then hesitated.

Should he go back into the laundry room? Would it be out of line for him to hang out at the counter? His eye caught the TV room door. "Do you allow food in there?" he said.

"Of course," she said. "Make yourself at home. No one's in there right now."

J.D. decided to throw caution to the wind. "Care to join me?" he asked.

She looked surprised, but nodded. "All right," she said. She came around the counter, followed by the old black Lab and the cat. J.D. hadn't expected it to become a party.

He set his cup down at a small table flanked by a pair of recliners and sat down. She sat in the other recliner and the cat jumped up on her lap. The dog flopped down at her feet and instantly began to snore. J.D. grinned. "Chaperones?"

Corrie laughed. "Just jealous," she said. "They hate for me to give my attention to anyone else."

Funny. They didn't seem to mind her giving her attention to the sheriff. "You really have a nice place here, Corrie."

She looked pleased at the compliment. "Thank you. I can't take all the credit; my father built the place into what it is, with my mother's guidance and the help of some really terrific people. I'm just picking up where he left off."

Her smile had faded. J.D. understood. "How long ago?" he said softly.

"A year ago last month. Stomach cancer."

"I'm sorry."

She inclined her head and took a sip of her coffee. "Me, too. My dad was a great guy." Her voice held only the slightest tremor.

"What about your mom?" J.D. asked. Corrie's lips twisted into a sad smile.

"When I was twelve. Heart aneurysm. She died in her sleep."

"Oh..." J.D. felt awkward. "I'm sorry." He took a huge swig of coffee and wondered what else to say. So far, it was looking like the weather might be the only topic that wouldn't be sensitive. Corrie saved him the trouble.

"It's okay," she said. "I don't mind talking about them. I'm not traumatized or depressed. I have a very good, very happy life. My parents taught me to appreciate what I have and not grieve over what

I don't have."

"That's very wise," he said, impressed by her serenity.

She shrugged. "It just makes sense."

"Dare I ask about a husband or boyfriend?" Where he got the audacity to ask that question he didn't know. He was almost afraid of her answer. The sharp look she gave him made him sorry he HAD asked.

"No to both. Can I ask YOU some questions?"

He tensed up; he knew she could sense it. "Like what?"

"Are YOU married? What about your parents? What do you do for a living?"

"No. Deceased. Not much," he deadpanned, but she didn't seem amused.

"You seem to be quite intent on being secretive," she said. "Don't you let anyone in to meet the real you?"

He hesitated, not sure how to respond at first. "I don't let everyone in to meet the real me, as you put it," he said. "Just people I like and trust."

"How do you know you'll like them and can trust them if you won't let them in?" she persisted.

He wondered. Could he take a chance with Corrie? Was she different... different than.... He heard voices in the laundry room, campers who were coming in to pick up the laundry they'd left in the machines, and he made up his mind. No chances. Not now.

He stood up and gave Corrie a grim smile. "If they want me to trust them, they'll just have to meet me out on the porch and wait for me to invite them in."

Corrie carried the third pan of enchiladas out to the patio serving table and sighed. Her mother's philosophy had always been that it was better to have leftovers for a week than to be short even one plate... but five pans had definitely been too many. The bike rally had drawn most of her guests into town for dinner.

She'd been pleased and relieved by the number of drop-in campers she'd signed in by four o'clock Friday afternoon. She and Dana and Red had been busy, so much so that she hadn't had time to check on Buster and see how he was getting along with the maintenance work. By six p.m., when the Friday night enchilada dinner was starting, all but one campsite was booked. However, the majority of campers had turned out to be bike rally participants who'd all roared out of the Black Horse, no sooner had they set camp up.

One notable exception had been J.D. He didn't seem to be in any hurry to make the acquaintance of any of the other bikers who flooded the campground. Nor did he seem interested in heading into town for the rally festivities.

Dana and Red had helped dish out generous helpings of enchiladas, beans, and rice and urged seconds and thirds. "I can freeze the other two pans, Dana," Corrie said. "I don't have a big enough stock of antacids on hand in the store if we keep pushing everyone to overeat!"

Now it was six forty-five and Corrie and the Myers sat down at one of the patio tables for their own meal. Corrie had wondered why Rick hadn't shown up, until she remembered that he was working the late shift, doing sobriety checkpoints at the county line, and had told her he wouldn't get his dinner break until seven. Now she looked over at J.D.'s campsite. He hadn't come over for dinner, but he didn't seem to be going anywhere. She didn't realize she'd been glancing over so often until Dana leaned across the table.

"He's a fine-looking young man," she said in a theatrical whisper. "Almost as fine-looking as the sheriff."

Corrie knew her face rivaled her enchilada sauce in color and heat. She wanted to make a careless, disinterested comment, but nothing came to mind. "I suppose," she said, taking a bite of food and quickly following up with her iced tea.

Red chuckled and said nothing. Dana shook her head. "I think he likes you, too."

Corrie had said nothing to Dana about the conversation she'd had with J.D. in the TV room. She shrugged, hoping Dana would drop the subject. "He's just friendly."

"With who?" Dana's green eyes widened and her brows rose. "I got the business from Rosemary Westlake while you were in the kitchen. She thinks there's something wrong with someone who won't take the time to be sociable. Of course, she could have been talking about Red," she added as her husband let out a snort. "He hightailed it for dear life when he saw Rosemary and Donald come up for dinner."

"I hate that stupid dog. Bon-Bon. What kind of crazy name for a dog is that?" Red shook his head in disgust. "She sat that dog on her lap all through dinner and all it did was whine, growl, snort, and drool. It would have put me right off my feed if I'd stuck around!"

"Well, lucky for me, your appetite survived or I'd have even more enchiladas to freeze." Corrie smiled. "Let's face it, Dana, if you weren't being paid to be here, if this was a relaxing weekend getaway for you, you probably wouldn't go out of your way to be sociable with everyone."

"I kind of got the impression that the sheriff didn't like him either," Dana went on. "Any particular reason why?" Corrie laughed shortly.

"No, nothing particular, just Rick being the sheriff," she said. "And the fact that J.D. made the mistake of showing up in a rather mysterious way. He's just a loner."

"A very attractive loner, you have to admit," Dana persisted. "What do you know about him?"

"That he likes to keep to himself. And that maybe he's not so anti-social as you think," she added, tilting her head in the direction of the campsite and getting up from the table.

J.D. walked through the patio gate, nodding a greeting and flashing a smile at Corrie. "I surrender," he said, holding his hands up.

"What?" Corrie said. He made quite a picture in his faded jeans and plain white t-shirt. He shrugged, his grin bashful, almost boyish, which did nothing to make him look less appealing.

"It was nothing short of an heroic effort for me to try to resist the lure of homemade Mexican food... after all, I am from Texas," he said. "But the breeze kept sending me hints about how good it would be, so if I'm not to late to partake...."

"Not at all," Dana said, jumping up and poking Red's shoulder. Red's mouth was full of enchiladas and he gave his wife a withering glare. She glared back and, resigned, Red got up as well. "Would you prefer red or green, J.D.? Or both? Don't you worry," she said to Corrie, gesturing at her to sit down. "We'll serve your guest. Would you like iced tea or lemonade or a soft drink?"

J.D.'s eyes glimmered with a laugh he was holding in. "Red would be good. And iced tea," he said and he shook his head as Dana scurried off, dragging Red after her. "Is there something about your friend I should know?" he asked as he sat down.

"Nothing I can think of," Corrie said, fighting back the embarrassed flush on her cheeks. "I'm glad you decided to join us. I thought you'd be heading into town with the other guests."

He shook his head but offered no explanation. Dana reappeared and set his plate and drink before him. She flashed a quick smile and disappeared before either J.D. or Corrie could say anything. J.D. picked up his fork, gestured at Corrie's plate. "Yours is getting cold," he said.

"Oh." Corrie glanced down. She'd helped herself to a small amount of food just to be polite and sit with the Myers. She had planned on eating a full meal with Rick, but she felt shy about telling J.D. that. "I... uh, I'll get more in a while. It's not like we're in any danger of running out."

J.D. nodded and began to eat. Corrie tried to think of something to say, but she had conversed herself out with the guests and she was enjoying the quiet. She relaxed and it seemed that J.D. was enjoying the silence as well. He looked up. "These are good," he said. "Very good."

Corrie blushed. "Thank you." She wondered why she felt so self-conscious about the praise. Every one of her guests always had scores of compliments on the food she served at her socials, but for some reason, she felt particularly pleased that J.D. had paid her a compliment. "It was my mother's recipe," she added. He straightened up and put his fork down.

"Do you always do that?" he asked.

Corrie stared at him, confused. "I'm sorry? Do what?" she asked.

He picked up his plastic cup of tea and stared at her over the rim as he took a long drink. His eyes were a dark, nickel gray, the color of storm clouds, and yet not ominous. She found herself unable to look away.

"What did I do?" she asked again. He set the cup down.

"So far, that's twice that I've offered you a compliment that you've handed off to someone else. The first time, you credited your dad for your having a nice campground, now you're saying your dinner is good because you used your mom's recipe for the enchiladas. Give yourself some credit. YOU run this campground, YOU made this dinner. Stop making it sound like you don't think YOU'RE good enough."

Her mouth dropped open. Was that his idea of flattery? She said the only thing that came to her mind. "You've got a lot of nerve! And anyway, it's not true." She wanted to get up and storm away, but she also wanted to burst into tears.

He noticed. "Hey," he said, lightly touching her hand with the tip of one finger, as if afraid she'd pull away if he did more. It felt like an electric shock to Corrie. "I'm not trying to put your parents down. Believe me, they've got to be special people."

"How would you know that?" she stammered, still fighting the urge to get up and walk away although she felt she couldn't if she tried. "You've never met them."

"I've met YOU," he said. "And if you're the product of your raising, then...."

"Then you're doing the same thing you're accusing me of doing," she said, managing a smile through tear-stung eyes. "Aren't you? Giving my parents the credit for who I am instead of to me?"

He stared at her, then his mouth twitched. "You're a sharp lady, Corrie Black."

She looked away, blinking. "I'm a smart aleck, that's what I am," she said. "I'm sorry if I was rude."

"No apologies necessary," he said. They fell silent again and Corrie glanced at her watch and grimaced before she could catch herself.

He noticed. "You got someplace to be?"

"No," she said, too quickly. "It's just that...."

Dana's voice floated out to them from the office. "...and I'm sure you've had a long, tiring day, SHERIFF..." Corrie winced, wishing Dana didn't try so hard to be subtle. J.D. grinned and pretended to be absorbed in draining his iced tea glass. Dana went on. "... and I'm sure there's plenty for you... I'll just get a plate and ... would you come give me a hand in the kitchen before you go out on the PATIO?"

"Is that my cue to leave?" J.D. asked Corrie in a stage whisper. Corrie fought down the embarrassment that was choking her.

"You stay put," she said firmly. He gave her a wink and a nod, but Corrie fixed her eyes on the doorway and watched Rick come out with his plate of food and his glass of tea, followed by Dana.

Rick didn't stop short or give any other indication of surprise at seeing J.D. and Corrie sharing a table. Dana gave Corrie an incredulous stare over Rick's shoulder before she turned and went back into the office, shaking her head. "Good evening, Corrie," Rick said. He looked like he usually did, his uniform neat and crisp, his face handsome and somewhat stern. "Wilder," he said, with a nod to J.D.

"Sheriff," J.D. replied, returning the nod.

Now Corrie wondered what would happen. She sat on one side of the picnic table, J.D. opposite her. Where would Rick sit? He never sat next to her, always across from her, but J.D. was already sitting there.... Her stomach fluttered.

Rick set his plate and cup down at the end of the table, walked over to one of the round tables that dotted the patio and brought over a molded plastic chair and sat on the end, between Corrie and J.D. He took off his cowboy hat, placed it on the bench next to Corrie and gave her his half smile. "You mind if I sit here?"

As if she would say, yes, she minded. Even if she had minded. Which she didn't. But she felt flustered. "Of course not." She looked across at J.D. who shrugged. As if she was asking HIM if HE minded. Which she wasn't. "Would you like seconds, J.D.?" she asked, feeling very much thrown off balance.

A fleeting expression of surprise flickered in J.D.'s eyes, but nothing else. "I wish I could," he said. "But I'm afraid I'd overdo it. Thanks, anyway." He stood up. "And thanks for the meal, Corrie. I've got to get going. I'll see you later." He nodded to Rick again. "Sheriff," he said and picked up his paper plate and cup, threw them away and headed back to his campsite.

Rick watched him leave. "Was it something I said?" he murmured. He glanced back at Corrie and raised an eyebrow at her. She was shaking her head. "What?"

"It's what you DON'T say, Sheriff, that puts the fear of the law into people."

"People shouldn't fear the law if they aren't doing anything wrong," Rick repeated his favorite refrain, digging into his meal. "It's great, as usual," he said after the first bite.

THAT was unusual. Rick rarely paid her compliments. Corrie pondered that while watching him eat. After a minute, he set down his fork.

"Is there something wrong, Corrie?" His dark blue eyes were clouded with concern. For once he didn't look stern and unfeeling. He looked worried.

"No. Why?" she asked, wondering what he would say. He shook his head.

"You're awful quiet. Are you upset with me?"

Corrie wanted to laugh. She and Rick had sparred verbally for years—hardly a day went by without them getting into some kind of argument or irritation with each other. And now, while they were sitting in relative peace, he thought she was angry with him. "Rick, if I was quiet every time I got upset with you, people would think I'd taken a vow of silence. Can't we just enjoy each other's company without having a big discussion going on?"

He looked unconvinced. "I thought you might have something on your mind."

Actually she did; something that had been bothering her for most of the day and, while she tried to dismiss it as trivial, she was glad he'd brought it up so she could air it out. "Just that I haven't seen the Landrys much since they got here."

Rick expressed no surprise at the unexpected subject. He nodded. "The weather's been nice."

"And I've always kept the grounds wheelchair-accessible for my guests' convenience," she added. "I'm just wondering if Betty's self-conscious about being seen in her condition."

Rick shook his head. "Some people might be, but not Betty. She's always been dignified and lady-like and never made a fuss about anything, but... well, I guess that could change, considering the circumstances," he added thoughtfully. "Maybe her son took them into town for the day and then out to dinner."

"Maybe." From what she had seen, it would be hard to imagine Marvin spending the day with Walter Dodson and enjoying it, even for Betty's sake. "But he'd have to have rented a car to do it and I haven't noticed any companies delivering one. I haven't seen him around today, either."

"Marvin hasn't even come into the store?"

"Not since they checked in," Corrie said. "And he used to always rave about my enchiladas, so it's odd they haven't come for dinner. I was wondering if I should go over there and check on them, maybe bring them a plate of food." She looked at Rick. "Or would that be too nosy?"

"If the question was coming from Dana," he said, keeping his voice low. "I'd say definitely nosy. But you're concerned. I'll go with you." He stood up.

"What, now?" she said. He indicated the meal with a sweep of his hand.

"What better time? We'll wrap up the food so they can put it in the fridge for tomorrow if they've already eaten dinner. Do you have any muffins left from this morning?"

"Four," she said, deciding not to tell him she'd planned on having them for a midnight snack. "I could wrap those up, too."

Ten minutes later, they were heading toward the Landrys' RV. As they walked up the path, they heard the sound of a motorcycle starting up. J.D. was on his Harley, dressed in black leather with a red bandana tied around his head. He slipped on his helmet and shades, gave Rick and Corrie a thumbs-up sign, and roared out of the camp.

"That's the most noise he's made the whole time he's been here," Corrie remarked. Rick grimaced.

"It's going to be loud when you get your bike rally guests back in tonight... and it'll be late, too."

Corrie shrugged. "I think everyone in the campground knows what this weekend is... and I've impressed it on my bike rally guests that courtesy demands they be considerate of the other guests." They had arrived at the Landrys' RV door and Rick climbed up the short steps to knock.

He stepped back and waited for the door to open. Nothing. He frowned and turned to Corrie.

"No answer. They probably did go somewhere."

"Not on foot. They didn't bring any other vehicle but the RV. Knock again," she said and he shook his head.

"They might be asleep," he said.

"At seven-thirty in the evening? Maybe they're just watching TV and they didn't hear you. You didn't exactly break the door down with that knock," she added.

"The door's closed and so are all the windows," he argued. "That's what people do when they go to sleep."

It suddenly occurred to Corrie what had been bothering her most of the day. She felt a chill. "Rick.... I don't remember seeing their windows or the door open today."

"Are you sure?"

"No... no, I'm not," she said, trying to think. "I was busy most of the day. All I noticed is that I didn't notice them around."

"If Betty's not feeling well...." Rick's voice trailed off. "Maybe Dana or Red saw them."

"Saw who?" Dana said, coming up the path behind them. "I saw you from the office window and wondered what was keeping you out here," she added.

"No one's answering the door," Rick said curtly. "Have you seen the Landrys today? Or Mrs. Landry's son? You do know them, don't you?" he added.

Dana nodded, then pursed her lips up and frowned. "Let me think... I thought I saw the son—thinning hair, about forty-something, right?—leave the RV this morning, walking toward the dog yard... not that he had a dog, I think he was just going for a walk. He seemed annoyed when I said 'good morning' to him, didn't even answer. Then I saw Marvin—he's the older, shorter man with the bald head, isn't he?—heading toward the bathrooms... no, wait, that was around twelve-thirty and the bathrooms were closed then. Maybe he was going to the camp store."

"He never came in. At least I never saw him," Corrie said. Dana glanced between the two of them.

"You think something's wrong? Oh, God... Betty...." Her face paled.

"Let's not jump to conclusions," Rick cautioned them. "I told Corrie they're probably asleep and...."

"And surely would have awakened by now with all the ruckus we're making out here," Corrie said in exasperation. She shifted both plates of food to one hand, brushed past Rick and pounded on the RV door. "Marvin! Betty! Are you—What the...?" In shock, she watched the door swing open and she stepped back. Without a word, Rick took a firm hold of her shoulders and moved her aside, pushing open the screen door, and stepping into the RV. After a split second, Corrie handed the foil-wrapped plates of food to Dana and followed him in.

She wished she hadn't.

Chapter 9

Marvin lay sprawled on the floor of the living room near the door, as if he'd been on his way to answer it. At first Corrie thought he'd passed out and fallen, but he didn't seem to be breathing, and there was a dark stain under him on the floor, and then Rick reached to check the pulse in Marvin's neck ....

She gasped and Rick spun around and grabbed her arm.

"Out! Now, Corrie! You don't need to see this!"

She shook off his hand. "Betty!" she cried and, to their surprise, a faint voice called from down the hall.

"In here...."

In two strides, Rick had crossed the living room, Corrie right behind him, even as Dana was crying, "What happened? What's going on? Corrie, what's wrong?"

Rick reached the bedroom at the end of the short hallway and slid the pocket door open. His broad back and shoulders blocked the way and Corrie couldn't see into the room. He turned to her. "She's not here."

Corrie spun and went back to the bathroom door they had passed. She grabbed the knob, but it wouldn't turn. "Betty?"

"In here... I'm in the bathroom...."

"Betty!" Corrie cried, twisting the door knob. "Open the door!"

"I can't," came Betty's feeble voice. "It's locked from out there."

"What...?" Corrie looked down at the knob she was gripping with both hands and she heard a stifled curse from Rick. He pushed her aside, none too gently this time.

"How can it be locked from out here? Bathroom doors don't...," he muttered. Then they both saw the lock button on the door knob. Rick motioned Corrie back, removed his handkerchief from his back pocket and carefully turned the lock.

He pulled the door open, using the handkerchief, and Corrie ducked under his arm. "Betty!"

Betty Landry sat on the closed commode lid, her usually composed face tight with fear. She was shaking. "Corrie! Oh, thank goodness! I thought no one would ever come let me out! Where's Marvin? Is he all right?"

Rick spoke up before Corrie said anything, although he allowed her to step into the tiny bathroom and wrap her arms around the shivering old woman. "Mrs. Landry, what happened? How did you get locked in here?"

Tears flooded Betty's eyes. "Marvin?" she asked, her voice quavering. Corrie gave Rick a pleading look. He seemed to understand and he took a deep breath.

"Mrs. Landry... Betty, he's... he's been shot. He's dead. I'm sorry," Rick said, glancing back toward the living room.

"Oh, no!" Betty dropped her head, covered her face with her hands, began to cry. Corrie held on to her, careful of her frail bones. "He can't be dead!" Betty moaned.

"Betty," Corrie said, keeping her voice low and soothing. "What happened?"

From outside the RV, Dana's shrill voice could be heard, pleading to know what was wrong and no doubt attracting more attention than Rick wanted. He muttered again and stepped back into the living room, from where he barked instructions at Dana to go into the office and call the sheriff's department. Corrie couldn't hear all the details, but she surmised that Rick was giving Dana a brief summary of what had happened and was cautioning her to keep calm and not spread the word all over the camp. Within seconds, he was back in the bathroom doorway. "Mrs. Landry... Betty... are you hurt?

Do you need an ambulance?"

Betty shook her head, her face still in her hands. Corrie looked up at Rick and she could see the impatience, tempered by compassion, in his eyes. The grim set of his lips told her he was itching to fire a barrage of questions at the weeping woman, but his innate decency wouldn't let him.

"Betty, you have to tell Rick what happened," Corrie urged her.

"I don't know!" Betty cried out suddenly, with more energy than Corrie had seen her exhibit since the Landrys had arrived. "I was in here, washing up, and I heard the front door open and I heard Marvin say, 'What's going on?' I reached for a towel and suddenly the door shut behind me and I heard the lock and then I... I heard...." Her lips trembled and tears spilled down her cheeks again. Her face was white and she looked like she was going to faint. Corrie spoke to Rick.

"We need to get her out of here," she said, her tone low but urgent. Rick gave a quick nod, then turned down the hall and brought Betty's wheelchair from the bedroom at the back of the RV. Corrie helped the old woman stand and then turn and seat herself. Now the problem was how to get her out of the RV without having to see Marvin's body. Rick looked at Corrie, as if asking her if she had any ideas, but Betty spoke up first.

"Marvin had a door installed in the bedroom with a wheelchair lift. That's how I get in and out. He said it was best to put it in the bedroom, in case of a fire at night, for my safety...." She began sobbing again and Corrie quickly grabbed the wheelchair handles and pushed her toward the bedroom.

By the time they had Betty settled safely on the ground, two sheriff's department cars had shown up. Corrie recognized the two deputies, Andy Luna and Daniel Klinekole, who had graduated from high school with her and Rick and had followed Rick into the law enforcement field with the same eagerness that they had followed him onto the football field during their junior and senior years of high school. Rick went to go talk to them while Corrie wheeled Betty into the camp store and into the TV room. Dana and Red had shooed a couple of guests out and Dana made a fresh pot of coffee. Red went out to disperse the curious guests that still lingered outside the office and Dana kept a watch on the doorway to head off any overly persistent ones.

Corrie waited until Betty had sipped some coffee. Her face was still pale, she still trembled, but she seemed to have gotten over the initial shock. "Betty," Corrie said, not sure if she was doing the right thing and not sure at all what Rick would think. "Do you have any idea who came into your RV?"

Betty shook her head. "All I heard was a voice... I didn't really hear what was said... I had the water running...." She pressed her lips together. "Marvin had that way about him, you know. Sometimes he'd bark a greeting at people, and if you didn't know him real well, you'd think he was angry. So I couldn't tell... if it was someone he knew and he was just kidding with them, or if someone was breaking in, or...."

"I'll ask the questions, Corrie."

Corrie jumped. She turned and cringed at the look on Rick's face. He wasn't happy. She started to say something, but Rick jerked his head toward the door. "It's time you left, Corrie. I have some questions for Mrs. Landry."

"Oh, please!" Betty cried, grabbing Corrie's hand. "Oh, please, Sheriff, please let Corrie stay with me. I... I'm not thinking straight... the shock...."

"I understand, Mrs. Landry, that you're upset," Rick said, his eyes still shooting darts at Corrie. Corrie bit her tongue before she said something that would only upset Betty—and Rick—even more. Rick's gaze flicked to Betty Landry's trembling lips and he gave an exasperated sigh. "All right, I'll allow her to stay, but...." He motioned Corrie to step out of the room with him for a moment.

Corrie was sorely tempted to play dumb, but at the risk of being kicked out, regardless of Betty's wishes, she got up and followed Rick. Before she could say a word, he held up a hand and glared at her. "I expect you to tell me everything she said to you while I wasn't around to hear." Corrie's mouth dropped open.

"What makes you think I wouldn't?" she snapped. He shook his head, but now he looked more worried than angry.

"Corrie, no secrets. You understand? Things aren't adding up and I don't...." He didn't slap a hand over his mouth, but the effect was the same. "Never mind," he muttered. "Let's get on with it."

Corrie's tongue itched with questions, but she kept quiet and preceded Rick into the TV room. Betty looked up in apprehension, relaxing only slightly when Corrie came and sat beside her and took her hand. Another deputy stepped in and quietly sat off to the side. Corrie recognized Dudley Evans, Rick's usual right-hand man and unofficial under-sheriff. He seemed unmoved by the whole situation, his smooth coffee-colored face calm and his dark eyes deceptively sleepy-looking. Corrie envied him.

"All right, Mrs. Landry," Rick said. "I want you to tell me, from the beginning, what happened."

"Well, as I was telling Corrie," Betty began and Corrie winced, although this time Rick didn't look at her, "I was washing up in the bathroom and I heard Marvin call out, 'What's going on?'...."

"What time was this?" Rick asked. Betty looked at him blankly.

"I... I'm not sure. Sometime today, before lunch time." She sounded vague, as if trying hard to remember, then she inclined her head meekly. "I never looked at the clock. We rarely do when we're on vacation," she added as an explanation. "I was in the bathroom, washing up for lunch. Sometimes it's early, sometimes it's later. I really can't give you an exact time."

Corrie knew Rick was a stickler for accuracy so his patience was nothing less than heroic. He nodded. "Go on, Mrs. Landry."

"Well, I grabbed a towel and started to dry my face and hands, because I thought maybe someone was dropping in, then I heard voices... Marvin's and somebody else's... then the door shut behind me and I didn't hear what was being said." She shook her head, bewildered. "I shut the water off and tried to open the door, but it was locked. I couldn't imagine why Marvin would have shut the door in the first place. I called out to Marvin, 'Who is it?' but he... he didn't answer."

She sat silent for a few moments, composing herself. Rick waited and then asked, "Did you hear a shot, Mrs. Landry?" Betty's face paled again.

"I... I didn't know it was a shot," she whispered. "I heard a loud noise, like a loud pop, and then I heard the front door slam and then it was quiet and I called out to Marvin again and he didn't answer. I got scared. I didn't know what was going on. I didn't know if he'd gone off with somebody, but then why would he lock me in the bathroom? And then I thought maybe he'd fallen and gotten hurt...."

"That still wouldn't explain you being locked in the bathroom," Rick pointed out and Betty nodded.

"I just never imagined it was... he was shot," she said in a haunted, quavering voice.

Rick gave her a few seconds to pull herself together. "Mrs. Landry, your son... Walter is his name, right? Where is he?"

"Walter?" She gave a start. "Walter... oh, he went into town this morning. Right after breakfast. I'm not sure what time, exactly," she added quickly, as if guessing at Rick's next question.

Rick waited while Betty took another sip of coffee and then set her cup down. Her hands still shook, but not as badly as they had before, and she clasped them in her lap. "Betty," he said, using her first name and the gentlest voice Corrie had ever heard him use, "I need to know... did you recognize the voice that you heard talking to Marvin?"

She shook her head. "No," she said.

"Did you hear what was said? Was it a man's voice or a woman's voice? Could you make out any words?" Rick persisted.

Betty stared at him with tear-glazed eyes. "Sheriff, I didn't hear actual words... I had the water running in the sink. I just heard a voice... I think it was a man's voice. But I didn't recognize it."

Rick nodded. He straightened up and looked at Dudley. "I think it might be a good idea for Mrs. Landry to be checked out at the hospital, just as a precaution," he said and Deputy Evans nodded. Betty started to protest, but Corrie spoke up.

"Betty, please, it would set us all at ease to know you're all right," Corrie said. "Rick—the sheriff—knows what he's doing."

Betty hesitated. "All right," she said wearily, as if too tired to protest. "But I'll need to get a few things from...." She broke off, her lower lip quivering.

Corrie squeezed her shoulder. "Just tell me what you need and I'll get it," she said soothingly.

"I'LL get it," Rick jumped in. Corrie flashed him a look of annoyance and Betty spoke up, her face reddening.

"Sheriff... I know it will seem foolish to you, but ... I would much rather you—or any gentleman—didn't go rooting through my... my undergarments," she stammered. "I'd rather Corrie..."

Rick tried not to let his exasperation show and Corrie could see it was a losing battle. "I'll be standing right beside her while she...." He took a deep breath as if realizing he'd just agreed to Betty's request and heroically regained his calm. "All right, Mrs. Landry," he said.

He waited impatiently while Corrie got a short list of what Betty wanted before she joined him outside on the patio. He jerked his head in the direction of the Landrys' RV, a silent command, and started walking. Corrie practically had to run to keep up with him.

She was fuming, but she waited until they were well away from the office before she said anything. "Why are you angry with me? And don't say you aren't," she said, trying to match his strides. "And it's something besides me asking Betty questions! What is it?"

He stopped and she nearly went right past him. He was chewing on his lower lip and Corrie knew that was something he did when he was either furious or terrified. Since there seemed to be no reason for him to be nervous, let alone afraid, she surmised he was upset beyond words and it had to be at her.

She said nothing, just looked at him with her hands on her hips, trying to catch her breath, and he seemed to be just as intent on avoiding her eyes. Finally he said, "I just wish you hadn't grabbed that door knob."

For a moment she didn't know what he was talking about, then the memory of her grabbing the bathroom door knob when Betty called out to them came to her and she felt heat rush to her face. "It was sheer instinct, Rick! I never stopped to think...."

"I know," he said, holding up his hands and looking at her. "I'm not mad at you, I'm mad at myself. I should have thought of it first. And I shouldn't...." he broke off.

Corrie could finish the sentence for him: he shouldn't have let her in the RV in the first place. Sometimes it was hard for her to separate Rick Sutton from Sheriff Rick Sutton and she knew that this was on of those times when she knew it was the Sheriff speaking... but that didn't make her feel any better.

"I'm sorry," she said, trying not to sound stiff and hurt. Rick either didn't notice or chose to ignore it.

"Let's get Betty's things so she can get to the ER and get checked out," he said.

Chapter 10

Crime scene tape had been stretched around the perimeter of the Landrys' campsite and Marvin, thank goodness, had already been taken away. Corrie waited while Rick spoke to the deputy guarding the scene then he motioned for Corrie to follow him.

"They'll need your prints to compare to the ones they find after they've dusted. Don't touch anything," he told her, leading the way up the steps. She made a concerted effort not to look at the dark stain on the living room floor and she kept her arms folded stiffly across her chest. "Have you been in the Landrys' RV?" Rick asked.

"Not on this visit," she said, as they reached the bedroom door. "Why?"

"Could you tell if something was missing?"

"Robbery?" she said, and frowned. Rick shrugged.

"It doesn't seem likely... I mean, if so, the perpetrator must have been fairly new at this to go about it the way he did—barging in and shooting like that. And he had to have known there was something worth stealing." Corrie shook her head; the Landrys were retirees, but she was certain they weren't much more than moderately well-off. Their RV was definitely no top-of-the-line model... in fact, Betty had once confessed, with a great deal of reluctance and embarrassment, that they had bought it used. Corrie mentioned this to Rick and he shook his head. "Then it's not likely it was a robbery," he said.

They went into the bedroom and Rick stood by the door and waited while Corrie gathered up a couple changes of clothing for Betty from the tiny closet. She turned toward the dresser and stopped. The top drawer was pulled open about six inches. She moved closer and stood staring for a moment at the disarray.

"Are you almost done?" Rick said impatiently. "I need to...."

"Rick, come tell me if this seems odd to you," she interrupted. In an instant he was at her elbow.

"What?"

She indicated the lingerie drawer. "This was already open and I haven't touched or taken anything from here," she said. "Look."

The left-hand side of the drawer was stocked nearly to the top with neatly folded ladies' undergarments. On the right-hand side, however, there was a gap and clothes were strewn as if someone had reached in and pulled something out of the drawer and hadn't bothered—or had time—to replace the items or even push the drawer completely shut. She looked at Rick and his face grew even grimmer.

"We'll have to ask Betty what she kept in this drawer. Don't take anything out," Rick warned and Corrie bit back a retort. She stepped back as he went out to the living room and told the fingerprint men to get the bedroom as well. Rick hadn't said a word about the apparent contradiction between the condition of the room compared to the drawer and the maddening thing was she didn't know if she should mention it to him.

"Corrie?" She started, so lost in her concerns that she'd almost forgotten about him. He stood in the doorway. "Come on."

They left the RV and, as if by mutual agreement, stopped at the edge of the campsite. Corrie said, "Rick, Betty's wheelchair was in the bedroom when we found her, wasn't it? Did you notice nothing else was out of place in the bedroom? As if whoever...."

"Corrie," Rick said, so sharply it made her jump. "Don't," he said.

"Don't what?"

Rick pushed his hat back and his gaze seem to bore right through her. "Don't get mixed up in this. I'm the professional here, not you. I've noticed plenty... maybe more than you have. And it's best that you stay out of this until the investigation is complete."

Corrie's jaw dropped; Rick had never spoken to her like that before. And she didn't like it one bit. Her temper flared. "And just how do you propose for me to stay out of it, Sheriff?" she snapped. "This murder took place on my property, to friends I've known for years! You can't...."

"I can," Rick said, his tone not only calm but professionally impersonal, which only infuriated her more. "I know you feel responsible, but you have to leave this to me to worry about. I don't want you going around trying to find out anything on your own."

"Are you going to have someone watching me every second?"

"Do I need to?"

She bit her tongue before she said anything else, but her hands clenched into fists. She told herself that antagonizing Rick was a sure-fire way to not get any information at all, so she tried a different tack. "Rick, this is my home, not just my business. I can't help but feel responsible, not just for my guests, but for my employees' sakes. I have a right to know what's going on in my own home, don't I?" The slightly wheedling tone she adopted was nothing like herself, but she didn't like Rick's official sheriff persona and she was willing to try anything to get him back to being Rick, her old friend since childhood. She had never tried to sweet-talk anyone, not even her father, in her entire life, and she felt like she was trying to fool herself and doing a terrible job of it.

Rick's mouth twitched; she wasn't fooling him, either. "Corrie," he said with great deliberation, "let me spell it out for you in no uncertain terms. I don't want you investigating this. I mean it."

"Why?" she said, angry at his condescending tone. "Are you afraid I'll mess it up or interfere?"

"You've already destroyed evidence by grabbing the bathroom door knob," he said and the split second the words left his lips, the look of dismay flashed in his eyes. NOW the old Rick she had always known made an appearance.

But the damage had already been done.

Corrie had vowed, years ago, on the day that seventeen-year-old Rick Sutton told her it would be better if they went back to being just friends, that she'd never, NEVER let him see her cry. Only once had she broken that vow and it was the day Billy died, but only because

Rick had tears in his eyes, too.

She wasn't going to break it again.

She turned and strode into her office, holding her tears locked in until she got up to her room and tried not to think about the fact that he hadn't even tried to call her back.

Chapter 11

The Myers insisted on Corrie taking a rest in her room while they took care of the office and the campground for the evening. She would have been content to do just that and brood, except that she got a surprise while the crime scene team was wrapping up business in the Landrys' RV. Dana called up to her, "Corrie! Jerry and Jackie are back!"

Quickly she threw cold water on her face and hurried down the stairs, relieved that her trusted friends were back, and worried that something had happened to them to make them return so quickly. Surely they wouldn't have heard of Marvin's murder by now? "Jackie!" she cried, shocked at the near-hysterical pitch in her voice.

Dana had been talking a million miles a minute as Jerry and Jackie got out of their Bronco, but now Jackie broke away and limped toward Corrie, hurrying as much as her recently replaced knee allowed, and enveloping her in a fierce, protective hug. "Oh, honey," she said, taking note of the glassiness in Corrie's eyes. "It'll be all right."

And with that, Corrie melted into Jackie's ample bosom and allowed herself to give way to tears.

A few minutes later, she, the Pages, and Dana were sitting around the table in the TV room and she filled Jerry and Jackie in on the recent events, starting when the Landrys had arrived. Corrie couldn't very well ask Dana to leave them alone—she'd been doing so much to help out. But Dana had a habit of embellishing the story, which only confused Corrie's telling it.

Jerry and Jackie listened, without interrupting, until Corrie was done. Then Jackie shook her head, her long, silver-gray ponytail swaying vigorously. "Something's not adding up," she said. "Don't you think?" she asked Jerry.

Jerry's forehead was wrinkled in confusion and impatience. "What is the sheriff doing about this?" he asked. Jerry had been an investigative reporter for twenty years before an ulcer forced him to retire and he and Jackie became a part of the Black Horse staff. Corrie knew he was upset because he never called Rick "the sheriff" unless he felt the law was moving too slowly or withholding important information.

"They're investigating," Corrie said, as soothingly as possible, although she wasn't exactly happy with Rick herself at the moment.

"They're doing nothing, I'll bet," Jerry said grimly. "Have they questioned anyone yet?"

"Me, unofficially," Corrie said. "They started to question Betty, but Rick decided it might be best for Betty to be seen at the hospital." She was dying to tell them about the mysterious gap in Betty's lingerie drawer. She shot a sideways glance at Dana who had gotten up to get the coffee pot and looked at Jackie. Jackie gave a barely perceptible nod; they would talk later.

Jerry was still muttering. "How can someone just walk up to an RV in broad daylight and shoot someone and then just walk away and nobody see anything? When did this happen?"

Dana came back and filled coffee cups around the table. "It had to have happened sometime this afternoon," she said. "I saw Marvin on his way to the bathrooms around twelve-thirty or so," she added.

"I thought you said he was heading to the office?" Corrie asked.

"I said I thought he was going to the bathrooms or to the office. But since you said you never saw him come in, then he must have been heading to the bathrooms."

Jackie frowned. "The bathrooms aren't open then. Marvin knows that. Are you sure you saw him?"

Dana laughed. "I caught a glimpse of him from behind as I was coming from our RV. Now that I think about it, he HAD to be going to the bathrooms, not the camp store. He was wearing an old bathrobe that looked like Joseph's 'coat of many colors'. It was hard to miss. He seemed in such a hurry I didn't call out to him."

"In a hurry?" Corrie echoed. Dana blushed, but she was still laughing.

"Well, you know that funny shuffle people get when they, uh, really have to go?"

Corrie nearly spit her coffee out and Jackie gasped. Jerry smiled. Corrie grinned.

"So that's how you figure he was heading to the bathrooms!"

"Well, if you think about it, where else would he be going? And anyway, only a cold-hearted person would refuse to let him in if it was an emergency!"

"That's true. Which reminds me," Corrie said. She glanced at the clock. "Has anyone seen Buster? He should have gone home hours ago and I haven't seen him since before lunchtime."

Jackie sat up straighter. "Wait a minute. Today's Friday, right? It's Myra's day off, so Buster would have been the one cleaning the bathrooms. If Marvin went in there at twelve-thirty, then Buster should have seen him!"

Corrie felt a prickle of unease crawl down her back. The fact that deputies had been all over the campground earlier and Buster hadn't appeared was unusual. She debated calling Rick. Part of her said it was the thing to do, but another part was still sore over his comment that she had muddied the investigation.

The door opened and Rick walked in. He paused when he saw Jerry and Jackie then gave them a half-smile. "I thought you folks were in Arizona this weekend," he said by way of greeting.

Jackie stood up and gave him a hug and Jerry shook his hand. "We haven't had a chance to tell everyone what happened with all the excitement going on. But I'm glad we came back!" Jackie said.

Rick gave Corrie a brief nod but she didn't acknowledge it, nor did she get up to get him coffee as she usually did. He went to the courtesy table and helped himself. Jackie's brows went up and she looked at Corrie, but Corrie just shrugged and shook her head. That was another explanation that would have to wait until later.

Rick came back to the table and took a seat. He looked at Dana. "Is Red busy right now?"

"He just went to do a sweep around the campground. He'll be back any minute."

"Buster with him?"

So Rick HAD noticed Buster's absence. Corrie could kick herself for not noticing earlier, but she still said nothing.

"We were just talking about that," Jackie offered. "It seems no one's seen Buster since he went to clean the bathrooms."

Rick set his coffee down, took out the small memo pad he carried in his shirt pocket, and flipped it open. "The bathrooms are closed from eleven to one, right?"

Corrie couldn't keep giving him the silent treatment; the situation was too serious for her to complicate matters with her hurt feelings. "Yes."

"And he hasn't been seen since?"

"Not by us," Corrie said. "The guests might have seen him around the campground, but it's not like him to miss the Friday dinner hour."

There were nods around the table; it wasn't like Buster to miss ANY meals, especially free ones. Corrie still hadn't shaken off the chill she'd felt earlier and then Dana spoke up. "Sheriff," she said. "I don't know if this is important or not, but as I mentioned earlier, I saw Marvin Landry heading to the bathrooms about twelve-thirty this afternoon... and he's been coming here long enough to know that they'd be closed at that time."

Rick was about to say something when the buzzer from the laundry room entrance sounded, Renfro let out his customary "woof" and Red walked in, looking irritated. "Corrie! You're gonna have to... oh, hello, Sheriff, I didn't know you'd come back."

"Time for asking questions, Red," Rick said, shooting Jerry a look as if he'd heard his complaint earlier. "I was hoping to catch the entire staff at once, but it seems Buster's missing in action."

"Buster's missing in action even when he's here!" Red snapped. He turned to Corrie. "Have you seen the condition of the bathrooms?"

"No, I haven't," Corrie said, half rising from her chair. "What's the matter?"

"They haven't been touched today! The waste basket in the men's room is overflowing. I got a complaint from one of the guests that he went in to take a shower and there was trash all over the floor and mud in one of the shower stalls."

"What time was this?" Rick slipped the question in adroitly. Red rubbed his chin and frowned.

"I think the fellow said he went in a little after one-thirty... you know, so that he could use the bathroom while it was just cleaned. He said it didn't look much better than his at home."

Corrie looked at Rick. His jaw was set and his eyes were grim. "So when was the last time anyone actually laid eyes on Buster?"

"I guess that would be me, around ten-thirty," she said. "He came in to get a cup of coffee and I told him to be ready to get on those bathrooms right at eleven. He didn't say a word, just nodded, got his coffee and left."

Rick nodded then turned to Dana. "And you saw Marvin Landry head into the bathroom at twelve-thirty?"

"Yes. Well, actually...." Dana bit her lip and wrinkled her nose. "Actually, if you put it that way, Sheriff... I never actually SAW Marvin go IN to the bathrooms. He was heading that way and I just assumed he went in."

"And you're sure it was Marvin?"

"Oh, yes, I was just telling everyone how he was wearing a bathrobe I'd call 'Joseph's coat"... you know, his coat of many colors? I saw him from behind as I was coming up to the patio, walking toward the bathroom, and... Oh!" Dana cried suddenly and both Corrie and Jackie jumped.

"What is it?" Corrie asked as Dana put a hand to her cheek.

"Well, isn't that odd? Think about it. Why would Marvin go to the campground bathrooms? They have an RV; why not use their own bathroom?"

Corrie looked at Rick and his expression never changed. "The RV bathroom might have been occupied," he said.

"True," Jackie put in. "You said yourself Marvin looked like he couldn't wait, Dana. Maybe Betty was in the RV bathroom and... well, in her condition, she couldn't have hurried, so Marvin...."

"How's Betty doing?" Corrie broke in to ask Rick as he was jotting things down in his memo pad. His eyes met hers briefly.

"She's all right. The shock was a little too much for her. They've given her a mild sedative. I'll have to ask her a few more questions, but they can wait for morning." He stood up. "I'll need a list of all your guests. And I need you and Red and Dana to tell me which ones you remember being in the campground from twelve-thirty onward."

"Have they determined the time of Marvin's death, Sheriff?" Jerry asked. Rick gave him a look Corrie knew too well.

"They're working on it," he said.

"Surely Betty would know, wouldn't she?" Dana put in. "I mean, after all, she was right there when it happened... well, not RIGHT there, but you know what I mean."

"Betty was too upset to think straight. And I'm sure the stress of having to answer too many questions all at once can't be good for her," Corrie said and she looked at Rick. A lot of speculation was going on and he wasn't ready to answer a lot of questions, but he needed their cooperation and if he played the heavy-handed "long arm of the law", he might cause some hurt feelings. He nodded, as if thanking her for cutting short any more conjecturing.

"We'll take Betty's statement in the morning, after she's had some time to recover. Right now, I want to know where everyone was and what they were doing from noon on." He turned to Corrie, and despite the fact that he was just doing his job, she did feel a tiny twinge of resentment. But she couldn't avoid answering him. It was Rick Sutton, the sheriff, asking, not Rick Sutton, her old friend.

"I didn't leave the office all day... too much paperwork to catch up on and customers coming and going. Plus, I had to get the enchiladas made for the Friday dinner." From the stiff way she answered, it was a wonder Rick didn't question her more closely. He nodded and made a notation in his memo pad then looked around the table. Apparently, questioning her was just a formality. Jackie spoke up.

"Well, Sheriff, we were somewhere between here and Phoenix. We stopped for gas in Las Cruces about five o'clock. I have a receipt in the Bronco with the time on it. And we got a bite to eat while we were there... what?" she asked Jerry as he took her arm and cleared his throat.

"Honey, I think we've established that we weren't here, but the Sheriff is too polite to interrupt," he said.

"That's all right, Jerry," Rick said. He almost smiled. "I'm glad to not have to drag it out of you." Again, he made a brief note. He turned to Red and Dana. "And you folks?"

"Well, let me think," Dana said, and it occurred to Corrie that Rick wouldn't have to worry about having to drag any information out of her. "After I saw Marvin—which, as I said, was about twelve-thirty—I came in to the laundry room, transferred my clothes from the washer to the dryer—it wasn't that much, really, just some bedding and towels... I did a huge load of our clothes when we got here because the washers at the campground we stayed at in Winslow were out of order for almost a week before we left...." Red cleared his throat sharply. Dana stopped, shrugged apologetically and wrapped up her narrative quickly. "And then I went into the store and helped Corrie with the dusting and restocking. That must have been a little bit before one o'clock."

"Until what time?" Rick asked.

Dana looked at Corrie. "About three, would you say?"

Corrie nodded. "We had a few customers for the store and a few more people check in, but at four I went to the kitchen to start putting the enchiladas together for the dinner tonight."

Rick nodded then looked at Red. Red looked sheepish. "Well, after doing a trash sweep, around one, I went back to our RV and fell asleep watching the game."

"That's the real national pastime, not baseball," Dana said, rolling her eyes. "You could've come helped us out."

"What time did you wake up?" Rick asked.

Red raised his brows. "I don't know... about four, maybe? I didn't look at the clock."

"Where are you parked?"

"At the end of the row by the office."

"Did you hear anything unusual this afternoon?"

"You mean like a gunshot?" Dana asked. She frowned. "Red wouldn't. Not if he had the TV on. He always has it on too loud."

Red shook his head. "Sorry, Sheriff. If I'd heard anything, I'd probably have attributed it to the TV."

Rick closed up his memo book and sighed. "I guess that's all for now. I'll have to ask you for that list of guests, Corrie."

It was a signal for everyone to leave. Jackie stood up with a grimace and that was when Corrie noticed that the cane, which the doctor had prescribed for Jackie to use while recovering from her knee replacement surgery a month earlier, was missing. She glanced at Jerry who rolled his eyes and shook his head. Jackie noticed.

"I know, I know," she said, waving off Corrie's concern. "The doctor said six weeks, minimum, using the cane, but it gets in my way more than it helps. Jerry's been giving me grief since we left the other night because I forgot to take it with me."

"'Forgot', my foot!" Jerry muttered. "She'll break her neck because she thinks that cane makes her look old! I told her she's going to mess up that knee even worse than it was before and it's gonna serve her right if she ends up in a wheelchair then!"

Corrie cringed, not because of the idea of her dear friend ending up in a wheelchair through her own impatience, but because she had caught a glimpse of Rick's face as the Myers immediately began sympathizing with both Jackie and Jerry about the situation and then launched into a general discussion about knee surgery, physical therapy and recovery time. She cleared her throat and fixed a stern glance on Jackie. "Well, I happen to agree with Jerry and I think it's best that you get yourself home and get some rest. I'm sure you're tired from all the traveling you've done today and you probably haven't done your therapy yet."

"You got that right," Jerry said. Jackie started to protest, but she must have seen the look of desperate pleading on Corrie's face and she understood.

"Well, we're all tired, especially Corrie," Jackie conceded. "It's been quite an exhausting day and I'm sure it's best if we all get some rest now." They filed out, Jerry and Jackie out the front door, Red and Dana through the laundry room, saying good-night to Corrie and Rick and each other as they went. Rick was cordial, but his curt responses indicated that his patience was wearing thin and Corrie felt a surge of irritation. Couldn't he see how this tragedy affected her and her friends... his friends, as well? She got up and started to walk past him on her way to the office desk and he caught her arm in a gentle grasp. "Don't be that way," he said quietly.

She resisted the urge to shake off his hand. "What way?"

"Look," he said, letting go of her arm and stepping back. "You have every right to be upset about what I said earlier, but don't shut me out. I need your help with this."

"Why? You're the professional," she said, folding her arms across her chest. She could be as stubborn as Rick, but the look in his eyes wasn't just from official police business. He was worried. As much as she wanted to stay mad at him, she allowed herself to thaw. "I'm sorry. I just... what do you need?" she asked, deciding that neither of them was in the mood for her to fumble through an apology.

He motioned her to the desk in the front office, where they would be far enough away from anyone walking in on their conversation or overhearing it from the laundry room or TV room doorways. She sat behind the desk and he pulled up another chair after dislodging a protesting Oliver from the seat. "Corrie, we both saw that gap in Betty's drawer. I did manage to ask her about that before I left the hospital. She said there should have been about twenty-five thousand dollars in cash in that drawer."

Corrie was stunned. She had expected that something of value had been taken from that place, but she couldn't comprehend someone stashing twenty-five thousand dollars in their underwear drawer. She drew a breath. "Where on earth did they...?"

"Dee Dee saw them at the bank yesterday morning, remember?" Rick said. "I called Wes Parsons, the bank manager, at home and he was none too happy to be disturbed at dinner, but I told him I needed information and it would be easier if he'd just give it to me without having to go through the hassle and time of getting a court order. From what he told me, the Landrys had been maintaining a joint bank account that was solely from Marvin's pension from the post office."

"I never knew Marvin had been a postal worker," Corrie said, then she snapped to attention. "What do you mean, 'had been' maintaining?" she asked.

"This is strictly between us, Corrie," he warned. "They closed that account out yesterday morning and Marvin wanted it all in cash."

Corrie shook her head numbly. "But how... why...?" She took a deep breath. "Where on earth did Marvin get such a big bank account?"

"According to Wes, that account used to be much, much bigger. He wouldn't tell me just how big, but he did say that it's been shrinking steadily over the last twenty-some years."

"They must have opened it shortly after they started coming here,"

Corrie murmured, still reeling from the news. "They would have been in their fifties, then. Maybe life savings? I mean, it couldn't have been from a pension? I thought they just retired a few years ago."

"Betty and Marvin both retired from the postal service. Marvin's been retired twice... from the postal service when he was barely thirty-nine," Rick said. "And from civil service about eight years ago, plus retirement from the reserves. Marvin actually had another account that was solely in his name, worth over fifty-thousand dollars and still growing. Betty's pension and Social Security has been paying the bills all these years. They were pretty well-off... a lot more than they seemed to be."

Corrie shook her head. "And what was they reason they closed out the account?"

"I don't know," Rick said. "Betty became agitated when I asked that question... wanted to know why the reason they closed it mattered. I'm not sure she'd be happy to hear that I know a lot more about their financial situation than they've let on."

Corrie stared at him. "Why are you telling me all this, Rick? I thought you wanted me out of the investigation."

"Because I don't know who murdered Marvin Landry... but Marvin must have known that person," Rick said flatly. "The way Marvin was laying on the floor... whoever it was that shot him was standing inside the RV, close enough to shoot Marvin point-blank. Marvin knew them and, to a certain extent, trusted them enough to let them get that close to him." His eyes drilled into Corrie's. "If that person knew Marvin that well, then there's a good chance that you know that person... or, at least, that that person knows you."

Corrie drew her breath in so sharply her chest hurt. "Rick, I have no idea who could have...."

"I'm not saying you do, Corrie," he said. "But there was no sign of someone searching for that money. The RV wasn't ransacked; whoever took it knew exactly where it was. So it only makes sense that whoever took it...."

"Had to know the Landrys pretty well," Corrie finished. "They knew they had the money and they knew where they'd hide it. They must have been in the RV before." She shivered.

"What is it? Are you all right?" Rick asked and Corrie stared at him bleakly.

"It's just that... whoever did it, had to know the Landrys. It might have even been a friend of theirs." Rick's lips tightened into a grim line.

"Or a relative."

Corrie felt her stomach do a somersault. "Walter Dodson? Betty's son?"

"You know I can't speculate, Corrie, but think about it...."

Corrie felt even queasier. Who better to know what was hidden in the drawer or that the Landrys had so much cash in their possession? And it was no secret that Walter Dodson didn't get along with Marvin.

She wondered where he was right now.

"Did you have any luck with fingerprints?" she said before Rick could finish the sentence. She didn't want to think about what might have happened to Betty. Or maybe that proved it was Walter. No matter how much he may have hated his step-father, he wouldn't hurt his own mother... would he?

Rick shook his head. "Not enough on the lock button to be able to make an identification match, but the crime lab will try. It was pretty badly smudged." Corrie winced.

"Rick, I'm sorry about that," she began but he cut her off.

"Forget it. There probably wasn't enough on there anyway and the only other ones on the bathroom door were the Landrys' and Walter Dodson's. The lab's still working on a few other unidentified ones in the living room." He shook his head in frustration. "Besides, who expects a bathroom door to have a lock on the OUTside? That's one thing Betty's going to have to explain."

Corrie nodded. "What about the gun?"

Rick's frustration seemed to multiply. "That's another thing. So far no one's admitted to hearing a gun shot anytime this afternoon."

"You've interviewed my guests?"

"Most of them. The ones that were here during the day, which isn't that many. I think all your biker guests will be in town until late tonight. There's a concert and party going on until two in the morning."

"And I think all of them left well before eleven o'clock. Registration for the rally started at ten this morning and... what?" she broke off as Rick's steady gaze drilled into her face.

"Not all of them did." He raised a brow. Corrie didn't bother to hide her exasperation.

"If you mean J.D., just come right out and say so. Surely you don't consider him a serious suspect," she said with a sigh.

"I'm not crossing him off my list just yet. Twenty-five thousand dollars is a good enough motive. So why not him?"

"Well, for one thing, we've already said whoever did it had to have known the Landrys, since they knew exactly where to find the money. He's never met them."

"Are you sure?" Rick pressed.

"I guess I couldn't swear to it," Corrie admitted. "But he doesn't seem to be the type of person they'd normally socialize with, right?"

"True," Rick nodded, and Corrie felt her temper flare. It was easy to forget Rick's well-bred background, which contrasted sharply with his chosen line of work, but sometimes his mother's snob side came to the surface. She bit back a sharp comment.

"Besides, he sat with you at the same table having dinner. That's a little too bold if you ask me," she said.

"Whoever did it had to be pretty brazen," Rick pointed out. "They committed murder and robbery in broad daylight! Sitting down and having a plate of food and a few laughs with the sheriff might be the kind of thing they'd do for a kick after doing something like that."

Corrie refrained from pointing out that neither J.D. nor Rick had appeared to be in a particularly humorous mood at dinner. "What about Buster?" she asked. Rick frowned.

"That's what's really worrying me. Did you notice if his car was gone?"

"I never looked." She got up and peered out the window. Buster usually parked his car on the far side of the maintenance shed. She could make out the gleam of the headlights under the safety lights and realized with a start how late it actually was. "Looks like it's still there."

"I'm going to go check it out," Rick said, getting up. Corrie spun toward him.

"By yourself?" she asked, surprised at how shrill her voice came out.

Rick gave her an amused look. "Corrie, I am a law enforcement officer, you know." He cocked his head to one side. "If it'll make you feel better, you can watch from the window, but you're not coming with me. Got that? If there's a problem..." He rested his hand on the butt of his gun, holstered on his side, and then he pointed at the phone behind the desk. "You can call for help if you think I need it."

Corrie nodded. Rick went out the door and headed toward Buster's car. As soon as the door clicked shut behind him, Corrie grabbed the cordless phone off the charger and held it, wondering if she should turn it on and have it ready just in case... Rick was almost to Buster's car, he had his flashlight out, was shining it on the car, in the windows, Corrie leaned closer against the office window, straining to see....

"What's going on?"

She half-gasped, half-shrieked and spun around, realizing that she was trapped in the space behind the desk.

J.D. Wilder was staring at her, his face half-amused, half-puzzled.

Chapter 12

Corrie's heart was pounding so hard she was certain J.D. could hear it. She clutched the phone and willed herself to calm down. J.D. gave her a quizzical smile.

"Were you going to make a call or hit me with that?"

"How'd you get in without me hearing you?" she managed to gasp and, for a split second, wondered if Rick was all right and how soon he was coming back. She didn't dare take her eyes off J.D. to check.

J.D. frowned. "I just came in through the laundry room. Should you have heard me come in?"

The security buzzer hadn't gone off. It was supposed to go off every time the door opened. Despite the nerve storm that gripped her at J.D. having walked in without her hearing or seeing him, it occurred to Corrie that she had forgotten to lock up after everyone else had left earlier, but she had no time to kick herself mentally. "It's after eight and the store is closed. Did you need something?" she blurted.

"I think you need to take a deep breath and calm down," he said, holding his hands up and taking a step back. "I just got back and saw the yellow police tape around the Landrys' RV and wondered what was going on. Did something happen to Mrs. Landry? Is she all right?"

"She's fine, I guess," Corrie said, still watching J.D. warily and not loosening her grip on the phone. "The doctors had to give her a sedative, but they say she'll be all right eventually...."

"Whoa," J.D. said, interrupting her. "Doctors? Sedative? You're talking like she's in the hospital." His brows rose in a quizzical look.

"Well, after a shock like that, Rick thought.... Oh, my gosh, J.D.," Corrie breathed as he frowned. "You don't know, do you?"

J.D. shook his head. "Fill me in. What happened to the Landrys?"

Corrie finally set the phone down and rubbed her forehead. "I guess there's no way to say it but straight out. Marvin was murdered earlier today. Someone walked into their RV and shot him, locked Betty in the bathroom, and robbed them."

J.D. let out a low whistle. "What time did all this happen?"

Before Corrie could answer, the front door opened and Rick strode in. His eyes narrowed at the sight of J.D. standing in the office, but he gave him a curt nod before he turned to Corrie. "I need to see you for a minute." He gave J.D. a sharp glance. "Don't go away, Wilder. I'll need to ask you a few questions."

Corrie tried not to think about the look of apprehension that crossed J.D.'s features before he gave a carefully careless shrug and sauntered toward the TV room. She was immensely relieved that Rick was back, but her relief was short-lived. "Did you find out anything about Buster?" she asked, keeping her voice low.

Rick shook his head. "Not really. There seems to be a bundle of clothing in the back seat of his car—his work clothes. Any reason why he would change clothes in the middle of the day?"

Corrie frowned. "Not that I know of. I mean, maybe if he'd cleaned the bathrooms and spilled bleach or ammonia on his clothes or gotten them wet, but since it doesn't look like he did that...."

Rick nodded, then jerked his head toward the TV room. "When did he come in?" he said quietly. Corrie glanced at the clock.

"Just a couple of minutes ago."

"You want to tell me why you looked so relieved when I walked in?"

Corrie hesitated. It was possible she was overreacting, but then she remembered about the laundry room door. "Rick, I turned around and he was there all of a sudden. When the office and store close at eight, I'm supposed to lock all the doors that lead in here, but with all that's been going on, I forgot. He said he came through the laundry room door but the security buzzer never went off. Unless the door's propped open...."

Rick's brows rose. "Propped open?" Corrie nodded. "By whom?" Rick asked.

"That's what I mean. I mean, he couldn't have done it, because he would have set off the buzzer when he first opened it. But someone must have left it open on purpose. That door shuts automatically as a safety precaution."

Rick rubbed his chin. "What were you talking to him about when I came in?"

"The Landrys," Corrie said. "He was concerned because...." She stopped, her eyes widening as Rick's narrowed. "He knows them!" she blurted out.

Rick's jaw tightened and he looked toward the family room. "I think I'd better ask Mr. J.D. Wilder some questions," he said.

J.D. sat in a wooden straight-back chair at one of the smaller tables in the family room and he looked up from the magazine he was pretending to read as Corrie and the sheriff entered. He forced an expression that he hoped was neither too calm nor too wary. "What can I do for you, Sheriff?" he asked.

The sheriff didn't beat around the bush. "How do you happen to know the Landrys?" he asked, point-blank.

J.D. set the magazine down and sighed. "What a surprise... I'm a suspect," he said. He glanced at Corrie, but she avoided his eyes.

The sheriff waited, not exactly tapping his foot, but his impatience was quite evident. J.D. reined in his sarcasm. "I just met them this morning. I was passing by on my way to the bathrooms and the old man called me over."

"What time was this?" the sheriff asked.

J.D. shrugged. "Maybe nine-thirty. The red-haired dame with the pug, Mrs. Westlake, was out for her morning constitutional, and I made an excuse not to have to stand and talk with her. I grabbed my towel and headed to the washroom." He noticed Corrie bit back a smile and it gave him a lift.

"Why did Marvin Landry call you over?" The sheriff's sharp voice intruded on his momentary feeling of relief. He grimaced inwardly. This wasn't going to sound good.

"He was trying to move some of the furniture around in the RV... said he wanted to make room for his wife to be able to maneuver her wheelchair around in there. He had me move that TV stand twice before it ended up right back where it was to begin with, then he had me carry a couple boxes to the bedroom. His wife watched me the whole time, like she was...." He stopped, then continued with a grim smile. "Like she was afraid I was going to steal something."

The sheriff's face was an impassive mask. J.D. glanced at Corrie. She seemed stricken by what he'd said. The sheriff's words were an indication that he didn't believe for one minute that J.D. hadn't robbed the Landrys. "What reason would Betty have for looking at you that way?" he asked.

"Hell if I know," J.D. said, recalling how the old lady's watchful gaze had given him the creeps. If anything, he was surprised that she hadn't told the sheriff about him being in the RV that morning and that the entire sheriff's department hadn't been out looking for him. "Her husband thanked me for helping him, cussed out some guy named Walter who seemed to be missing-in-action from the old man's point of view, and tried to give me some money. I told him, no, thanks, it was my pleasure, but he kept insisting. Finally he stuffed a twenty into my front jeans pocket." Both Corrie and the sheriff looked surprised and J.D. felt his face redden. "Told me to have a beer on him at the rally. I just said thank you and didn't argue anymore."

"You didn't see a middle-aged man who's traveling with the Landrys?"

"I presume that's the Walter that Old Man Landry was ticked off with. Thinning hair and miserable face. Saw him going for a walk earlier this morning, but other than that, not at all."

The sheriff said, "And the last time you saw the Landrys was when you helped Marvin move stuff in the RV?"

"Absolutely."

"Can you tell me what you did the rest of the afternoon, until the dinner hour tonight?"

"Other than avoiding Madame Westlake?" J.D. grimaced. "I kicked around my campsite, pretty much."

"Anyone see you?"

"Besides Madame Westlake?" He shrugged. "I don't know. I didn't see Corrie around, but I did see her helper friend there."

"Buster?"

"No, not him. The lady with the frosted blond hair. She's just as nosy as Mrs. Westlake, but a lot more refined."

The sheriff's demeanor grew grimmer. "When was the last time you saw Buster?" he asked.

"The big bearded guy?" J.D. shrugged. "I saw him emptying trash this morning. He kept eyeing me like he wasn't sure he liked me much. I guess he's still sore about me coming in at night without a reservation. Other than that I haven't seen him at all." He noticed the look in the sheriff's eyes. "Why?" he asked sharply.

"He hasn't been seen around the campground most of the day," Rick said and J.D. was surprised that he shared that much information with him. "I was just wondering if you knew where he might be."

J.D. shook his head. "Not a clue. After dinner, I went into town to see what was going on at the rally, but I didn't stay... only long enough to have a beer or two. Then I stopped in Ruidoso to pick up a few things, but the lines at the checkout stands were crazy. I just got back about fifteen minutes ago," he finished. Sutton nodded.

"So." The sheriff's manner became brisk. "If we were to find your fingerprints in the Landrys' RV, we have a perfectly reasonable explanation as to why they're there."

J.D. tried to remain relaxed. "That almost sounds like a suggestion that I get an attorney, Sheriff," he said.

"That's your right, Mr. Wilder," the sheriff said smoothly. "But because your prints will be at the scene of the crime, I will have to ask you not to leave town and tell you we will have to search your possessions."

"I've got a reservation through Sunday night," J.D. said, his heart thudding even as he managed to appear cool and unconcerned. "And I've got nothing to hide, Sheriff." He cocked his head on one side and gave what he hoped was an innocent look of inquiry. "Mind if I ask what it is you're looking for?"

He hadn't expected an answer—not a straight one, anyway—and Corrie looked just as surprised as he felt when the sheriff said, "The gun used to kill Marvin Landry and twenty-five thousand dollars."

Crash! J.D. had leaned over in his chair to replace the magazine on the wall rack behind him and when he heard the amount that was missing, he started and the chair tipped over backward. Corrie gasped, but the sheriff made no move to help J.D., just raised an eyebrow.

"That seemed to surprise you," he commented as J.D. got to his feet.

"Well, yeah," J.D. said, his face burning with embarrassment... and a sudden onslaught of nerves. "I mean, who carries that kind of cash with them?"

"Apparently, the Landrys do," the sheriff said. "There will be a couple of armed deputies patrolling the campground tonight and they'll begin a search in the morning. I suggest you turn in for the night, Mr. Wilder."

"Rick!" Corrie hissed at him and he gave her a ferocious glare. J.D. got the message loud and clear.

"I've got nothing to hide," he said again. He gave them a brief smile. "I suppose I'd best turn in. Tomorrow promises to be a busy day."

"Were you coming into the store to get something?" Corrie asked. "I mean, we are closed, but if you needed something...." J.D. welcomed the sound of her voice.

"No, not really," he said. He looked at her and smiled and it made her blush. "I was just stopping in to say good night."

"Good night," the sheriff said before Corrie could respond and J.D. took the hint. He left.

Chapter 13

Rick and Corrie were silent as J.D. headed out the side door back to his campsite, then Rick went to the laundry room door and, using his handkerchief, picked up the pen that had been used as a door stop. He showed it to Corrie. "Recognize it?"

She shook her head. "Not unless you count the two dozen or so I've got in my desk drawer and on the counter. Someone could have just dropped it."

"Sure. And it conveniently fell right where it would keep the laundry room door from buzzing when it opened. I used to believe in coincidences, too, Corrie. But I've been a cop too long."

"And when do you think J.D. would have had the opportunity to prop the door open without us seeing him?"

"I didn't say J.D. did it."

Corrie frowned but before she could say anything, she heard the sound of motorcycles entering the campsite. She glanced at the clock. "It's early for them to be getting back. They must have heard about the murder."

"I'm sure it's the biggest news in town," Rick said. In silence, they watched the parade of motorcycles rumble into the campsite, not loudly but subdued, as if out of respect for Marvin. Suddenly Rick stiffened and motioned to Corrie to join him at the window. "Look over there!" he said.

Corrie looked and saw, to her surprise, a Harley cruise right up to Buster's old Pontiac. Two riders were astride the bike and, as it glided to a stop, the one on the back of the bike, a burly man, dismounted. Neither wore a helmet; that much, and the fact that the driver had long blonde hair, Corrie could make out in the darkness, but the faces were in shadows. Then she saw the two riders move in for a long kiss.

Rick had already slipped out the door and it only took Corrie a second to decide to join him. He didn't try to stop her. Silently they crept up to the maintenance shed and stood in the shadows. The two motorcyclists were engaged in quiet conversation spiked with occasional laughs, then the driver gave the man standing beside her another kiss and she turned the bike and roared away. The man waved and then pulled off his do-rag and Rick stepped forward.

"What the hell do you think you're doing, Buster?"

The effect was extraordinarily comical. Buster jumped and let out a squeak and nearly fell down. Corrie emerged from the shadow of the maintenance shed and joined Rick as he strode toward her truant maintenance worker.

"Sheriff! Corrie! I... I ... what's up?" Buster said, forcing a weak smile. It was hard for Corrie not to stare. Buster in black leather biker gear was something to see. He looked as if he were ready for Halloween.

Rick said nothing, but Corrie stepped forward. "What's up?" she repeated. "Right now, I'm so mad at you I can hardly remember why I was so worried about you earlier! You've got a lot of explaining to do!"

"I'm sorry, Corrie," Buster muttered, shooting nervous glances at Rick, who still maintained an ominous silence. "I can explain the whole thing, really. You see, I...." He looked at Rick again and cleared his throat. "Uh... does HE have to hear this?"

"Yes," Corrie and Rick both responded, which made Buster jump again.

"Okay, okay! Sheesh!" Buster muttered. He shot a glare at Rick and straightened up. "I had a date."

"Since eleven o'clock this morning?" Corrie said. She folded her arms across her chest and looked at Rick, who said nothing but shrugged.

Buster let his breath out in a sigh, looking thoroughly defeated. "Okay, so I was stupid to think you wouldn't have noticed. But yeah. I've been at the rally all afternoon. Noreen said she'd pick me up at the front gate at eleven and bring me back. That was her, she just dropped me off," he added, then regained a little of his bravado. "We didn't do anything wrong, except for me ditching work and I don't see why the sheriff has to be involved in all this!"

"Buster, I couldn't care less what you've been doing for the last ten hours," Rick said, putting his hands on his hips and causing Buster to take an alarmed step back again. "But your being gone without an explanation during a murder investigation has made you both a prime suspect and a feared possible second victim. Quite frankly, I think the majority vote was that you might have been in the wrong place at the wrong time and ended up dead somewhere, but now, you'd better have a damn good alibi and reliable witnesses that actually saw you at the rally this afternoon!"

"Whoa, back up, back up. 'Murder investigation'? What murder investigation? Who was murdered? And why am I a suspect?" Buster's eyes had widened and his face had turned a sickly shade of pale green. His glance darted back and forth between Corrie and Rick.

Corrie looked at Rick. "Marvin Landry was found murdered this afternoon, Buster," she said quietly. "It looked like someone tried to rob him and...." Buster's mouth had dropped open and his eyes bulged.

"No way. You're kidding me! When did this happen?"

"Sometime between eleven a.m. and one p.m. today," Rick said and Corrie stared at him. She hadn't heard that the time of Marvin's death had been definitely established. Though she was itching to throw questions at Rick herself, she bit her tongue and kept quiet. She merely gave Buster a look as if she had known this information all along.

"Well, I met up with Noreen at the campground gate right at eleven on the nose," Buster said, visibly relieved. "So I couldn't have done anything to Marvin, even if I wanted to! And why would I have wanted to kill him? Why would anyone?"

"Twenty-five thousand very good reasons are missing from the Landrys' RV," Rick said, his face impassive despite Buster's increasing shock.

"Twenty-five thousand... you mean, dollars? You're kidding me! Where the heck did they get that kind of money?"

"That's not important, Buster. What's important is that the money is gone and Marvin is dead."

"Man, twenty-five grand," Buster said. He shook his head and let out a low whistle. "I guess I shouldn't be surprised. I thought the old guy was a tightwad, and that's probably where he got his money from!"

"Wait a minute," Corrie said holding up a hand. "What do you mean, Marvin was a tightwad? How do you know?"

Buster blushed and shuffled his feet. "Well, uh, you know, Corrie, sometimes the old man—Mr. Landry—would ask me to help him out around the RV," he mumbled. "You know, hauling out trash, helping with the hook-up, moving stuff around. And he'd sometimes, you know, uh, give me a little something...."

Corrie could tell from the way Buster shrank back that her eyes were blazing like machine guns. "Buster, you KNOW it's against our policy to receive tips from the guests!" She shook her head. "And you have the nerve to call the poor man a tightwad?"

"Hey, come on, if he had twenty-five grand just sitting around his RV, he could have been a little more generous," Buster protested. "I didn't shake him down for the money, Corrie, honest! He'd offer and I'd take it. I've been doing it for years and no one's ever had a word to say about it. No harm done."

Before Corrie could say anything else, Rick spoke up. "Just how much did he give you, Buster?" There was a curious tone in his voice, one Corrie couldn't make out, and she wondered what Rick was really wanting to find out.

Buster looked uneasy. "Not much. Five bucks at the most. I know it seems like a lot for taking his trash to the dumpster or moving furniture around the RV...."

"You went into the RV to help him out?"

"Not this time! I swear it, Sheriff! He gave me five bucks to help him set up that wheelchair ramp when they first got here, but I never went inside!"

Buster looked like he was on the verge of a heart attack and Corrie almost felt sorry for him. "And that's it?"

"That's it! I promise! He'd call me over and say, 'Son'... he always called me 'son' and I never liked that, but what the heck, I'd try to be nice... he'd say, 'son', give me a hand over here, would you?' And I'd go help him with whatever he needed help with, then he'd pull a few bucks out of his pocket and tell me to go buy myself a beer." Buster took a deep shaky breath. "I promise you, Corrie, I'd swear on a stack of Bibles, I never did anything to those old folks and I sure as heck didn't try to rob them. You've gotta believe me!"

She did; Buster was a bundle of nerves and there was no way he'd have kept his cool long enough to pull off the caper. She looked at Rick. His face wasn't giving anything away. "I don't suppose you happen to own a gun, do you, Buster?"

Buster's answer surprised Corrie. "Yeah, I do."

"You own a gun?" Corrie couldn't hide her incredulity. The way Buster was acting, he'd probably end up shooting himself if he tried to use a gun. Rick pressed on.

"What kind and where is it?"

"Am I gonna need a lawyer?" Buster asked plaintively. He looked terrified and Corrie felt sorry for him. She gave Rick a nudge and he seemed to back off.

"Only if it's the gun that killed Marvin," Rick said. "Where is it?"

"Here. Right here, in my car," Buster said, almost too eagerly, then looked stricken as Rick stepped between him and the car door.

"You have a permit for this gun, right, Buster?" Rick asked and Buster's face once again took on a look of panic. Rick sighed. "Never mind. Forget I asked that. Let's just take a look at it."

Corrie stood back, glancing over her shoulder toward the campground office as Rick checked out Buster's firearm. She thought she saw a shadow move from the patio toward the shed, but then again it might have been her imagination. She turned around as Rick shut the door on Buster's Pontiac. He was shaking his head and Buster was stammering, "I swear, Rick—Sheriff—you gotta believe me! It was there! I never use it! I swear I've never used it and I wouldn't do anything to anybody!"

"What's wrong?" Corrie said, giving her full attention to the two men. Buster seemed to be on the verge of tears. She couldn't decipher Rick's expression; in fact, he looked like he wasn't sure how he felt, either.

"The gun's not there," Rick answered her. She stared at him. Buster burst into speech again.

"Rick—Sheriff—I'm serious! I haven't touched that gun since I put it in the car and I never...."

"When did you put it in the car, Buster?" Rick broke in as Buster threatened to hyperventilate.

"I don't know... three months ago? Maybe four? I can't remember... I just know I'd never...."

"Buster, you need to calm down," Corrie said, trying to sound more soothing than snappish. "Now take a deep breath and think. If you didn't hurt anyone, you've got no reason to be nervous. You're making the sheriff think you did something wrong by acting like this."

Buster gulped and took a deep breath and let it out slowly. "Okay," he said though his voice wasn't quite steady. "Okay. It was just after Christmas. I remember now. My uncle gave it to me. He said it was my dad's and that he'd found it with my dad's things, you know, after my dad died, and he—my uncle—thought I'd want to have it."

"So you're telling me you haven't touched that gun since December?" Rick said, his skepticism unmistakable. Buster swallowed hard.

"Not really touched it, you know, not like shooting it or anything. I don't even know if it was loaded. I mean, he gave me a box of bullets for it, but I don't know if there were any in it. I never checked... I wouldn't even know how! I... I don't know nothing about guns, but I didn't want to tell my uncle that. I just... my uncle gave it to me and I stuck it in that space under the seat and that was it."

"You ever show it to anybody?" Rick asked. "Told anyone about it?" When Buster didn't answer, he went on, "Did you know carrying a concealed weapon without a permit is against the law, Buster?"

"I don't think Buster thought about it as a weapon," Corrie said, ignoring the glare Rick gave her. Buster jumped on the suggestion gratefully.

"That's it! That's right, Corrie! I didn't think of it as a gun, Rick—Sheriff. I thought of it as just one of my dad's things... you know, a memento...."

"Right," Rick said shortly. "So, DID you ever show it to anyone or tell anyone about it?" Rick repeated.

Buster swallowed hard. "Uh," he said. "Well...."

"Good God, Buster, let's not go through this again!" Corrie snapped. "Just answer the question honestly!" Buster straightened up, his eyes looking like those of a man facing a firing squad.

"Okay," he sighed. "Yeah, Sheriff, I did tell someone about it... Marvin Landry. He said he was looking to buy a handgun and wanted to know if I knew anyone who'd be willing to sell him one cheap. He offered me a hundred bucks for it."

Chapter 14

Both Corrie and Rick stared at the burly man, and Corrie's heart sank. She had no idea how Rick felt. His voice was just as stony as ever. "You told Marvin Landry you had a gun and he offered to buy it from you for one hundred dollars. Is that correct?"

"I'm gonna need a lawyer, aren't I?" Buster whispered. Rick sighed irritably.

"Buster, listen to me and answer me straight. What time did this happen?"

"I dunno. I'm not sure. Sometime this morning. I was doing a trash sweep."

"Did you happen to see Walter Dodson around?" Corrie asked suddenly. Rick cleared his throat, a subtle warning, but Corrie chose to ignore it.

"Who's that?" Buster asked.

"Betty's son. Mid-forties, thinning hair, bad attitude." She could feel Rick's irritation at her like heat from a fire, but she was tired of him dragging things on. This policy of his to suspect everyone, even though he had a prime candidate for Marvin's murder, was wearing on her nerves.

"Oh, that guy. I didn't know he was Betty's son... didn't know she even had kids. Yeah, I've seen him around. He was in the RV when the old man asked me to help him set up the ramp. I wonder why that Walter guy didn't do it... I mean, if he's Betty's son and all...."

Rick took control before Corrie could say another word. "Was that when Marvin asked you about buying a gun?"

"Huh? No! Not then. That was yesterday I set up the ramp, you know, right after the Landrys got here. It was early this morning when Marvin asked me about the gun."

"How early?"

Buster's forehead wrinkled as he strained to remember. "Right about seven-thirty. I remember 'cause I was listening for the 'Question of the Day' on the morning radio show... the prize was a pair of tickets to the concert tonight and I was hoping I'd win, you know, so I could take Noreen, but before they asked the question Mr. Landry called me over. I didn't expect the old folks to be up so early. Marvin kind of waved me over and we talked on the front steps of the RV. He asked me to come in, but I didn't... I had some mud on my shoes from the trash sweep. I know," he added hastily when Corrie let out an exasperated sigh. "I know, that was too early, but since I was supposed to meet Noreen at eleven, I wanted to get done early." He turned back to Rick. "Marvin, he wasn't too happy about that... about me not coming inside. It was like he didn't want to be heard."

"DID you get the gun to show Marvin Landry?" Rick asked. Buster shook his head.

"No. He said we'd settle up later. Said he was busy right then. I don't know what he was doing, but he didn't look busy. I just remember thinking it would have been nice to have that hundred bucks today when Noreen and I went out since I missed my chance to win the concert tickets."

"Did you tell Marvin where you kept the gun?" Rick asked.

Buster bit his lip. "Yeah, I told him I kept it in my car."

"Buster," Rick said, his voice quieter. "When you had this conversation with Marvin Landry, was anyone else around?"

Rick's near-whisper had an effect on Buster. He lowered his voice as well and, though she was only an arm's length away from the two men, Corrie had to strain to hear him. "I was standing at the bottom of the steps, Marvin at the top... but his wife, Betty, was in her wheelchair, in the hallway, behind him... I'm not sure he knew she was there." His face contorted. "But we weren't exactly whispering, Sheriff, even if Marvin was trying to keep his voice down. You know how loud he could be. Anybody could have heard us."

"Well?" Corrie asked.

She had, at Rick's request, gotten Jerry to drive Buster home since Rick wanted Buster's car dusted for prints, but he hadn't said much more to her besides that. She stood at the main door of the office and tried not to yawn. It was nearly midnight and it had been a tiring day, but Rick seemed in no hurry to leave.

He chewed his lip, as if he debating whether he should say something or not. Corrie was in no mood to play guessing games. "Will you just spit it out so I can get to bed?" she sighed. Rick shook his head.

"I don't like this, Corrie. Part of me says I should take Buster in for questioning—it's only logical—but my gut tells me someone else got hold of that gun and killed Marvin."

"If," Corrie added, "Buster's gun WAS the one used to kill Marvin." Rick scowled at her.

"Don't you think it's a mighty strange coincidence that Buster's gun, which none of us ever knew existed, suddenly disappears right after Marvin is shot to death?"

"Well, of course," she admitted. "But last time I checked, you're still innocent until proven guilty."

"I'm not talking about Buster being guilty," Rick countered. "I'm talking about that gun and where it is now." He paused. "And who else might have known about it."

Corrie leaned against the door jamb and rubbed her eyes, but Rick didn't take the hint. "It could have been a lot of people who heard them talking about it," she murmured.

Rick said nothing for a long moment. "There is actually one person more likely to have heard them than anyone else."

"Who?"

Rick jerked his head in the direction of the campground. "Who's got the site directly across from the Landrys' RV?"

Corrie came fully awake. "J.D.?" she said incredulously. Rick grunted.

"I know, you think I'm being paranoid, that I just don't like him and I've got something against the guy, that I'm not being fair. Fine. Admitted. Now let's be realistic. Marvin wasn't a quiet man, but he didn't have a bullhorn. The most logical person to have overheard Buster's conversation with the Landrys about the gun was J.D. He's already admitted to having been in the Landrys' RV, so his fingerprints are accounted for. And there's one more thing." He paused.

"I'm sure there's more than one thing," Corrie said, but she felt uneasy. Rick was making too many points that couldn't be ignored. "What is it?"

"He said Marvin gave him twenty dollars to help him move stuff in the RV. Buster just told us that Marvin never gave him more than five."

"So you think...."

"I don't know," Rick interrupted. "It's just something weird that doesn't make any sense and it's bothering me."

"Aren't you overlooking the obvious?" Corrie said wearily. "Walter Dodson could have overheard the whole conversation about Buster's gun. He could have been in the RV while Marvin was talking to Buster this morning, or else somewhere close by. He's still the most likely suspect. I don't understand why you insist on trying to pin this on someone who probably has absolutely nothing at all to do with this!"

"I'm not overlooking anything," Rick snapped, his eyes drilling into hers. "And whether you mind my saying so or not, I'm not the one with tunnel vision here, Corrie. Anything out of the ordinary, no matter how trivial it seems or to whom it happens, deserves my attention, regardless of my personal feelings."

Corrie said nothing. Normally, she'd have taken umbrage at Rick's accusation that she was biased, but she was too tired to continue arguing. And anyway, she couldn't see how the difference in what Marvin gave Buster and what he gave J.D. had anything to do with making J.D. more likely to murder and rob Marvin Landry. Rick broke into her thoughts.

"Look, I'd better get going go. It's been a long day for both of us. Are you going to be all right?"

"Sure," she said with a shrug. "You've got armed deputies around, right? I'll lock up everything tight...."

"I'm going to walk through the building and check your locks."
She stared at him. "Why?"

"I thought it'd make you feel better," he said, but he avoided her
eyes and her temper flared. She couldn't stand it when he wouldn't
be straight with her, no matter how trivial he thought it might be.

"I feel just fine, thank you very much. What's the real reason?" she
snapped.

He sighed and pointed to the pen that had propped the laundry
room door open. It was still lying on the top of Corrie's desk. "All
right, it'll make ME feel better, too," he said. "And while I doubt I'll
get anything from it, I'm taking that pen and seeing if there are any
prints on it."

Corrie had forgotten about the laundry room door. She had
planned to lock it right after Rick had gotten done questioning J.D.
earlier but the return of her motorcycle guests and Buster had
distracted her and she'd never gotten around to doing it. She
shivered. If she could forget something like that after the scare J.D.
had given her and everything else that had been going on all day, it
probably wasn't a bad idea to have Rick go through the building. "All
right, I guess I'll feel better knowing the place is secure." She went
around the desk. "Come on, Renfro, it's bedtime, old boy."

The old black dog blinked sleepily and yawned, his tail thumping
as he stood and staggered up the stairs to the living quarters, still
half-asleep. He never gave Rick a glance as he passed. None of the
excitement of the day seemed to have registered with him at all. Rick
chuckled. Corrie turned to him in surprise, but Rick had managed to
chuckle without smiling.

"Yes," he said. "I know you've got a state-of-the-art security
system, but I'll feel better once we catch Marvin's killer so Renfro
won't lose anymore sleep!"

Chapter 15

Jackie let herself in the front office at exactly six o'clock the next morning while Corrie was pouring her first cup of coffee. "You didn't have to come in today. You were supposed to have the weekend off," Corrie said.

Jackie smiled and locked the door behind her, then went to hang her jacket in the storage room under the stairs to the second floor. "Saturday's always a busy day. No sense in letting you deal with everything on your own while I just sit around... which I hate to do anyway. Besides," she added, raising her brows at Corrie, "we have some things to discuss."

Dana and Red weren't scheduled to come in to work until seven when the office and store opened, and Corrie was glad to have some private time with her old friend. "Dana's been a big help. Thanks for recommending her," Corrie said, then smiled wistfully. "But of course, she's not you."

Jackie accepted the compliment and a cup of coffee with a wink. She slid into a chair behind the counter, resting her leg on the footstool Corrie had provided for her after her surgery when she insisted on returning to work after two weeks. Corrie pulled up a high stool, noting that Jackie had, once again, neglected to use her cane, but she didn't feel like haranguing her over it at the moment, since there were a lot of other things she wanted to talk about. They could see all three doors that led into the office as well as the front walkway through the window, but they still kept their voices low. "So tell me what's going on," Jackie said.

Corrie almost choked on her coffee. "You're kidding, right? You know what's going on. There's been a murder here!"

"I don't mean that." Jackie said. "I mean, what's going on with you and Rick and your mystery guest. Dana told me, that's how I know," Jackie said, holding up a hand bejeweled with silver and turquoise. Corrie stared at her, open-mouthed, and then laughed.

"Well, tell me what Dana told you and I'll tell you what's true," she said.

"Just that this mystery man—a very attractive mystery man— shows up in the middle of the night," Jackie said. "And our sheriff seems to be none to happy about it. Dana says Rick acts like it's just natural, small-town suspicion of strangers, but she believes it's pure jealousy, plain and simple."

"And why would Rick be jealous of J.D.?" Corrie asked, keeping her voice neutral. "It's not like he and I have... anything going on. We're just friends, remember?"

Of course Jackie remembered. It was her shoulder that Corrie had cried on fifteen years earlier. Corrie's mother had been dead five years and Jackie had been a mother and best friend to Corrie during her teen years. She hadn't said "I told you so", she hadn't tried to make Corrie feel better by bashing Rick and pointing out that Corrie deserved far better and, in the long run, she would be grateful that things had ended when they did. For one thing, Jackie wouldn't lie— she'd been quite fond of Rick, and still was. And Corrie was sure that Jackie had been just as heartbroken and bewildered as she had been by the turn of events... even though, deep down, Corrie, Jackie, and even Billy, had always known that someday Rick would have to make a choice that was very difficult and painful—for both him and Corrie.

Jackie sipped her coffee and Corrie dragged her mind back to the present. "Oh, it's the way men are, honey," Jackie said. "As long as there's no threat, they're happy to just let things be, but the minute they think there's competition...."

"Right," Corrie interrupted. Jackie smiled and shook her head, but dropped the subject. Corrie went on, "So what's the reason you and Jerry came back from Arizona so soon? Something wrong?"

"Oh, that," Jackie said and rolled her eyes. "My granddaughter decided that a thirty-thousand-dollar wedding, complete with a dress with an eight-thousand-dollar price tag, was just a tad bit pretentious. So she eloped. Last I heard, she was in Vegas."

"Eloped?" Corrie gasped. "You mean after her parents spent a fortune on the wedding, she and her fiance just took off and got married in Las Vegas?"

Jackie grimaced. "Wouldn't that have been nice? No, honey, she eloped with the best man."

Corrie couldn't seem to get her mouth to shut. "But they were engaged for five years!" she sputtered. Jackie shrugged.

"I try not to say 'I told you so' .... I told my daughter and her husband that true love didn't require a huge, fancy wedding and that they were putting too much emphasis on the wedding and not enough on the marriage. But it's too late and what's done is done, and now we just have to deal with what's happened the best we can, but I'm not having much luck convincing anyone of that... especially my daughter. After all, there is the matter of the non-refundable deposits on the reception hall, the caterer and the photographer. And I don't suppose you know anyone in the market for a wedding dress?"

"Not an eight-thousand-dollar one!"

"Well, of course, they'd get a great deal on it... even though it's never been worn," Jackie sighed. She patted Corrie's hand. "Well, if you hear of anyone who might be interested, let me know. In the meantime," she said and fixed her sharp gaze on Corrie's face. "What are we going to do about this situation?"

"Marvin's murder?" Corrie said, hoping that Jackie wasn't tying the offer of a barely-used wedding dress to her perceived dilemma of Corrie being pursued by two men. After all, it was mostly wishful thinking on Jackie's part. She pushed all thoughts of love and relationships out of her mind and decided to focus on the present crisis.

Jackie nodded. "Tell me what YOU think about the whole thing, Corrie. Anything strike you as odd?"

"A lot," Corrie admitted. Rick would flip if he found out she was discussing it with Jackie, but he should be thankful it wasn't Dana. "For one thing, if you haven't heard, the Landrys were robbed." She told Jackie about the money that Marvin and Betty had withdrawn from the bank and how it had disappeared from its hiding place in Betty's drawer. "I know where the Landrys got twenty-five thousand dollars, but what I don't understand is what they needed it for and why they had it hidden in their RV. That's a lot of cash to keep stashed in a drawer with your fine washables, isn't it?"

"Myself, I only keep about ten thousand on hand," Jackie deadpanned then shook her head. "Corrie, NO one keeps that much cash around, even for emergencies. If they were going to put it in another bank, they could have done an electronic transfer or a cashier's check. There had to be a reason why they withdrew it all in cash."

Corrie nodded. "Rick says Betty refused to discuss it with him. In fact, it sounded like she told him it was none of his, or anyone else's, business."

"That doesn't sound like Betty." Jackie's brow furrowed. "Of course, some people don't like to discuss money with people outside their family. Your father was like that," Jackie said and Corrie nodded.

"The other thing is the lock on the bathroom door." She told Jackie about Betty being locked in.

"That really makes no sense," Jackie said, frowning. "You mean it was like the door had been put on backwards or inside out?"

"Exactly," Corrie said. "I didn't even realize at first that Betty was locked in the bathroom. I thought something had happened to her and that was why she couldn't open the door. I never dreamed the lock was on the outside." She didn't say that one of the reasons relations were so strained between her and Rick was the fact that she had, much as she hated to admit it, made his job harder by touching the knob, albeit unintentionally. Jackie nodded thoughtfully.

"I suppose it's occurred to you that Betty was lucky the murderer just locked her in instead of killing her?"

"That's what makes me suspect it's Betty's son... Walter Dodson."

"Betty's son," Jackie mused. "Now there's a interesting development."

"You didn't know about him?" Corrie asked. Jackie shook her

head.

"I've tried to recall if I've ever heard Betty talk about him... or even mention him, but I keep drawing a blank. Obviously, you've never heard of him either."

"No one seems to," Corrie said. "Everyone reacts the same when they hear about him: surprised, even shocked. It doesn't seem natural that you could know someone as long as we've known Betty and Marvin and not know about one of them having a child." Jackie nodded again and Corrie went on. "Since he was traveling with them, it would explain how he knew exactly where to find the money. He went straight to Betty's drawer and took it out... he didn't go searching for it and nothing else was out of place. And it would make sense why Betty wasn't harmed in the robbery and shooting," she said. "I mean, as obnoxious as Walter Dodson was, I don't think he'd hurt his own mother."

"If he needed money, though, why not ask her instead of killing Marvin and taking the money?" Jackie asked.

"Maybe that was why Marvin and Walter didn't get along," Corrie said. "The account Marvin emptied belonged to both him and Betty. Marvin had plenty of money in another account that was under his name alone, but Betty didn't have access to it—for all we know, she might not even know about it. Maybe Walter Dodson did ask and Marvin refused and...." But Jackie didn't seem to be listening. There was a faraway look in her eyes and she pursed her lips as if deep in thought.

"Okay, what is it?" Corrie sighed. "You've got that same look on your face that Rick gets when he lets me ramble on about something he already knows the answer to. What am I overlooking?"

"Nothing at all," Jackie said, her eyes coming back into sharp focus. "And that's the problem. It's too perfect. Can Walter Dodson be that stupid to commit a crime and leave evidence pointing at him from all directions?"

"No one's seen him since yesterday," Corrie pointed out. "He could be long gone by now. Part of his plan. Or maybe he didn't plan it... he and Marvin got into an argument that got out of hand. Rick says that whoever shot Marvin had to be standing inside the RV, practically right next to him—and he took off after...." Jackie shook her head.

"After he 'accidentally' shot his stepfather? You couldn't convince anyone that it was anything but premeditated... after all, he had to have taken Buster's gun, which no one even knew existed until that morning...."

"IF it was Buster's gun," Corrie interjected. "Anyway," she added, "you have to admit that he's the most likely suspect. It's ludicrous to even think anyone else could be involved."

"Rick suspects that mystery man, J.D. Wilder, doesn't he?" Jackie said shrewdly. Corrie felt her face grow hot.

"I guess he's got his reasons. But everybody's innocent until proven guilty, right?" she said coolly.

"In your mind, not if it's Walter Dodson," Jackie said, shaking her head. "Rick's right. You ARE smitten with that J.D. Wilder!" Corrie set her coffee cup down before she dropped it, only spilling a few drops. She pressed her hands together in her lap.

"Rick told you that?" she said, her words strangled. Jackie make a sound that could only be described as a cluck.

"Rick Sutton tells nobody anything," she said. "It's written all over his face."

To Corrie, Rick Sutton's face made the Sphinx look like a laughing hyena. "Well, if Rick's face is an open book, it's a blank one, for all I can see," Corrie said. "You're seeing things that aren't there, Jackie."

Jackie waved her hand and got up, dismissing Corrie's protests to sit still and let her help. "And you're not seeing things that are right in front of your face, Corrie." She brought the coffee pot over and refilled their cups. "Let's forget those two men for now, if we can," she said. "I think the first thing we have to find out is why Marvin and Betty had all that money with them."

"'We'?" Corrie said, then laughed. "Maybe I forgot to mention this, but Rick does not want me involved in the investigation unless HE involves me! He'll have a coronary if he finds out we're having this conversation." She looked over her shoulder as if Rick just might be standing outside the window, listening to every word, as Jackie returned the coffee pot to the courtesy table.

"Corrie, you and I have known Betty a lot longer than Rick has," Jackie said as she took her seat. "There's probably things she'll tell us that she won't tell him. I think we need to pay her a visit."

"All right," Corrie said. "I can get Dana to keep an eye on things for a while. Do you have any idea what time visiting hours are?"

Before Jackie could answer, there was a sharp rap on the office door. Both women jumped, Corrie stifling a gasp and Jackie clapping her hand over her mouth to stop a shriek. To Corrie's shock, Rick stood framed in the door's upper glass panel. He raised a brow and pointed to the door knob.

"What's he doing here so early?" Corrie muttered as she hurried to unlock the door. Her heart was pounding, but she was too concerned about what his showing up an hour earlier than usual meant to be annoyed with him.

"Everything all right?" Rick asked by way of greeting. Corrie stared at him. He looked like he hadn't taken time to shave and his uniform was rumpled. He nodded a greeting at Jackie who got up to get him coffee. Corrie locked the door behind him.

"I don't know, you tell me," she said. "Did something happen?"

His mouth twitched. "What makes you think something happened?"

"You're here at six-thirty and you didn't bring any muffins," she deadpanned. "Besides that, you look like you slept in your clothes... not that you look like you got much sleep. Have you been working all night?"

He accepted the cup of coffee from Jackie with a nod and took a huge gulp, grimacing as he burned his mouth. "I thought you were supposed to be using a cane, young lady," he said to Jackie, who rolled her eyes and shook her head. Then he took another swig of coffee. "You got it partly right," he said, turning his attention back to Corrie. "Nothing happened and I didn't work last night, but I did sleep in my clothes... when I did sleep." He looked from Corrie to Jackie. "Did I interrupt something?"

"We were just talking about going to visit Betty Landry and see how she's doing," Jackie said, her face all innocence. Corrie was grateful Jackie had brought it up when Rick turned to her and scowled.

"Sorry to burst your bubble, but Betty's being released today... and no, she won't need a ride, I'll be bringing her back as soon as I get done questioning her!"

Corrie knew her face betrayed her and Jackie's plans, but she mustered up a little bravado. "What are you implying?" she asked.

"Not implying a thing. I'm saying, flat out, that you—and Jackie," he added, turning to look at Jackie, "are NOT going to interrogate Betty Landry."

"The thought never crossed our minds," Corrie said, leaning on the counter and resting one hand on the back of her hip. Rick folded his arms across his chest.

"Uncross your fingers and say that to me... and look me in the eye when you do," he said. "But before you do, I should tell you that when the window behind your desk is cracked open, your voices can be heard all the way to the patio entrance."

Corrie thrust her hands into her pockets to hide the fact that it unnerved her that she HAD thought about him lurking outside her window, listening to every word she and Jackie said... and also to keep from throwing a punch at him. "And why is the window cracked open, SHERIFF?" she asked, fighting to keep her cool. "You made a big thing about securing my building last night and you're telling me you missed the front window?"

"On purpose," he shot back. "I had a feeling I might hear a lot more of what I need to know. And I was right. So no matter how much better you two ladies know Betty Landry," he said, bowing slightly to Jackie who looked sheepish, "you're not going to get anything out of her without my finding out about it. Clear?"

"As a bell," Corrie snapped. "And, by the way, just how did you get here, Sheriff? If you can hear us, then surely we should have heard your car drive in."

Rick Sutton's face turning red was a sight even more rare than a total solar eclipse. He cleared his throat. "My car hasn't moved since last night. Let's leave it at that. There's more important things to talk about." He pulled out his notebook and flipped a few pages, avoiding her glare. "First off," he said, "Buster's alibi checks out. He was seen at the rally in the company of his girlfriend, Noreen Adler, from eleven-thirty yesterday morning until well after nine p.m. In fact, he made it a point to be seen—his girlfriend's quite an attractive lady."

Jackie allowed a smile. "I guess Buster felt he had a good reason to brag."

Corrie couldn't help but ask, "How attractive?"

Rick didn't look up. "Apparently, Buster is attracted to statuesque blondes who wear leather and ride Harleys. Not my type."

Only the part about the leather and the Harleys, Corrie thought sourly. Rick's ex, Meghan, was nothing if not a statuesque blonde. "So Buster's out of it," she said.

This time Rick did look up. "He would be... if we knew where that gun was and whether or not it was the one used to shoot Marvin." He tapped his pen on his notebook. "And just to prove that I don't have tunnel vision, I did check on Walter Dodson's whereabouts. I called the dispatcher at the Harris Cab Company in Bonney and he said the log showed that Walter Dodson called for a cab at nine yesterday morning. Both of the company's cabs were busy, so Donovan Harris himself picked up Dodson in his own personal vehicle at nine-twenty and dropped him off at Findley's Hardware in Ruidoso. I'll start my questioning there this morning."

"So where was he all night?" Corrie asked. Rick glanced at his notes.

"The Snowcap Lodge in Ruidoso. Checked in at two-thirty yesterday afternoon."

"He stayed there all night?" Corrie reined in her impatience. She wasn't in the mood for a game of "twenty questions", but when Rick only answered the question he was being asked, without embellishing, it was because he was feeling pressured to reveal more than he felt was necessary. And while he might not agree, Corrie felt that any and all information pertaining to a murder that occurred on HER property, to HER guests, was necessarily HER business.

"Apparently." Rick shrugged. "He called the sheriff's office himself about twenty minutes ago. Said he'd just heard about Marvin's death on the morning radio news show."

"Did he say where he'd been all day yesterday?" Corrie could hardly contain herself. Rick sighed and shook his head.

"We just found the guy and while you might find it hard to believe, he appears to be in a state of shock and worried about Betty. He wanted to go right over to the hospital, but I told him to wait until eight-thirty when Betty will be discharged. I want to talk to her before he does."

Corrie bit her tongue before she said anything else. She knew Rick was doing his job and he didn't need her to tell him to make sure someone kept an eye on Walter Dodson, but it irritated her that Rick was being overly cautious in suspecting the most obvious suspect. Rick's voice broke into her thoughts. "I'm sorry I interrupted your litany of things that don't make sense, but there is one I'd like to get cleared up... and that's who propped open your laundry room door last night. Have you unlocked it yet?"

"No, we don't unlock any doors until seven," Corrie said. "And I haven't heard anyone come in to use the laundry this morning."

Rick nodded. "I'll get Dudley to dust the door handle for prints before you unlock it. He's on his way over."

"Won't he find just about everyone's prints on it? I mean, everyone who's staying at the campground and has used the laundry?" Jackie asked. Rick sighed.

"It's standard procedure... besides, I think we can get partials off the pen that was used to prop the door open. It's got flat sides."

"That pen's probably got just about everyone's prints on it, too," Corrie pointed out. "If it's one from my desk, anyone who's checked in for the last two days has used it to sign their paperwork."

"Well, it's the best we can do!" Rick snapped and Corrie drew back in surprise. Rick usually thrived under pressure. The investigation was taking a much bigger toll on him than he was letting on. He rubbed his eyes and took a deep breath. "Sorry," he said, in a much softer voice. "It's been a long night and the day won't be much shorter."

Corrie had taken his cup and refilled it without saying a word. He took it and thanked her silently with his half-smile. Finally Jackie cleared her throat. "Corrie, were you still planning to have the Saturday pancake breakfast this morning?"

"Yow," Corrie said with a grimace as she looked at the clock. "I'd better get moving. I should have had the batter made up by now!"

"I'll help," Jackie said. "Let me just give Jerry a call and get him going."

"Right," Corrie said. She turned to Rick. "Don't feel you have to stick around. You need to get some rest." She tried to sound matter-of-fact, but the truth was, her heart twisted at the sight of Rick's haggard face.

"I need to get this murder solved," Rick said, but there was none of the sharpness in his voice that there had been earlier. "Besides, I go on duty in another hour. I have to be at the hospital before Betty is discharged."

It had been ages since Rick had missed a Saturday pancake breakfast. He seldom worked weekends, and not just because he was pulling rank as sheriff; any kind of crime, especially murder, was rare in Bonney County. Corrie knew there would be no rest for him until Marvin's murderer was brought to justice. "Why don't you run home and grab a shower, then stop back here before you go to the hospital? I'll have some breakfast for you. You have to eat, you know," she added before he had a chance to argue.

He was silent while Jackie hung up the phone and said she was going over to her RV for a minute, then she and Jerry would be back to help Corrie get breakfast started. "And I'll get Dana and Red to come over and help, too," she said as she bustled out the door.

"Don't forget to bring your cane," Corrie called after her. Jackie waved back, resignedly.

Rick watched her leave then he stretched and yawned. Corrie bit back a smile; Rick was so conscientious of presenting a professional lawman's image he wouldn't even let an old friend like Jackie see him yawn. "Well, what do you say, Sheriff?" she asked.

Rick gave her his half-grin. "I've got a spare uniform in the car. If you'll loan me a towel and let me grab some basic toiletries, I'll use the campground showers and be ready to help out by the time you get the batter and the sausage ready. I can't see Betty until after eight, anyway."

Corrie's mind went blank for a second, then she swallowed hard. "I don't use girly-scented shampoo or soap. You can use my shower upstairs and just get a razor and shaving cream, on the house. I have no idea what condition the campground showers are in and Myra won't be here before ten-thirty...." Her voice trailed off as Rick nodded.

"All right," he said. "Just make sure your man-eating watch dog doesn't go all 'Cujo' on me when he hears me come up the stairs." Corrie laughed and Rick's smile almost grew wider. He turned to go out the door when something occurred to Corrie.

"Hey, Rick?" she said. "What did you mean when you said your car hasn't moved all night?"

He stopped with his hand on the doorknob, but didn't turn around. He looked over his shoulder. "Think about it," he said.

She did and she blushed.

Chapter 16

J.D. forced himself to show up for breakfast, even though he wasn't hungry. Despite the fact that the aromas of Corrie's pancakes and sausages were teasing his senses, he felt he had a lump of concrete sitting in his stomach. And it didn't make him feel any better to see the sheriff was present... in full uniform, no less.

Of course, the sheriff hadn't left the campground all night. J.D. had seen him sitting in his Tahoe, just out of sight from the windows of the office, keeping an eye on the place. He wasn't sure, but he suspected that the second-floor window under which the sheriff kept his vigil was Corrie's bedroom window.

"Long night, Sheriff?" he asked casually as he helped himself to a cup of coffee. Sutton had done a good job of washing the tiredness off his face, but J.D. could see the circles under his eyes, though he doubted anyone else would notice. The sheriff fixed his steely gaze on J.D.

"Same number of hours, whether you're sleeping or working, Wilder," Sutton said.

So much for small talk. J.D. lifted his cup to the sheriff and moved on. He fought the urge to look back, but he could feel Sutton's eyes following him as he filled a plate and took a seat. He didn't see Corrie and he surmised that she might be in the kitchen.

There wasn't much talk and laughter on the patio, though almost every seat was taken. It could have been the early hour, but J.D. guessed it had more to do with the murder. He grimaced as he overheard the six people at the table behind him discuss, in low tones, cutting their stay short and checking into a motel in town... if they could find a vacancy. This whole thing could hurt Corrie and her business badly. There had to be some way he could help....

He looked up and caught the sheriff's vigilant stare. It was apparent the law had already convicted its main suspect and only lacked probable cause and evidence to arrest him.

J.D. set his jaw. Despite his resolve to keep his distance, Corrie needed him and, no matter what Sheriff Rick Sutton thought, he wasn't going to back off... no matter what it cost him.

Rick had left shortly after eight to go to the hospital and talk with Betty after her discharge. It was now nearly ten and Corrie was growing impatient. She had tried to stay busy, but with both Jackie and Dana helping out, she found herself with very little to do after the Saturday breakfast had been cleaned up.

"Staring out the window at the highway isn't going to make him get here any faster," Jackie had murmured to her while Dana was helping a couple of guests in the laundry room. "Why don't you go upstairs and get a little rest? We've got everything under control here."

Corrie sighed. "I'm all right, Jackie. I just feel frustrated. This is my home, my place of business... and I could be losing it, little by little, every minute that goes by and this murder isn't solved! I can't believe that Rick doesn't understand that!"

"Oh, honey, I'm sure he does," Jackie said, patting Corrie's shoulder. "And you haven't lost any guests so far." Corrie gave her a skeptical look.

"You mean no one's even expressed any concern over the fact that a guest was shot to death in broad daylight in his own RV? I find that hard to believe."

"I didn't say THAT," Jackie said dryly, leaning on her cane which she was using more to keep everyone from fretting about her than because she felt she needed it. "We've been doing some damage control and reminding folks that we have armed deputies keeping an eye on things. A few of them fussed over being questioned and searched, but they'd be the first ones to raise a fuss if something happened to them." She gently urged Corrie to the door. "Look, if you won't go lie down for a while, then why don't you go for a walk and get some fresh air? You look like you could use it and it wouldn't hurt for the guests to see you out and about."

Before Corrie could argue, the front door opened and Delbert Otero, the mail carrier, walked in. He gave Corrie and Jackie a solemn nod instead of his usual cheery greeting, apparently feeling that it wouldn't be appropriate in light of the recent tragedy. Corrie returned his nod just as solemnly as he deposited her personal mail and the campground's business mail in two neat piles on the counter before turning to the mailboxes to the right of the entrance. Corrie kept a few for her long-term tenants to be able to receive mail while staying at the campground. None of the boxes were very big. The Pages had had the first box for years, the one next to theirs belonged to the Westlakes. It was when Delbert opened the Westlakes' box that he broke his silence.

"What the...? Hey, Corrie, the Westlakes go on vacation or something?"

She turned in surprise. The Westlakes' box was crammed full of mail. Delbert stood with another small bundle in his hands and a perplexed expression on his broad face. He looked at Corrie for an explanation and she turned to Jackie.

"Did you see the Westlakes at breakfast this morning?"

Jackie shook her head. "I haven't seen them since Wednesday before we left for Arizona," she said. "When was the last time either Rosemary or Donald picked up their mail?"

Corrie tried to think. So much had happened in the last few days that she couldn't remember right away. "Rosemary comes in almost every day," she began then stopped and exchanged a look with Jackie. "She hasn't been inside the office since the day the Landrys arrived!"

"That was two days ago," Jackie said, her brow furrowing with concern. "When was the last time you actually saw them?"

"They were both at the enchilada dinner last night," Corrie said. "Right before we...." She paused, suddenly aware that Delbert was still standing in the office holding the Westlakes' mail. Corrie made a decision and held out her hand. "Let me have it, Delbert. I'll take it over to their RV."

"Uh... I dunno, Corrie," Delbert said uneasily. "I mean, you know, postal regulations...."

"Delbert, I have a key to all the mailboxes," Corrie interrupted him. "I think that gives me a legal right to accept their mail." She had no idea if it did or not, but she was hoping Delbert would cooperate without question.

He still didn't look convinced. He looked at the bundle of mail in his hand as if it would give him an answer and bit his lip. "Well...."

Corrie threw up her hands. "Never mind, Delbert. Just put it in their box," she sighed. Delbert was a trusting soul who took everyone's word at face value and he exhaled with relief as he jammed the mail in his hands into the Westlakes' overflowing box and then left, giving Corrie a grin of thanks. She had a momentary twinge of conscience at taking advantage of Delbert's simple faith, but it passed quickly.

No sooner was he out the door than Corrie pulled the keys out of her desk drawer and opened the box. She resisted the temptation to look at the mail itself, but she gave Jackie a grim smile. "Hold the fort till I get back."

Corrie hurried down the walkway to the path and nearly collided with Dana who had just stepped off the patio, coming from the direction of the laundry room. "Where are you headed in such a hurry?" Dana asked.

Corrie hoped Dana hadn't overheard her exchange with Delbert and she really wanted to make her visit to the Westlakes' RV without Dana's knowledge, but to try to come up with an excuse while holding three days' worth of mail in her hands was beyond Corrie's capabilities. Besides, Dana spent a lot of time socializing so she, of all people, would be able to tell Corrie if the Westlakes had been around. "Have you seen the Westlakes lately?" she asked.

Dana's expression became guarded. "Last night, at the enchilada social," she said promptly. Usually she had to stop and think and muse and embellish. Corrie raised a brow.

"That's it?"

"I think so," Dana said, edging toward the office door. Corrie stared at her.

"Did you see either of them at all before that?" she pressed.

Dana grimaced, her fingers twining together. She was torn. Part of her didn't seem to want to discuss the Westlakes, but there was another part of her, the part Corrie—and all Dana's friends—knew so well... the part that was dying to talk about something that she shouldn't be talking about. Her next words confirmed this. "I probably shouldn't say... I'm probably wrong... and it's probably nothing at all, just a misunderstanding...."

"What is it?" Corrie asked bluntly. It was all the encouragement Dana needed.

"Well, I'm probably out of line saying this, but I don't think things are quite as rosy at the Westlakes' as Rosemary would like us to think," she said. "In fact, Corrie, you might think I'm crazy for saying this, but... I think Rosemary had something going on behind Donald's back."

That wasn't what Corrie expected to hear. "Something...? You mean, an affair?"

Dana nodded vigorously. "And you won't believe with whom!" she said, keeping her voice low. "Marvin Landry!"

"WHAT??" Corrie squawked, nearly dropping the bundle of mail. Dana's finger covered her lips as she looked around.

"I know, it's crazy, isn't it?" she whispered, unable to contain herself any longer. "But I saw them—Rosemary and Marvin—the day the Landrys arrived. They were talking over by that stand of trees by the dog yard. They looked guilty when they saw me. Well, Rosemary did," she amended, while Corrie wondered why Dana had been over by the dog yard herself. "I wondered why Marvin Landry was heading that way... he doesn't have a dog, after all, and he kept looking around and back over his shoulder as he went. It just seemed odd, so I thought I should see if there was a problem or if I could help. I stayed back so he wouldn't see me," she added unblushingly. Corrie clamped her lips shut to keep from remonstrating with Dana about interfering with the guests' personal business. She couldn't be THAT hypocritical. Dana went on, "Marvin looked perturbed when he saw me... he left right away. Rosemary made a big thing of telling me that Marvin was inquiring about pugs—when Bon-Bon was going to have another litter, how much would they cost, how much maintenance they require. She made it sound like he was thinking of getting one for Betty... you know to keep her company."

"Did you believe her?" Corrie asked. Somehow she couldn't picture Marvin being remotely sentimental enough to consider getting Betty any kind of gift, much less a puppy. Dana sniffed.

"No way Betty would be able to look after a dog in her condition... and can you really picture MARVIN doing it?" She shook her head. "I think Rosemary made that up, you know, to cover up whatever she and Marvin were really doing by the dog yard."

Corrie stopped herself from commenting that even Marvin, for all his gruff and unsentimental ways, would have surely found a better place for a romantic liaison than the dog yard. "So then what happened?"

Dana shrugged. "Then Rosemary said she had to get home and so I left, too." She grimaced. "I saw Donald coming back from the restrooms on my way to our Airstream. He looked upset... shaking his head and muttering to himself. I wonder now if maybe he ran into Marvin on his way."

"Did you see Marvin after that? Or hear anything?"

"No...," Dana said thoughtfully. "At least, it wasn't Marvin I saw."

Corrie felt her head spin. "What are you talking about? Who did you see? And where?" It occurred to her that anyone else but Dana would have become suspicious of her sudden interest in the private affairs of her campground guests, but Dana was only too eager to have a receptive ear to bend.

"The next morning," Dana went on, as if she hadn't heard, and her eyes widened. "I'll bet that's where he was going!"

"WHO?" Corrie said, barely refraining from taking Dana by the shoulders and shaking her. Dana nodded vigorously.

"Corrie, remember I told you I saw Walter Dodson going for a walk yesterday morning? He was heading toward the dog yard... I'll bet you anything that he found out or suspected that Marvin and Rosemary were seeing each other and he went over there to either confront Rosemary or tell Donald!"

Corrie turned the thought over dubiously. "Why wouldn't he just confront Marvin?" she asked. Dana grimaced and shrugged.

"Maybe he didn't want to upset Betty by bringing it up in front of her."

To Corrie, the Walter Dodson she had met didn't seem the type to be overly concerned about anyone's feelings, even his own mother's... or that he would want to protect Marvin's reputation. She reminded herself of her errand at hand. "Well, I wouldn't say too much about it, Dana... it might stir up trouble."

"Oh, I agree," Dana said. "Especially if the sheriff found out!"

Especially, Corrie agreed to herself and decided that, whether Rick liked it or not, she was going to find out if either of the Westlakes had a reason for being curiously absent... or for wanting to get rid of Marvin Landry.

She slowed down as she approached the Westlakes' RV. She could hear voices through the half-open window. Angry voices.

"What on earth were you thinking anyway, Rosemary? Marvin Landry, of all people?" Corrie cringed. She couldn't recall ever hearing Donald Westlake raise his voice in all the years she'd known him.

"Why not Marvin? If not him, then who else?" Rosemary replied shrilly. Bon-Bon punctuated her words with a sharp bark.

"ANYone else! Anyone we don't know personally would have been just fine!" Donald bellowed. His words brought Corrie up short. Surely this wasn't the way she would have expected a husband to react to his wife's dalliances with another man. She decided that this wouldn't be a good time to drop in on the Westlakes and she began to back away from the RV as quietly as she could. Rosemary's next words stopped her cold.

"He had the money, Donald, and he had it in cash! It was too good to pass up... it was a perfect opportunity!"

"Until Marvin ended up dead!"

Corrie stood frozen, her heart pounding so hard she was certain the Westlakes could hear it. Although she wanted desperately to hear what else would be said, she knew that getting caught eavesdropping—with her hands full of their mail, no less—was going to get her into more trouble than she bargained for. She would have to call Rick and report what she heard.

Her eyes still fixed on the Westlakes' RV door, she took another step back, and tripped over one of the solar lights that illuminated the walkway. She gasped, stumbled backwards, and fell onto her side, the Westlakes' mail flying out of her hands.

The RV door swung open as she sat up. Donald and Rosemary Westlake stared at her and she managed a stiff smile.

"Hello," she said, trying to sound nonchalant. They continued to stare at her as she got to her feet. "Guess I should pay attention to where I'm going," she said with a laugh. "I was just bringing your mail over...."

"The mail?" The word burst from both Donald and Rosemary and they exchanged an alarmed glance.

"Uh...." Corrie's mind went blank as she began gathering up the envelopes that had scattered along the ground like autumn leaves. "Delbert couldn't fit anymore into your box, so...."

"I'll get those, Corrie," Donald Westlake said as he scooped up several pieces of mail and practically snatched the ones Corrie had picked up out of her hands. "Thanks for taking the trouble to bring it over."

"Oh, no trouble at all. My pleasure," she said lightly. Donald avoided her eyes as he bundled the mail so that the addresses couldn't be seen. For once, Corrie deplored her aversion to snooping in other people's business. But it was too late now. She looked up at Rosemary. The woman's face was so pale, her lipstick, rouge and eyeshadow looked more like clown makeup than ever. "Well, I guess I should be going," Corrie added.

Neither of the Westlakes responded. Rosemary turned and went back into the depths of their RV, ostensibly attending to Bon-Bon's fevered yaps. Donald stood with the mail clutched in his hands and a grim look on his face as Corrie turned and headed back to the campground office.

Chapter 17

Corrie forced herself to walk at a normal pace although her impulse was to run as fast as she could back to the office, where Jackie and Dana waited for her, where Jerry and Red were nearby, where she could call Rick if he hadn't already come back....

"Miss Black!"

She had gotten as far as the corner of the tall wooden fence surrounding the pool and Deputy Dudley Evans came up to her from the direction of the restrooms. Myra Kaydahzinne, one of the campground's maintenance workers, was with him, her pretty bronze face pale with shock, making her brown eyes darker. Since Myra was the epitome of Native American imperturbability, even for a young woman barely out of her teens, Corrie's heart pounded with dread. The grim set of Dudley's jaw only increased her apprehension. "What is it?" she asked.

Before Dudley could say anything, Myra burst into speech. "Corrie, Dudley—I mean, Deputy Evans—was just telling me about Marvin Landry and that I shouldn't be nervous or scared because he's keeping an eye on things... him and the sheriff and some other deputies, that is," she added quickly when Dudley cleared his throat and blushed... something Corrie had never known a black person was capable of showing. Myra went on, "And I know Buster didn't do his job yesterday, which doesn't really matter because whoever searched the bathrooms made such a mess that you couldn't tell anyway, but I don't imagine anyone would think to look in this." With that, she stuck out a vinyl-gloved hand which Dudley intercepted with a plastic evidence bag.

"I'll take it from here, Myra... Miss Kaydahzinne," Dudley said, adroitly taking command of the situation and slipping the bulky white plastic bundle she held into the evidence bag.

Corrie's nose wrinkled as she caught a whiff before Dudley sealed the bag and the expression of distaste on his face confirmed what she had initially thought. "Is that a diaper?" she asked, not sure if she believed what she was seeing.

"Oh, yeah," Dudley said, with a triumphant gleam in his eye. "And you won't believe what's inside of it!"

"Buster's gun?"

Rick shrugged. He had arrived at the campground just before Corrie had returned from her visit to the Westlakes' RV and the two of them were in the family room, seated at a small table in the furthest corner from the door, away from all windows. Dudley and Myra had given Rick their statements and had left, Myra to return to her duties and Dudley, presumably, to do the same... although Corrie wondered if there was a possible romance blossoming between Dudley and Myra. Dudley's usual phlegmatic attitude, which Corrie suspected was his way of emulating Rick, was missing and he had shown an unusual amount of concern and attention to Myra. Despite Deputy Evans' reputation as one of the county's most professional and experienced lawmen, he wasn't more than a few years older than Corrie's employee. She pushed any further speculation about their relationship aside and focused on what Rick had discovered from his questioning of Betty Landry.

Rick was being guarded in his revelations—even more so than usual. "Until the lab gets through with it, I can't say for sure. I can't even say yet if it's the gun used to shoot Marvin... and I'm not holding out much hope for fingerprints. I'd be very surprised if the killer wasn't wearing gloves." He tapped his pen on his notebook. "I don't suppose you have any guests who have a child in diapers?"

Corrie shook her head. "I couldn't tell you the last time I did... so now we have to find out where that diaper came from as well."

Rick flashed her a look. "*I* will be sending deputies around to find that out."

Corrie stared at him. "I thought you said you needed my help!"

"I need your help HERE, not out THERE," Rick said, jerking his head in the direction of the campground. It sounded like a reminder that she had botched things up before and he wanted her where she would do the least amount of damage. She felt her cheeks grow hot. Despite his earlier apology, Rick would never let her live it down. He went on. "It was clever... pure luck that the garbage bag ripped apart when Myra pulled it out of the can and that she noticed that diaper was unusually heavy. The gun would have ended up in the county landfill and been lost for good."

"You talked to Betty and her son, didn't you? She's all right, isn't she?" Corrie asked, trying to shrug off the sting of Rick's blatant demand that she stay out of the investigation.

Rick didn't look up; he continued to make notes in his memo pad. "Yes."

Corrie waited, but he didn't go on. She wasn't even sure which question he had answered. She didn't want to prod, but her curiosity was increasing as fast as her patience was decreasing. "Well, what did they say?"

Rick still didn't meet her eyes. "Corrie," he said and it was a clear warning.

"Don't tell me!" she snapped. "It's 'official sheriff's department business' and, therefore, none of mine!" She stood up, nearly knocking her chair over. Rick looked up at her, but gave no indication that he was going to speak. She went on. "You've got a lot of nerve, Sheriff, keeping me in the dark about what's going on! I have a right to know...."

"...how the investigation is progressing, not every detail that could compromise it," he finished her sentence for her. His eyes drilled into hers. "Corrie, I know it's hard for you to sit by and let someone else take care of what you believe is your business. But finding Marvin's killer is MY business. If I need your help, I'll let you know. Believe me, I do appreciate the help you've given me so far."

"Oh, do you?" she asked bitterly. "Well, then show me a little consideration, Rick. This is my home, my business, my friends! I think I deserve...."

"It's not a question of what anyone deserves!" Rick shot back, his eyes blazing despite their blue iciness as he stood up to face her. "If it comes down to it, Marvin didn't 'deserve' to be murdered, Betty didn't 'deserve' to be widowed like that, and you don't 'deserve' to have this whole mess happen right in front of you in addition to...." He stopped and looked away.

Corrie stared at him. "In addition to what?"

He didn't answer at first, but then he sighed. "The pen and door knob to the laundry room turned out negative for prints... that is, prints that you'd normally expect on a door that's used as frequently as that door is," he said.

It took a moment for his meaning to sink in. A chill trickled down her spine and she slowly sat back down. "They were wiped clean?" she said, her voice barely above a whisper. Rick nodded. "So that means...."

"Somebody thinks you know something," Rick said, his voice a low rumble like distant thunder. "Everyone involved here knows you and I are friends and if they think we're discussing the case, that you know what the police know...."

"Then it couldn't have been Walter Dodson?" Corrie said. "If he was in town all night...."

"And all day." Rick gave a slight shake of his head and looked up at the ceiling. "Ah, what the hell, Corrie," he sighed. "I guess I can tell you this much. Donovan Harris dropped Dodson off at Findley's Hardware in mid-town Ruidoso yesterday morning. Three customers and Art Findley himself saw him there until ten-thirty." He tossed his pen onto the table and sat down, his forearms resting on the table in front of him. "The mystery of the backward bathroom door has an explanation. Seems that after Betty became wheelchair-bound—"

"When DID that happen, anyway?" Corrie interrupted. For once, Rick bore an interruption patiently. He checked his notes.

"About two months ago. Betty wanted the bathroom door in the RV to swing open the other way—easier for her to get in, Dodson said—and Marvin didn't get around to it right away because he eventually wanted to put in a pocket door at some time in the future. So when Dodson joined them on this trip a week ago, she asked him to do it... probably trying to boost his image in Marvin's eyes. Well,

Dodson apparently isn't much of a handyman; he put the door on wrong and Marvin hit the ceiling. Art said Dodson was griping about how he wasn't appreciated, that if Marvin was so smart why didn't he do the job himself when Betty first asked, and he was tired of Marvin sniping about it so he said he'd go into town and buy a replacement door. Art said he spent most of his time talking to him about prices and delivery and installation costs."

"Where did he go after that?"

"Kokopelli's Koffee Kiva for a bagel and coffee—cinnamon raisin bagel with fat-free cream cheese and a no-fat, no-foam latte, to be exact," Rick said dryly. Corrie bit back a grin; she was sure the young counter girl at Kokopelli's—who usually had to be summoned twice before she attended any female patrons—had to be all but tasered to leave Rick alone after she answered his questions. Rick went on. "After that, he wandered around mid-town Ruidoso for a couple of hours. Five different merchants identified him as having been browsing in their shops. He went to The Quarters for a beer and a sandwich a little before one o'clock. He asked the waitress and bartender about a place to stay and they recommended the Snowcap Lodge. So unless eleven witnesses are lying or hallucinating, Walter Dodson was nowhere near the Landrys' RV at the time of Marvin's murder... he wasn't even in the county."

Corrie let her breath out, not realizing she had been holding it. She looked up; Rick was studying her, his dispassionate calm masking a deep concern. "So if it wasn't Walter Dodson...?"

Rick stood up and wandered over to the door. He glanced around and Corrie assumed he was checking to see if Jackie was still keeping watch over things. He came back and sat down again. "We're back to suspecting everyone, Corrie," he said quietly. "Buster is the most obvious suspect—if it is his gun—because he had access to the weapon and the hiding place."

"Except for the diaper," Corrie pointed out, adding wryly, "If I can't even get him to throw trash away, I doubt he'd have much interest in looking through it for something like that!"

"And the fact that he wasn't here to prop your laundry room door open. Besides all that, there's a question of motive." Rick cleared his throat. "The other obvious suspect...."

"Is J.D. Wilder," Corrie finished. "Right?"

"We have to suspect everyone, Corrie," Rick said. "He admitted that he was in the Landrys' RV, he could have propped open your laundry room door...."

"How?"

"I don't know," Rick answered, still remaining patient. "What I do know is that there was only one set of prints on that door knob... and they belong to J.D. Wilder. Of course," Rick continued, "it's odd that his prints are the ONLY ones on a door knob that's been used by at least a dozen people in the last few days. I'm not sure just how thoroughly you and Jackie and Dana dust and polish door knobs." She looked at him sharply. He was being too patient.

"What else did you find?" she asked bluntly.

He cleared his throat and flipped a few pages in his memo pad. "Corrie, keep in mind that J.D. Wilder is a total stranger who appeared mysteriously in the dead of night. I'm sure you understand that it only makes sense that I ran a check on him."

Of course he had to. It would have been irresponsible for Rick not to, seeing as how a crime had been committed shortly after J.D.'s mysterious appearance and, Corrie admitted grudgingly, his suspicious behavior. "You found something," she said.

Rick fished a couple of folded-up copies of newspaper clippings from the back of his memo pad and pushed them across the table toward her. They were from two different news sources. The first was from the Houston Chronicle, dated three days before J.D.'s appearance. The headline read "Prosecutor in Drug Dealer's Trial Missing". The second was from the El Paso Times, dated the day J.D. arrived at the Black Horse. It read "Missing Prosecutor Found Dead". Both clippings featured the same photo of an attractive woman, identified as Tricia Powers, a rising star D.A. in Houston, with a reputation for being merciless when it came to pursuing convictions of drug dealers. Corrie barely skimmed the stories: the woman was set to prosecute an extremely slippery drug dealer, with connections to a major cartel, who had eluded capture for several years and had recently been apprehended by detectives. She had been receiving death threats; thanks to the evidence gathered by the narcotics squad when they made the bust, it was a sure thing that she'd be able to pull off a conviction. But then she had left Houston without permission from the D.A.'s office on the eve of the dealer's trial. She had also cleaned out a personal bank account, the amount of which was not disclosed, and disappeared, only to reappear in El Paso, dead, three days later, the victim of a mysterious gas explosion in a house that was suspected of being used by the drug dealers as a safe house. The money from the bank account was missing. Corrie remembered hearing about it on the morning news show. She looked at Rick.

"What does this have to do with J.D.?"

"The Houston Metro police are looking for him, Corrie. They want to ask him some questions," Rick said quietly. "He knows the murdered woman."

"Knows her how?" Corrie asked, her stomach twisting into knots. Rick shook his head.

"They're not saying... they just asked me to try to keep him here without arousing his suspicion. It's a federal case, so the FBI is on the way to take him back to Texas."

"They think he...?" She couldn't bring herself to complete the question.

"I don't know," Rick said, and it occurred to Corrie that those had to be the hardest three words for Rick Sutton to say. "But until those agents get here, I'm keeping a close eye on J.D. Wilder... and you're going to stay as far away from him as possible."

"How, Rick?" she said, her eyes stinging, mostly from her annoyance at her fear. "He's a guest here... in my place of business." Her home, she wanted to add, but she knew that was already in the forefront of Rick's mind.

"You're not to be anywhere where he can get you alone, Corrie," Rick said, his voice edged with granite. "Not you or any other of your employees, not until we know what his connection is with that D.A. or those drug dealers."

"But even if there is a connection... that doesn't mean he has anything to do with Marvin's murder," Corrie said.

"It doesn't matter," Rick snapped. "A woman he was seen with is dead, and now Marvin is dead, just after J.D. Wilder arrives here and makes his acquaintance. Maybe it's a coincidence, but I don't like coincidences where people end up dead!"

Corrie said nothing. They were both silent for a minute, before Rick spoke up again. "I have to admit I can't find a connection between both cases, except for the fact that money was missing in both instances. I can't find anyone, besides us, who knew that the Landrys had that money in their possession."

Corrie sat bolt upright in her chair, her fear vanishing in a wave of chagrin. "Rick, that's what I wanted to tell you before Dudley and Myra found the gun!"

"Donald and Rosemary Westlake? They knew about the money?"

Corrie had never seen Rick look as shocked as he did at the information. "That's what I heard, Rick. I know I wasn't imagining things." She took a deep breath. "I just don't know that you'd be able to get them to admit to anything."

"It still might not have anything to do with Marvin's murder," Rick said. "There could be other reasons they knew about the money."

"You mean you don't suspect them in the least?" she said, hardly able to believe what she was hearing. Rick shook his head.

"I'm not saying that," he said. "I'm just saying that a lot of things don't add up to the Westlakes being involved in Marvin's murder."

"Like?"

"Like the fact that it sounds as if the Westlakes—or at least, Rosemary—had talked to Marvin about the money and that it seemed that he was about to enter into some kind of business deal with them. Which means they knew about the money legitimately."

"Donald Westlake didn't sound too happy at the idea," Corrie pointed out. Rick nodded.

"It could be Donald hadn't planned on getting the Landrys involved and Rosemary went ahead and made arrangements without consulting him. You have no idea what kind of business the Westlakes are in?"

Corrie shook her head. "Donald has a lot of computer knowledge... he helped us set up our website. I assumed it had something to do with computer, maybe technical support or something like that. I never see them leave the campground except to go into town once a week."

"They get a lot of mail, don't they?" Rick persisted.

"After three days, Delbert couldn't cram any more into their box," Corrie said. She was relieved that Rick hadn't taken her to task for intercepting the Westlakes' mail. "I never paid any attention to how much they received and I didn't look at any of the envelopes I took over to them today."

"That's one less thing for you to get into trouble over," Rick said, raising an eyebrow at her. She didn't know whether to laugh or be annoyed until Rick winked at her and she knew he was simply trying to calm her nerves. She laughed, despite her annoyance.

"So now what are you going to do... besides not tell me what you're going to do," she added. Rick flipped his memo pad shut and slipped it into his shirt pocket.

"I'll have to talk to the Westlakes... and they probably won't have too much trouble figuring out who talked to me. Be prepared to have them be upset with you. Maybe enough to leave."

Corrie felt a twinge. Naturally, she deplored the idea of losing any of her guests, but she couldn't see how the Westlakes could blame her for reporting what she'd heard. "I didn't have much choice," she said.

"And I'll be sure to impress that on them," Rick said. He stood up. "There's no reason why you can't carry on with the usual campground activities you have on the weekends. You have plenty of help and I want you and the Pages and the Myers to work together and within each other's sight...."

Corrie tuned him out. The thought had occurred to her that the Westlakes had the site at the furthest end of the campground that bordered on National Forest land and private residential property. Just beyond the campground's fence was a picnic area adjacent to a few homes that belonged to residents that had owned the land long before it became part of the National Forest. The picnic area had a playground, picnic tables, and at least one dumpster. It was easy enough to get there from the Black Horse without being seen... and if anyone had observed families with small children using the picnic area, it would be easy to find what was needed to conceal the murder weapon.

"Corrie?"

She looked up; she hadn't heard most of what Rick had been saying. And he had noticed. His eyes narrowed with suspicion. "Is there something going on in that head of yours that I should be aware of?" he asked.

"Absolutely nothing," she said. She stood up, her chair scraping across the floor and almost falling over. "So are we done here?" Rick continued to look at her, his pen tapping on the table. Despite the frost that had descended on the room along with his silence, she felt herself grow hot and prickly. "I have a lot to do before the pizza party this afternoon, Sheriff," she said, hoping to get him to leave without seeming to rush him.

"And I just got done telling you to have the Pages and the Myers help you out," he said. "Or were you thinking of something else while I was talking?"

"Jerry and Jackie go to Saturday evening Mass," Corrie said. "They take care of Sunday mornings so I can go to Mass, while I take care of Saturday evenings. It's been the way things have always been around here... for years," she added.

Rick leaned toward her, resting his hands on the table between them. "I'm well aware of that, Corrie, but it's still five hours till the pizza party gets underway and you seem to be in an awful big hurry to get started on... something."

She didn't answer, but her eyes locked with his and for a long minute, neither of them said anything or moved. Corrie told herself that she would not, could not, let Rick win this round, she had to....

Rick straightened up. He seemed satisfied and Corrie held her breath. Had it really been that easy? Was that all she'd had to do, stand her ground and he would back off? Then Rick's lips twitched.

"I'll have Dudley check on that dumpster in the picnic area... the residents aren't supposed to be using it for their own personal trash, but I know the lady with the newborn twins in the neighborhood fills her trash cans a lot faster than most of the other residents do and she has a hard time taking her own trash to the dump." Rick put his hat on and tipped it at Corrie before he turned and walked out, leaving her with her mouth hanging open.

Chapter 18

"Hey, Corrie! Can we talk a minute?"

Corrie looked up; she was alone in the office area of the camp store, having finally talked both Jackie and Dana into going and spending an hour or two visiting with their spouses before they had to begin getting ready for the pizza party, and none of the doors had sounded a bell or buzzer to signal someone entering. She started to get up from her seat behind the desk when she heard a tap on the window behind her and she spun around.

"Buster? What are you doing out there? You're not scheduled to work today. Myra's already here and...."

"Yeah, I know," Buster said, keeping his voice down and glancing over his shoulder, as if afraid that his hiding under the office window and talking to Corrie through it would attract attention. "Listen, I need to talk to you. Can I come in?"

"Sure," Corrie said. Buster hesitated; he pressed his forehead against the window screen so hard that it nearly popped out. "What are you doing?" she asked, perplexed. Buster gave her a weak grin.

"Uh, your dog... is he in there with you?"

Corrie sighed. Buster's phobia was getting more and more annoying. She leaned over and gave the old dog a gentle pat to wake him. "Come on, old timer," she said. "Buster's afraid of the Big, Bad Wolf, so you'd better finish your nap upstairs." Renfro sat up groggily, yawned, then gave Corrie a look that said he did not appreciate her interruption of his much-needed rest.

"Upstairs," Corrie repeated, pointing to the stairs. Renfro sighed, stretched, and then took his time ambling across the room, making low grumbling sounds in his throat as he passed her. Oliver, not pleased at all by the disruption in his daily routine, threw a glare in Buster's direction and hissed. Corrie shook her head, unable to help smiling. Her good humor vanished when she turned and saw Buster still hovering outside the window.

"Okay, it's safe to come in now," she said, rolling her eyes as Buster hurried up the walkway and slipped inside the door, still making a huge spectacle of himself as he looked over both shoulders and edged his way in backwards. All he needed was a ninja costume to make himself even more obvious.

Once inside, he made a quick circuit of the office and store, checking the laundry room and family room to see if anyone was in either place, then checking the side door that led to the patio. Corrie wouldn't have been surprised if he was humming the "Mission: Impossible" theme song under his breath and her patience lasted until he went to the bottom of the stairs leading to her living quarters and craned his neck to see if anyone was in the stairwell.

"Okay, Buster, what's going on and what are you doing here? I can barely get you to show up when you're scheduled to work, so I can't imagine what you're doing here on your day off." He returned to the counter, his finger to his lips.

"Listen, Corrie," he said, keeping his voice low. "I had a thought last night about everything that's been going on... you know, about Marvin being killed and all that?"

As if she could forget. She choked back an exasperated sigh rather than choke Buster. "And what did you think last night?" she asked, wondering if she should even encourage the conversation.

He rested his hands on the counter, his dark brown eyes pleading and puppy-like. "Corrie, you believe me when I say that I'd never do a thing to the Landrys, don't you? You know I didn't kill Marvin and steal all that money, right? Even if my gun is missing...."

"Of course, I believe you," she said and it was the truth. Not because she trusted his innate honesty; she just didn't think he'd have the intellect to plan the caper or the guts to pull it off. Buster might look like a bear, but he certainly wasn't a grizzly.

He took her words at face value. He cleared his throat. "See, here's the thing... between you and me, there's only one person who's the most likely suspect."

Corrie knew exactly who Buster had in mind, but she decided to see if he was willing to consider anyone else. "Walter Dodson?" she suggested.

"Huh?" Buster blinked, his confusion wiping the conspiratorial look off his face. "Walter Dodson? Betty's son?"

Corrie raised a brow. "Who were you thinking of?" she asked innocently.

"Well," Buster said slowly, the mention of Walter Dodson having opened up a different avenue of thought... one he was reluctant to consider. "I guess he might be a suspect, too... but actually, I was thinking of someone else...."

"J.D. Wilder," Corrie said and Buster nodded, beaming a huge smile at Corrie's astuteness. She suppressed an exasperated sigh. "Why him?"

"Well, think about it, Corrie," he said eagerly. "He shows up in the middle of the night and nobody knows anything about him, he's a total stranger...."

"Just like most of my other guests," Corrie said tiredly. "Including Walter Dodson."

Buster shook his head; apparently nothing she could say would dissuade him from his suspicions. "Yeah, but this J.D. guy? He's trouble. I mean, you can tell just by looking at him."

"Because he wears leather and rides a motorcycle?"

Her not-so-subtle jab went right over Buster's head. "He's sneaky, too," Buster went on. "He keeps to himself and he doesn't act sociable."

"You've been talking to Rosemary Westlake," Corrie said dryly.

"Why would he come into town for a motorcycle rally and not go to the rally?" Buster persisted, tapping his sausage-like fingers on the counter to emphasize his point. "Tell me that's not weird!"

"He HAS gone to the rally."

"How do you know?"

"Because he told me he had," Corrie said, wondering why she was even pursuing this conversation. Buster's eyes narrowed.

"I haven't seen him there," he said and raised a brow.

"Just because you haven't seen him there doesn't mean he hasn't attended," Corrie argued. Buster was probably too busy enjoying the attention from his girlfriend to notice who else might be at the rally. "Besides, are you telling me you're following him around and checking up on him? What he does with his time is none of your—or anyone else's—business!"

"Come on, Corrie, don't you think I've got a point or two?"

"So far, you haven't said anything that would prove that J.D. had anything at all to do with Marvin's murder." She stood up. "Look, Buster, I know you're concerned because it seems your gun is implicated, so let me just tell you this. A gun was found and it's believed to be the murder weapon...."

The blood drained from Buster's face so fast he nearly fell over. He took a step back and started shaking his head. "What do you mean? They found my gun? Who found it? Where was it? I swear I didn't...."

"Buster!" Corrie said sharply. "Listen! No one is saying you did anything. I'm just telling you they found a gun. They don't know yet for sure if it's yours or if it had anything to do with Marvin's murder. I can't tell you anymore than that. I'm just letting you know so you won't be caught off guard when the police question you."

Buster was almost hyperventilating. He shook his head. "Don't you see, Corrie? They're gonna think I did it! I have to prove I didn't! I have to show them it was J.D.!"

"Buster...."

"He was in the Landrys' RV, Corrie! He knew where the money was hidden!"

"Buster, you can't...."

"I found it, Corrie!" He reached into his jacket and pulled out a bulky package which he plunked down on the counter with such force it made Corrie's pen jump. She stared at the package, then at Buster.

"What is this?" she asked and her heart began to pound. She was almost afraid of his answer and she prayed feverishly that she was wrong.

"The money," Buster whispered. "Twenty-five bundles with one thousand dollars in twenty-dollar bills in each one." He paused, took a deep breath. Corrie couldn't. Her head was spinning.

"Buster, where did you get this?"

"I told you, I found it."

"WHERE?" She screamed the question at him in a whisper. He gave her a look, not understanding her near-hysteria.

"In Wilder's duffel bag. I hung around the fence behind the Landrys' RV this morning, waiting for him to leave his tent. I saw him go up to the bathrooms to take a shower. When I was sure he wouldn't come back right away, I snuck into his tent. Way down at the bottom of his duffel bag, he had this wrapped up in a saddle bag from his bike and that was wrapped up in a bath towel and.... What...?" he squeaked as Corrie lunged across the counter and grabbed him by the collar of his shirt.

"Are you out of your mind?" she hissed at him. "You snooped through one of our guests' possessions? And you took something out of his tent?"

Buster looked hurt. He backed away out of Corrie's grasp. "Corrie, don't you get it? Don't you see? This proves that J.D...."

"Buster, you had no right to do that! Even Rick can't do that without a warrant!"

The look on Buster's face told Corrie that he was very disappointed with her reaction. Why on earth wasn't she impressed with his investigating skills or happy that he had solved the crime?

And he was clueless as to how much trouble he was in.

"But, see, now we have proof," he said slowly, as if that would make it easier for her to understand. "Now we can tell the sheriff that Wilder had the money...."

"HAD the money, Buster," Corrie said, her stomach lurching. The incriminating evidence against J.D. was undeniable, but, unlike Buster, she understood that evidence had been tampered with—again—and Rick was going to go through the ceiling when he found out. She dropped back into her chair, shaking her head. "Buster, how do you expect me to tell Rick about this? 'Oh, hey, Sheriff, Buster just happened to find twenty-five thousand dollars in cash hidden in J.D. Wilder's tent. No, of course, it wasn't lying out in plain sight, Sheriff, he actually went inside J.D.'s tent—without his knowledge—

and went through his duffel bag to find the money!'"

Buster's face looked like it was melting. The realization of what Corrie was saying drained the last bit of triumphant excitement from him and his mouth dropped open. "Oh, man," he breathed. "You don't think... the sheriff's gonna think I shot Marvin Landry... and took the money... and then hid it in Wilder's stuff to frame him?"

Corrie didn't answer; the fact that Buster was able to finally make the connection meant that it wouldn't take anyone—especially Rick—long to do the same.

The question was, did Buster really have proof that J.D. had killed Marvin?

J.D. stood just outside the laundry room door, his heart hammering as he debated what his next move should be.

He'd returned from his shower earlier and noticed the flap that covered the screened zip-door of his tent hanging askew and no wind could account for it not being exactly as he'd left it. One look inside his tent told him that his belongings had been tampered with, even before he opened his duffel bag, cursing himself for not having taken the bundle with him for once. And once he saw Buster doing his best—and failing—to discreetly sneak into the campground office to talk to Corrie, it hadn't taken him long to figure what had happened.

He had sprinted silently across the gravel road and onto the patio outside the laundry room doors. He stopped just inside the doorway, letting his galloping heart slow down and his breathing return to normal before he slipped inside. The laundry room was empty. He had crossed the room in three strides and rested his ear against the door panels, hoping that no one would come upon him listening. Somehow, he had to get that bundle of money back and then, regardless of how he felt about leaving Corrie in the lurch, he had to clear out. Staying here had been a big mistake.

He strained to hear words through the closed door, but all he heard were muffled voices. He didn't dare attempt to open the door just a crack; he didn't know how far it would take to trigger the security buzzer. He edged back out onto the patio and made his way to the corner of the building near the front entrance. The office door was slightly open, and he would be able to hear through the screen, but there was no place for him to hide. He hoped he wouldn't have to wait too long.

Buster's voice, almost unrecognizably whiny, drifted through the screen door. "You mean, no matter what, Wilder's gonna get away with this, Corrie? You're sure the sheriff can't do anything about this?"

"I don't know," Corrie answered and J.D. could hear the strain in her voice. "I don't know what Rick can do with this information and I don't know if you're going to be in trouble as well. We don't even know if this proves anything about J.D. being involved in Marvin's murder...."

J.D. hadn't realized he'd been holding his breath. Corrie didn't believe he was guilty. Or rather, she didn't WANT to believe he was guilty. That was good, but that didn't mean that her sense of duty wouldn't prevent her from reporting Buster's find to the sheriff... and there was no ambiguity about how HE felt about J.D.

Not to mention he still had to get that money back somehow.

Buster's voice grew louder; he was moving toward the door, getting ready to leave. J.D. glanced around and, seeing no one, dashed toward the patio. He slipped around the corner and waited, watching until Buster had made his way to his old Pontiac, which he had parked behind the maintenance shed, and drove away. Buster hadn't been carrying anything in his hands; that meant he had to have left the bundle of money in Corrie's care. J.D. felt the sweat break out along his back.

He didn't have much time. He had to act fast.

Corrie pushed the door shut behind Buster and rested her pounding head against it. Just when she couldn't imagine this nightmare getting worse....

She turned around and slumped against the door, staring at the plastic-wrapped bundle sitting on the counter. She had to get it out of sight before anyone came in and saw it. And she had to call Rick and tell him about it, although she had no idea what she was going to say to him that wouldn't get Buster—and herself—into even more trouble.

She went behind the counter and looked from the bundle to the phone, trying to dredge up the motivation to do what she knew she had to do. She knew she should find a safe place to hide the bundle until she could turn it over to Rick, but her eyes moved dismally around the cramped area behind the counter, seeing nothing. She felt sick to her stomach and wanted to burst into tears.

Was it just to spite Rick that she'd refused to admit that there was something secretive and strange about J.D.? She had allowed herself to get so caught up in his apparent—and flattering—interest in her that she hadn't allowed herself to see the truth about him. Her mind went back to the newspaper clippings that Rick had shown her and she felt herself grow cold. Only a complete fool would ignore the overwhelming proof that was right in front of her. She and her stubborn pride had put her and her staff—her friends, the only family she had—in mortal danger. She couldn't hesitate any longer.

As she reached for the phone, she became dimly aware of the laundry room buzzer going off. She snapped to full attention as she turned in the direction of the laundry room.

J.D. Wilder stood a few feet away.

Corrie's eyes locked with J.D.'s for what seemed like an eternity, though it couldn't have been more than a second or two. Despite his disarming smile, she saw the wariness in his eyes that warned her that he was already on to her. Her heart leaped into her throat and began to hammer wildly.

"Hey, Corrie," he said, the friendly words not quite hiding the strain in his voice. He approached her slowly, his gaze darting toward the bundle, still lying on the counter. She could have kicked herself for not having stashed it away earlier. Did she dare reach for it now? Or should she just hit the speed dial for 911? Should she scream?

Amidst her scrambled thoughts, she suddenly realized he'd been moving closer the whole time and she stepped back, bumping into Jackie's cane that had been left leaning against the stool. She automatically reached for it to keep it from falling over and that was when J.D. lunged toward the bundle on the counter.

Corrie dropped the phone, snatched up the cane with both hands, and brought it down with a "thwack!" on the counter, right on the bundle of money.

J.D.'s eyes widened with surprise and he pulled back a split second before the cane could crush his outstretched hand. Corrie jerked the cane back and swung it like a baseball bat, directly at

J.D.'s head. "Corrie! Wait!" he yelled and ducked away, but she still managed to connect squarely with his left shoulder. He let out a yelp of pain and then a stifled curse as he stumbled backwards a step and Corrie seized the opportunity.

She flailed at him wildly, the cane slashing through the air with all the energy she didn't waste screaming for help. She edged out from behind the counter, J.D.'s own shock at her reaction aiding her in driving him back far enough for her to make a break for the door.

"Corrie!" he yelled. "Corrie, stop! Wait!" He managed to deflect a blow aimed at his head with his left forearm as he reached toward her. Gritting her teeth and fearing that he'd grab the cane the next time she aimed at his upper body, she switched direction and swung the cane down at his legs, feeling a satisfyingly sickening "crunch" as it connected with his right knee. He roared with surprise and pain as his leg buckled and he went down like a falling tree.

She froze, stupefied that she'd managed to bring him down, then made a dash for the door. She gasped as she felt his hand latch onto her ankle and she, too, went flat on her face, still gripping the cane with both hands. His grasp on her leg tightened and she felt him give a mighty tug. Terrified, she twisted onto her side and aimed the next swing of the cane at J.D.'s head. She hit him a glancing blow on the temple, not enough to knock him out as she had hoped, but enough to make him release her ankle. He grabbed his head and groaned, rolling onto his back as Corrie scrambled to her feet.

She backed toward the door, her eyes still on him, the cane upraised to strike if he made another move toward her. Should she run? Or finish him off? She found her voice and shrieked as the front door flew open and Rick burst in, his gun drawn. "Sheriff's department!" he shouted.

Corrie nearly fainted from relief. "Rick!" she half-sobbed, staggering behind him for cover. "Oh, Rick, thank God!"

"Yeah, thank God, Sheriff," J.D. moaned, dragging himself toward the wall away from them. "I can't believe I'm glad to see you!"

"That's far enough, Wilder," Rick warned, moving slowly toward J.D., his gun and steely glare unwavering. "Put your hands up where I can see them!"

J.D. slumped on his back, his arms bent at the elbows, his palms out. He took several deep breaths as Rick moved closer. "On your stomach, hands on your head," Rick ordered.

"Sheriff...."

"Now, Wilder!" Rick roared. Corrie jumped and tightened her grip on the cane she was still holding. She'd never heard Rick use that voice before, nor seen the expression on his face. He took his eyes off J.D. for a second to glance back at her and suddenly the Rick Sutton she knew so well reappeared.

"Could you put the damn cane down for a minute and call for help?" he snapped.

Stung, Corrie stared at him as he jerked his head toward the phone she'd dropped on the floor earlier. She put the cane down on the counter and stepped around him, edging as far away from J.D. as she could. She caught sight of the black, purple and red lump that was welling up on the side of his face. Her eyes met J.D.'s incredulous stare for a brief moment and she turned away to make the call.

"Sheriff," J.D. gasped. "Listen, we need to talk."

"You have the right to remain silent, Wilder. I suggest you take advantage of that," Rick growled.

"Yeah, I know the drill, believe me. Listen, there's something you need to know...."

Rick ignored him, keeping his gun aimed at J.D.'s back as he patted him down with his free hand. He removed the cuffs from his belt and proceeded to secure J.D.'s wrists behind his back before turning him over. J.D. groaned and managed to prop himself up against the wall and shook his head.

Rick turned his attention to Corrie. "Did he hurt you?" he asked, his voice taut. Corrie shook her head, willing herself to calm down. Rick relaxed slightly, but kept his eyes and weapon trained on J.D. "What happened?" he asked.

Corrie indicated the bundle on the counter. "Buster found that in J.D.'s tent," she said, not bothering to explain how he found it. "It's the money stolen from the Landry's RV."

J.D. shook his head and laughed weakly. "No, it's not," he said.

"Be quiet, Wilder. Explain it to your lawyer and then you can tell the judge and jury all about it when you go to trial," Rick snapped. J.D. scowled.

"Sheriff, this won't make it as far as a hearing before you'll be out of a job and Corrie will end up losing this campground. I'm telling you, this is a huge mistake and if you'll check my wallet, you'll see why!"

"Don't threaten us, Wilder," Rick said, his voice edged with ice.

"No threat, Sheriff. Consider it a warning." J.D. rolled to his side slightly, grimacing, and jerked his head toward his left rear pocket. "Go on, get my wallet, you'll see what I mean."

Rick hesitated then reached for the bulky leather tri-fold. He flipped it open, pulled something out that Corrie didn't recognize, then froze, his eyes darting from the item in his hands to the man on the floor. "You've got to be kidding," he said stonily.

J.D. shook his head. "I must say, Sheriff, I never dreamed I'd have my cover blown in such a dramatic—not to mention, painful—way."

"'Cover'?" Corrie repeated. She stared at Rick. "What is he talking about?"

For an answer, Rick tossed the item in his hands to Corrie. It was a shield with the words "Houston Police Department" etched on it. She looked at J.D., dumbfounded, then at Rick. He lowered his gun, pushed back his hat and sighed.

"Corrie, meet Lieutenant Jesse Dean Wilder, Narcotics Division, of the Houston police department," he said.

J.D. sat up, inclined his head in a painful attempt at a bow, and gave Corrie a lop-sided smile. "And up until about twenty minutes ago, it was a pleasure to meet you, too, Miss Black," he said.

Chapter 19

"Why, in the name of all that is sane, didn't you tell me you were a cop from the beginning?" the sheriff asked.

J.D. tried to find a comfortable way to sit in the recliner that Corrie had insisted he take in the family room. Despite himself, he'd been impressed at the way the sheriff had managed to call off most of the sheriff's department and any state police who were responding to Corrie's call for help. Now he sat with his right leg propped up, with an ice pack on his knee and one of the steaks that was to have been used for the Sunday night campground steak dinner pressed against his temple. His shoulder was throbbing as well, but with any luck, Corrie didn't do much more than bruise it. Fortunately, he was able to bend his knee and put some weight on it. He hoped he wouldn't have to present himself in the emergency room at the county medical center; he'd already attracted more attention than he ever wanted and his condition was sure to merit a lot of interest.

Not to mention he had no desire, whatsoever, to explain how he had acquired his injuries.

He sighed and waved away Corrie's offer of a fresh steak for his shiner. "Because I didn't come here as a cop, Sheriff. In fact, I am technically on LOA from the Houston PD. It's the reason I'm not carrying a weapon," he added. He looked from the sheriff to Corrie. "Look, I'm sorry about all this, but as suspicious as it looks, I had nothing to do with robbing the Landrys, much less with Marvin Landry's murder."

"Just how do you happen to be carrying the exact amount of money that the Landrys are missing from their RV?" Sutton asked. He'd asked Deputy Evans to run a check on the serial numbers of the money Marvin had withdrawn from the bank and they hadn't matched the ones in the bundles J.D. was carrying. Having to admit he was wrong was something the sheriff was apparently not accustomed to, but he was taking it in stride. J.D. had to admire him for hanging on to his composure while the case he had been successfully building crumbled into pieces right before his eyes.

Corrie, however, was feeling enough guilt for all of them combined. She finally stopped apologizing when J.D. assured her that he wasn't going to file a complaint against Buster or press assault charges against her. She slid into a chair, apparently hoping the sheriff wasn't going to ask her to leave while he and J.D. got this mess straightened around. J.D. didn't have a problem with her staying; it felt good to have someone in his corner. Even if she had tried to clobber him nearly half to death.

That didn't mean he was ready to drop his guard.

"I have a perfectly legitimate reason for having that money in my possession, Sheriff, and it has nothing to do with the Landry case. Can we leave it at that?"

"No."

"Didn't think so," J.D. muttered. He set the steak down on a plate on the table and wiped his face with the washcloth Corrie had provided him. "Look, Sheriff, it's a long story and, as bad as this is going to sound, I don't have time to explain. Apparently you've done your homework because I've got federal agents on the way to ask me questions I'm not ready to answer."

"Seems like you've got someone keeping you informed, Lieutenant." J.D. couldn't help but grimace when the sheriff used his rank. "The real question here is, whose side are you on? And why are you here?"

J.D. bit back a grim smile. "I know it doesn't look that way, Sheriff, but rest assured, I am on the side of truth and justice."

"But not necessarily on the side of the law."

This time J.D. allowed his smile to slip out. "I'm impressed," he said. The sheriff's expression didn't change.

"And I'm still waiting for an explanation." He pushed two photocopied newspaper clippings across the table at J.D. J.D. didn't bother to glance at them; he already knew what they were. "What's your involvement with this case?" the sheriff repeated.

"What do you think?"

"That you had a hand in busting open this case and somehow got on somebody's wrong side. Same goes for this prosecutor. I'm still working on figuring how you ended up with that particular amount of money in your possession."

"The money has nothing to do with that case, or the Landry case, for that matter," J.D. said flatly. "You're just going to have to take my word for it."

"Right," Sutton said dryly. He tapped the woman's photo. J.D. sighed.

"She was in bed—literally and figuratively—with the drug dealers she was prosecuting. She was supposed to drop the ball on this case; the dealers would have walked, which would have been career suicide for her, but made her ten million dollars richer. Problem was, her husband didn't like the idea much... he'd spent the last three years working to bust this drug ring."

"He was a member of your vice squad?"

"Yeah," J.D. said shortly. He shrugged. "Can't blame him for not liking the whole scheme... especially since the wife decided to make HIM the fall guy while she headed off to Mexico or the Caribbean, or wherever, with her drug kingpin boyfriend, after cleaning out their joint bank account... of course, her plan all along was to knock off the husband and plant evidence to prove that he was in league with the dealers. She tried to make it look like an accident."

The sheriff raised a brow. Corrie leaned forward in spite of herself. "The fire in El Paso?" she asked.

J.D. nodded. "The idea was to lure her husband to the 'safe house' the dealers had in El Paso, ostensibly to show him proof of their connection with a major cartel. She didn't know he was already on to her... and she sure as hell didn't know that the ringleaders had already decided she was too much of a risk. Her husband found her car parked two blocks from the safe house, with her luggage in it, along with the cash from their personal account and a plane ticket to Cancun. Lucky for him it took a while to stash the money in his travel bag and he was late to his meeting with his wife. The gas explosion went off right on time, while he was still at the car."

"And his wife didn't get out in time?" Corrie asked incredulously. J.D. gave her a glance; he didn't like what he was about to tell her.

"I told you the dealers were on to her. They showed up before her husband did, then made sure she *wouldn't* get out." He reached for his throat and made a curious twisting motion, then cocked an eyebrow at the sheriff. "You follow?"

Corrie gasped. Sutton shot her a glance then turned back to J.D. "You're giving me an awful lot of information," he said. "Almost too much. How do you happen to know such intimate details about this woman and her husband?"

J.D. said nothing for a long moment. He touched the photo of the woman gently with one finger and his jaw tightened. "When she went to work for that law firm in Houston, she went back to using her maiden name professionally. Said that 'Wilder' didn't convey the image she wanted to project."

"Oh, my God," Corrie said, catching her breath.

J.D. pushed the clipping away.

Chapter 20

Corrie gladly gave over the running of the Saturday evening pizza party to Red and Dana. Rick had asked J.D. to accompany him to the sheriff's office to discuss a few things. Naturally, the invitation did not extend to Corrie. Once Dana and Jackie had heard what had happened, they insisted that Corrie let them take care of the pizza party. There were few people who would be attending; the majority of guests that were bike rally participants would be gone until the early hours of Sunday morning and Jackie said there was no reason for Corrie to knock herself out after all that had happened. She made up the dough and the sauce before she and Jerry left for Saturday evening Mass and Dana chopped all the toppings. Red confessed to always wanting to try tossing a pizza. After a few near-misses, including one that almost landed on the roof, he was able to assume Rick's usual role of amusing the guests at dinner.

Corrie leaned against the counter, staring up the drive to the highway. Her guests seemed to be perfectly content with the way things were going and, being reassured by Red and Dana that they had the pizza party under control, she had returned to the office. There wasn't much more to do in there, since most of her guests were otherwise occupied, but at least she would be easy to find. Just in case. Although the truth was that she really didn't think Rick would return to fill her in on all the details. But she could hope.

Her coffee had grown cold in the cup in her hands and she was thinking about refreshing it when the bell rang over the side door. She turned and nearly dropped the cup when Walter Dodson walked in. "What are you doing here?" she blurted.

"Glad to see you, too," he snarled, his face growing a more pronounced shade of red than usual. Had he gone grayer in the last couple of days? Corrie stopped herself from fingering the end of the braid of her own dark hair.

"I didn't know you were back," she said, gathering her scattered thoughts. For some reason, the sight of Walter Dodson unnerved her, despite Rick's repeated assurances and proof that he was innocent of Marvin's murder. "How's Betty?"

"How do you think she is?" he snapped and then seemed contrite. He stuck his hands deep in his pockets and rocked back on his heels. "She's all right," he mumbled. "The sheriff told her she should check into a hotel until the arrangements can be made," he said. "She wanted to come get some stuff out of the RV. I told her I'd take care of it, but she insisted." He shook his head and prowled restlessly around the camp store.

"She's there now?"

"Yeah. I wanted her to wait till tomorrow. Told her I had some stuff to take care of first and I didn't want to leave her here alone. But she insisted," he repeated. His gaze darted toward the front door, then the TV room and the laundry room door.

Corrie's guard went up and she wished she'd remembered to let Renfro back downstairs. "What stuff are you taking care of? Why are you here now?"

He looked at her, his eyes narrowing, as he moved toward the counter. "I was kind of curious," he said, his voice lower than usual. "How much do you know about the Westlakes?"

"The Westlakes?" Corrie raised a brow. "What about them?"

Walter shook his head irritably. "Don't be as cagey as Ma," he growled. "I mean this home-based business they're in. Ma says she isn't sure what it is... something to do with Internet sales. Marv wanted in on it, thought it would make them a bundle. A lot he knew about making money... he was better at blowing it!"

"'Blowing it'?"

Walter sneered. "Don't play dumb. I know the sheriff's probably filled you in on Marv's and Ma's financial picture. You two are pretty cozy, aren't you?"

"Not really," she said coolly, not sure which statement she was answering, although the heat in her face probably gave away the fact that she wasn't being completely honest in either case. "I always assumed the Landrys were fairly well-off but frugal."

"*They* were fairly well-off? Or Marv was?" Walter shook his head. "Ma had no choice but to be frugal, but Marv was just a tightwad, plain and simple, unless he got hold of some get-rich-quick scheme. He lost more money on wild investments, crazy business deals, and gambling losses than he's ever made. Know why they stayed in RV parks? Marv lost their home, all their retirement savings. That RV is the only property Ma's got... except for the money that's gone missing!"

Corrie reached for the counter to steady herself, hoping the action looked casual. "But how could they afford to travel...?"

"They didn't 'travel'," Walter said. "Except for coming here every summer—for which Ma footed the bill out of her retirement—they kept that RV parked in my driveway all winter long, every year, for the last ten years!"

With an effort, Corrie managed to close her mouth and swallow. How was it possible that people she considered good friends had managed to keep their true lives such a secret? "I'm sorry... I didn't know...." She wasn't sure why she was apologizing, but she didn't know what else to say.

Walter shrugged. "Sure, you didn't. Why would you? That's how Ma was... all about keeping up appearances. She'd have died if any of her friends knew the way things really were." He sighed. His mask of bravado slipped; Corrie wondered if she was seeing the real Walter Dodson for the first time. "Dad wasn't rich but his life insurance left Ma pretty comfortable... she'd never would have had to take that postal service job if she hadn't married Marv. Didn't take him long to drain Ma of every penny Dad had left her... and me." His expression hardened and he threw Corrie a sharp glance. "I guess that sounds like I have a real good motive for knocking off Marv... maybe I do, but that doesn't mean I did." He moved toward the counter. "I know these people, the Westlakes, are making money... they offered Marv a chance to buy into their business, told him that he'd be able to make all kinds of money. Ma didn't like the idea. She had managed to keep Marv from spending too much in the last couple of years, hoping they'd be able to build up a nice nest egg. She was tired of living hand to mouth at their age... she wanted to enjoy life instead of pinching pennies. She felt this investment was too risky for the amount of money they had left... and for the kind of financial savvy that Marv had, which was zilch. But Marv wouldn't listen. He never listened," Walter said bitterly.

Corrie shook her head. She couldn't believe she was actually beginning to feel sorry for Walter Dodson. And Corrie's heart went out to Betty; she couldn't believe that Marvin could have been so self-centered. And what's more, she was feeling sorry for Marvin... for his need to prove himself and for his failures to succeed. However, she was sure that Walter wouldn't share her sympathy for his step-father, so she kept her feelings to herself. "So what's Betty going to do now?" she asked, training her gaze out the window, searching in vain for Rick's Tahoe.

Walter Dodson shook his head. "Not sure yet. She's gotta see how deep in debt Marv left her and how much of it is her responsibility. Then we'll see. I'm hoping she might be able to enjoy the last few years of her life doing what she wants to do... travel, go shopping, gardening...."

"Gardening?" Corrie's head jerked around. She managed to catch sight of the deep flush on Walter's face before his usual scowl replaced it.

"Ma loved puttering around in her garden... she had one in my backyard," he said quickly. "That was before she ended up in that wheelchair. That was Marv's fault, too, you know. He took everything from her that she loved." He stopped abruptly and shook his head. "You sure you don't know anything about the Westlakes' business?" he snapped.

"If you want to know so badly, why don't you ask them yourself?" she fired back, forgetting to feel sorry for him.

"It doesn't matter anymore," he muttered. "Ma's out of it now and all she needs to do is get her money back and things will be fine."

"'Fine'?" Corrie repeated incredulously. "Her husband was

murdered! How can things be fine?"

Walter Dodson moved toward the door. "Call me heartless if you want to," he said. "But the truth is, in the long run, Ma's far better off without Marv. I'll take care of her."

His ominous words gave her a chill. She made an attempt to sound casual. "Betty has always been more like a friend than just a guest here," she said. "I'm more than happy to help her with whatever...."

"Ma'll be just fine," he interrupted, shooting her a venomous glance. "She needs some time alone, that's all, and she'll get things sorted out soon. Don't trouble yourself."

"It's no trouble," Corrie said, watching him closely.

He went to the front door and paused with his hand on the knob. "I said I'd take care of her and I mean it. Don't bother her and let her work things out. That's what I'm here for." He gave Corrie a grim smile and he went out the door.

Corrie watched him get into his rental car and drive away. He hadn't gone back to the RV... whatever "stuff" he'd told Betty he had to take care of, it was obvious that it was information he didn't want her to hear about. And it had to do with the Westlakes.

Corrie made up her mind. She went out the side door and moved quietly to the gate that opened onto the patio area. She could hear conversation, cheers, and applause—apparently Red had perfected his pizza-tossing. One thing she did not hear, however, was a dog barking. She peered around the corner and confirmed what she had suspected... Rosemary Westlake never went anywhere without Bon-Bon. Neither Rosemary nor Donald were in attendance for the pizza party. Perhaps they had slipped away from the campground and gone to town for dinner, just to avoid any questions, but Corrie doubted that. Now would be a good time for her to pay them a visit.

She headed down the gravel path that took her past the Landrys' RV and her steps slowed. She looked at the RV's darkened windows—the blinds were all down and closed, which seemed odd to Corrie. There was a nice cool breeze that most people would have welcomed on a warm spring night. A light showed dimly from the bedroom area. Betty might be in there resting or sleeping or maybe sorting through paperwork. Corrie's heart ached; even if Marvin had been no

Romeo, surely Betty had to be missing him terribly. She fought the urge to go up to the RV and knock on the door. Betty needed her privacy right now. She started walking in the direction of the Westlakes' RV.

Walter Dodson's concern for Betty seemed out of character for him. Betty and Marvin had never been openly affectionate and it had seemed to Corrie that it was no different between mother and son. Betty had never so much as mentioned Walter in all the years Corrie had known her, even though, according to Walter himself, Betty and Marvin had spent all their winters parked in his driveway. Why had he been such a secret for so many years? Did he resent that as much as he seemed to resent the way Marvin had treated his mother? Then why suddenly all the consideration and hovering over Betty? Was it because now Marvin was gone and he felt free to do so? Or was there a different, more sinister reason? It was one thing to want to be able to take care of one's mother, but something else to prevent anyone, especially an old friend, from even approaching her. Corrie wondered what it was he was afraid Betty would say to her... and about what. From the day they arrived, Betty was ill-at-ease around her son and anytime his name was mentioned, her manner became alternately guarded or vague... as if she were afraid she'd say the wrong thing.

Corrie's steps slowed to a halt. Was it possible that Betty had always been afraid of Walter? Was that why she never talked about him? And if it was true that they were so short of money that they had to spend the off-season parked at his home, did she now feel that she owed him something—loyalty, perhaps? And was all that because she knew he had murdered Marvin? But his alibis checked out...

Only because Betty had vouched for the time he had been gone, Corrie thought. *And only Betty had heard the voice in the RV before Marvin was shot.* She had been vague about both... perhaps deliberately vague....

Corrie looked up as Rick's Tahoe pulled into the campground. Abandoning her idea of questioning the Westlakes, she hurried back to the office to see what information Rick might be willing to give her.

She entered the side door just as Rick and J.D. were coming in the front door. J.D. gave her a grin which helped alleviate the pang of guilt she felt at seeing him still limping on the knee she had attempted to shatter. The swelling on his face had gone down, too, as well. Rick nodded to her and stopped her from getting him any coffee.

"Any more coffee and I won't be able to close my eyes for a week," he said. She shot a look at J.D. whose expression had sobered.

"What's wrong?" she asked.

"Besides the fact that Marvin Landry's murderer is still at large, absolutely nothing," Rick snapped then looked contrite. "Sorry. I told you I've had too much coffee," he said.

"Blame me for his bad mood," J.D. volunteered, resting his hip on the edge of the courtesy table to take the weight off his injured knee. "I was too perfect a suspect to be innocent. Maybe if I'd been straight with the sheriff from the get-go, he wouldn't have wasted so much time on me."

Rick shrugged. "Playing the blame game won't get us anywhere, Wilder. We need to go back to the beginning and see what we missed."

We? Corrie hid her surprise at the use of the word; better to capitalize on it before Rick realized what he'd said and changed his mind. "Mind if I ask where Walter Dodson is on the suspect hit parade?" she asked.

Rick gave her a look of resigned patience. "He'd be at the top of the charts, if it weren't for his iron-clad alibi. There's no way all those witnesses in mid-town could be wrong in exactly the same way." He stopped abruptly and his eyes narrowed. "Any reason why you brought him up?"

"You just missed him. He was here a little while ago, asking questions about the Westlakes."

"The Westlakes?" J.D. said, raising his unbruised brow. Rick nodded.

"Apparently, the late Marvin Landry was thinking about entering a business arrangement with the Westlakes."

"The missing money?" J.D. asked.

"That's our guess," Rick said, and the fact that he called it "our guess" made Corrie feel one-hundred percent better than she had in days. J.D. nodded thoughtfully.

"And what kind of business venture are the Westlakes running?"

"We have no idea," Corrie said, but then she glanced at Rick. "Or do we? Do YOU?"

Rick cleared his throat and Corrie did a double take. She'd never seen him look so uncomfortable. "Actually, that was what I was coming over to talk to you about when Mr. Wilder here distracted us." He cleared his throat again and, to her shock, his face turned an alarming shade of brick red. Corrie waited but when Rick didn't meet her gaze she gave up waiting for his answer and her heart dropped into her stomach.

"Don't tell me—they're dealing drugs. Or laundering money," she said, slumping against the counter. The last thing she wanted to hear was that, not only were two of her long-time guests involved in an illegal business right under her nose on her own property, but they had tried to involve two other long-time guests... one of whom had ended up murdered. Rick cleared his throat again.

"No...." He chewed his lower lip and gave J.D. a quick glance. J.D. shrugged. He obviously had no clue as to what kind of business the Westlakes were running. Rick sighed and shook his head. "Okay," he said. "Let me just say it. They own a business called 'Romance Enhanced' and they specialize in... uh...." He cleared his throat. "Lingerie, perfumes, and... other items of an extremely personal nature."

Corrie's jaw went slack. For what seemed like an eternity, she could not speak. Finally, two incredulous words burst from her lips. "The WESTLAKES?" From the way Rick was avoiding her eyes, she could tell he was just as flabbergasted—not to mention mortified—as she was. J.D.'s eyes went wide and he spun on his heel and went toward the laundry room door. At first Corrie assumed he was checking to make sure no one walked in on this highly sensitive conversation. Then he turned and Corrie could see from the way he was biting his lip that he was struggling to keep from bursting out laughing.

Rick cleared his throat yet again, shooting a venomous glance at J.D. "It seems that they didn't have any actual 'hands on' involvement in this business," he began, flushing at his own choice of words. "It started as a multi-level marketing enterprise that they got into at ground-floor level years ago. They're now at management level and in charge of several distributors who do the actual hosting and selling. Donald and Rosemary just handle the paperwork, fill the orders on-line, sign up more people to become distributors and party hosts... and collect pretty hefty paychecks."

Corrie shook her head. "And Marvin Landry was going to pay them twenty-five thousand dollars to get into this business?" she croaked. Rick shrugged and looked at J.D. who was still fighting back laughter.

"It doesn't usually work that way in multi-level marketing," J.D. said, making a concerted effort to pull himself together. "The way it works is that the Landrys—or rather, Marvin—would sign up to become a distributor, either by direct sales or setting up a website... or hosting a home party, in this case. The first level usually isn't the most lucrative; mostly you'd get steep discounts or free merchandise, depending on the company you're dealing with, or you'd get a percentage of what you sell. In Marvin Landry's case, he might keep a portion of the profits, but his main goal would be to get others to sign up under him to sell the products and he'd get a portion of their profits. Then they'd do the same and so on. Every level you go up, the more money you make. The goal is to get as many people under you as you can, as quickly as you can. If he was offering the Westlakes a hefty sum of money, I suspect it was because they were thinking of getting out of the business and he wanted to buy in at their level instead of starting at the bottom."

"That's it exactly," Rick said, nodding. "Donald wanted out of the business. He told me they'd made a substantial amount of money over the years and invested it well and they were set for a cushy retirement. When Rosemary discovered last summer that Marvin was a sucker for get-rich-quick schemes, she figured it was a golden opportunity. And since it was a lucrative business, she didn't worry that Marvin wouldn't be able to recoup the money plus a lot more. The problem, she said, was that Betty was dead set against it."

"I don't blame her," Corrie said, feeling her cheeks grow hotter by the second. "I can't imagine someone like Betty...." *Or Marvin, for that matter!* she thought. Her voice trailed off and she looked at Rick. "So she did know what Marvin was trying to get into, but she was too embarrassed to tell us. Or her son."

"So Dodson didn't know the nature of the Westlakes' business," J.D. said. He looked at Corrie and she shook her head.

"Not from what he told me earlier. He was trying to get me to tell him and he didn't believe that I didn't know."

"Well, needless to say, he wouldn't be any more thrilled at the idea of his mother getting herself involved in this kind of business than Betty herself was," Rick said dryly. "If he finds out, he might want to kill Marvin all over again."

They were silent, then Corrie said, "Do you think it might be a good idea to talk to Betty again... I mean, if we let her know that we know what Marvin was planning to use that money for... and let her know that we won't let anyone else know...."

Her voice trailed away as Rick's gaze met hers. "What else did Walter Dodson tell you?"

Corrie took a deep breath and gave them a quick rundown of what Walter had told her about Marvin and Betty's financial situation and how it affected their lives... and how he made it sound like Marvin's death wouldn't exactly be such a heart-rending tragedy for Betty in the long run.

"Damn the alibi, Sheriff," J.D. said, folding his arms across his chest and shaking his head. "This guy has 'prime suspect' written all over him!"

"I can't ignore the fact that eleven people, six of whom are respected business owners, and all of them complete strangers to Walter Dodson, have stated without question that he was in Ruidoso, twelve miles away, at the time Marvin was shot!" Rick snapped. "Unless you're suggesting mass hallucination or that Dodson has the ability to bilocate, there's no way that he's guilty of Marvin's murder!" Rick shook his head. "I've got to get back to the office," he said. "I was supposed to have gotten word back from the medical examiner's office about the exact time of Marvin's death by now and the crime lab was supposed to put a rush on the ballistics tests on the gun—not to mention all the tests they were running on the trash in the can where the gun was found, all the debris they vacuumed out of Buster's car, and all the prints and other evidence they got from the Landrys' RV. Either they're really as swamped as they claim they are or else they figure a murder in Bonney County isn't as important as one that happened anywhere else in the state." He looked at Corrie, then at J.D. "You going to remain for the rest of your scheduled stay, Wilder?"

J.D. shrugged. "Why not? It's paid for through tomorrow. Might as well hang around and see if this case gets wrapped up before I have to go."

For some reason, those words caused a slight pang in Corrie's chest. She'd gotten used to J.D. being around and, now that she knew he wasn't a murderer, didn't want to think about him leaving... or think too much on why she felt that way, either. She swallowed hard and avoided J.D.'s gaze. "Want some pizza before you go, Sheriff?" she said. "I think Red's pretty pleased with himself and wants your expert opinion."

Rick half-smiled—the first time he had in a long time. "Only if I can get it to go," he said. "It's going to be a long night. Corrie," he said, stopping her as she headed for the patio. "You're still going to the eight o'clock Mass tomorrow?"

"Of course," she said, perplexed. She never missed the early Sunday morning Mass... and neither did he. He nodded.

"Just checking," he said. Corrie wasn't sure she believed him, but decided that that was one mystery that she'd have to let go for the time being.

Chapter 21

J.D. made himself at home in the straight-back chair he favored in the TV room and waited for Corrie to finish getting the sheriff his pizza. He was debating whether he should honor the sheriff's request to not say one word to Corrie about his request and risk Corrie's wrath when she found out—and she WOULD find out—or make his own life easier and be completely honest with Corrie.

Sheriff Rick Sutton, on an otherwise silent trip back to the campground, had finally let J.D. know exactly what his feelings were regarding Corrie. The man was completely in love with her and had been for a long, long time. Not that he had come right out and said so. All he said was, "Wilder, I'm sorry about your wife. And I know you've got a lot going on that you have to deal with. But I need to know that I can count on you to keep Corrie safe until we find whoever murdered Marvin. I've got an entire county to take care of and, much as I want to, I can't be at the campground round the clock... but you can. However long you're going to be there, don't let her out of your sight. Please."

It was the "please" that got to J.D. He had stared at Sutton's face for a few seconds. He never turned to look at J.D., but the set of his jaw and the determined stare out the windshield told J.D. more than words could.

"You got it, Sheriff," he said and only then did Sutton turn to look at him and give him a nod of thanks. "Just remind me to stay away from her when she's got some kind of stick in her hands, all right?" J.D. added, rubbing his shoulder ruefully.

The sheriff let out a short laugh and shook his head. "She's a much better fielder than batter, Wilder. You're lucky she was swinging a cane at you instead of lobbing rocks!"

J.D. knew that Corrie would have a fit if she thought the sheriff was having someone watch her. But if he didn't tell her and she found out that she'd been watched, she'd be mad at both the sheriff AND him. Either way, she'd be mad at the sheriff, so J.D. decided to save his own tail. He gave her an affable grin as she entered the TV room after the sheriff left.

She stopped and her eyes narrowed. "What?" she asked.

He gave her a wide-eyed look. "What, what?"

"What are you up to? Or rather, what has Rick put you up to?" She folded her arms across her chest and the warmth in her coffee-colored eyes was missing. J.D. had never been fond of iced coffee and now he knew why.

"Okay," he said, realizing that Corrie had probably suspected all along what the sheriff had planned, but waited until he was gone to corner J.D. "The sheriff wants me to keep an eye on you. Not," he said emphatically, "because he's afraid you're going to go poking into something you shouldn't, but because he's worried that whoever killed Marvin thinks that you might know too much."

He braced himself for a barrage of angry and hurt words, but Corrie merely bit her lip and cast a quick glance back toward the office. Her eyes drilled into J.D.'s but her voice was softer. "Are you being completely honest with me? You're not saying that to spare my feelings?"

"Corrie," J.D. said as he stood up and moved toward her. "I don't think you realize just how much danger you're in... and it's precisely because you HAVE been a lot of help. Maybe more help than the sheriff would like to admit," he added. "Consider yourself in a sort of 'witness protection program' for the next couple of days."

"Thanks. I think," Corrie said, forcing a smile. She sighed and shook her head. "I don't know why Rick wasn't straight with me about it. I had a feeling he was up to something, but I also knew he'd never admit it, so I let it go."

"Maybe he knew you'd blow up at him if he told you?"

"So he threw you under the bus? That's not like Rick."

J.D. shrugged. "We both know he's got a lot on his mind. Maybe he just wanted to avoid an argument. He didn't want to be worrying about you being upset at him on top of everything else."

"Rick's used to me being upset with him," Corrie said dryly. She spread her hands out. "So what's the plan? Are you going to spend the night in your tent, or should I pull out the rollaway bed for you to stay in the office or the TV room?"

Well, THAT was easier than he had expected. J.D. quirked an eyebrow and smiled. He wasn't sure which one of the options Corrie had offered the sheriff would prefer, but he decided to err on the side of caution. "Let me head over to my tent and make it look like I'm turning in early... if anyone asks, I wiped out on my bike—I sure look like it," he added, grinning as Corrie's face reddened. "Don't worry about it," he said sternly. "Just think of it as a disguise, adding to my cover story. No one will question why I'm not at the rally or hanging around the patio socializing. Or why I don't feel like staying up late. What time do you lock up the office and store?"

"Eight, sometimes eight-thirty on a Saturday," she said.

"I'll make a late trip to the mens' room about eight-thirty, eight-forty-five," he said. "I should be able to slip into the laundry room without being seen and once you let me in, lock the door behind me. We'll make sure no one will be leaving the door propped tonight," he said.

Corrie nodded, her lips set grimly, but he noticed her give a slight shake of her shoulders, as if his words had given her a chill. His heart twisted. Try as she might, she couldn't hide the fact that she was afraid. "Should we tell the Pages and the Myers? I mean, they live on site, too... and they're my friends. They should know what's going on." J.D. nodded.

"I agree," he said. "They need to be on alert, also. I'm sure that the sheriff doesn't want to risk losing any of you," he said, mentally adding, *But especially you.*

"Okay," Corrie said. "The pizza party will be wrapping up in the next hour or so."

"That gives me time to check all your windows and doors and take a look around the campground." He nodded toward the stairs. "I take it that leads to your living quarters?"

"Yes."

"Anyone but you ever go up there?"

"Nobody," Corrie said with a firm shake of her head. J.D. raised an eyebrow.

"Nobody? You never entertain guests at home?"

She raised a brow back at him. "All right. My apartment isn't much more than a bedroom, a kitchen, and a bathroom. Only my best friend, Shelli Davenport, comes up once a week, and the Pages for dinner on very rare occasions. I'd like to keep my private life just that, J.D.," she said, pronouncing every word clearly. "This entire campground is my home. Any other entertaining I do takes place down here... not in my bedroom. Is that clear?"

J.D. nodded. "Crystal clear." He had half-expected Corrie to tell him that her social life and entertainment habits were none of his business, but it made him happy to hear that she rarely brought anyone into her inner sanctum—not even the sheriff, apparently. "So, you have any objections if I start by checking your bedroom windows?"

Corrie smiled. "No objections, but it might be a good idea if I go up first and disengage my security system."

"Security system?" J.D. frowned. "What kind of security system do you have?"

"One with four legs, a tail, and lots of fur," she said with a laugh. J.D. grinned.

"And you want to make sure he doesn't bite me?"

"Oh, no danger of that," she said with a wave of her hand as she started up the stairs. "But if I let you walk in on him while he's sleeping, he might keel over from a heart attack!"

Corrie sighed and looked at the clock, positive it had to be broken. Surely it had been longer than two minutes since the last time she looked at it... it couldn't only be a quarter to three in the morning. She couldn't be THAT nervous.

She sat up and listened. J.D. had insisted on securing her windows, so she couldn't enjoy the spring night breeze or the sound of the creek nearby. Other than Renfro's steady snores and Oliver's little cat-motor rumbling steadily, the only other sounds were the occasional footsteps of J.D. Wilder as he made his circuit around the camp store and office. His steps were interrupted by soft rattling sounds as he checked doors to make sure they were still locked and not tampered with. At longer intervals, she heard a slight creak as he settled onto the rollaway bed to rest in between patrols—but certainly not to sleep. He had declined the offer of using the Barcalounger in the TV room for that very reason. Comfort wasn't a option; he was going to stay awake and alert.

Corrie drew her knees up under her chin. Normally she would have thought that Rick was being overly cautious in insisting that she have someone watch her round-the-clock and, under normal circumstances, she would have resisted any attempts for him to have anything but a deputy patrolling the campground. But he had asked J.D. Wilder to watch out for her—and that made a difference. He might not like J.D. personally and he might still be sore over the fact that J.D. kept his status as a law enforcement officer under wraps, but he apparently trusted J.D.'s abilities and instincts. Which made Corrie fully appreciate just how much danger she was in.

Restlessly, she got up and threw on a pair of jeans and a sweatshirt. Oliver and Renfro, awakened by her abrupt movements, looked at her curiously as she crept, barefooted, to the top of the stairs leading down to the office and sat down on the top step. The door at the bottom of the stairs was open and she no sooner settled down when J.D. appeared in the doorway. His face was in shadows except for his eyes. "Something wrong?" he asked, his voice taut with tension.

She shook her head and brushed her hair back from her face. "Can't sleep. It's a little stuffy with the windows shut."

He gave her a grim smile. "Sorry about that. Not taking any chances."

"I know," she said. "See or hear anything unusual?"

J.D. shrugged. "Depends on your definition of 'unusual'... looks like the Westlakes got home and went straight to bed. Most of your bike rally guests are tucked in for the night and no one seems to have needed to make a nighttime trip to the restrooms. Only Walter Dodson hasn't come back yet."

Corrie got up and went down the stairs. "Is the light still on at the Landrys' RV?" She and J.D. moved to the side door and peered out into the darkness toward the Landrys' RV. A dim light still showed through the blinds of the bedroom window.

"She probably sleeps with a light on. For safety reasons. Most elderly folks do," J.D. said.

"Yeah," Corrie agreed. "I just hate the thought of her being there alone... not that I think I'd feel better if her son was there." J.D. turned to look at her.

"You think he had something to do with Marvin's murder, don't you?" he said. Corrie shrugged.

"I think Betty's afraid of him... I think she knows a lot more than she's admitting... and I think she's trying to protect her son." J.D. nodded and motioned her away from the window.

"You might be right—and the sheriff might be inclined to agree with you—but there's still a lot of things that don't add up."

"I know," Corrie said. She slipped onto her stool behind the counter. J.D. took the chair Oliver usually occupied.

"You should probably go get some sleep," he said. "You've got to be tired."

"Not as tired as you must be," Corrie argued. "I've only been losing sleep a couple of nights. You've been living a nightmare for a while."

J.D. cocked an eyebrow at her. "It comes with the territory, Corrie. Being a cop's not easy."

"But... losing your wife in such a horrible way?" She hadn't meant to blurt it out. J.D. looked away and said nothing for nearly a full minute. "I'm sorry. I just... I'm sorry," she repeated softly.

He stared out the window, his hawk-like profile outlined in silver from the moonlight. The usual glimmer in his eyes had dulled and his gaze seemed fixed on a point a million miles away. He sighed. "You get tired of living a lie after a while, Corrie. But never, in a thousand years, would I have wanted it to end the way it did." He turned back toward her, folded his arms across his chest, and tilted his chair back against the wall. "I did four years in the Marines right out of high school before I decided to become a police officer. I was a rookie cop in Dallas when I met Trish," he said. "She was a first-year law student. We were both young and on fire to right the wrongs of the world, eager to fight for truth, justice, and the American way... just a crazy couple of idealists." He smiled tightly and shook his head, his eyes misty with memories. "I moonlighted as a mall security guard to help her get through law school, and she worked as a clerk in a law firm, trying to learn all she could, getting her foot in every door she could. She was offered a position in the district attorney's office... not a lot of money, of course, but she had a chance to make a difference, be one of the good guys, lock up the scum—especially drug dealers and pushers—that was destroying society.

"By that time, I'd been a cop for five years and getting disillusioned. I was catching the bad guys but she couldn't get them convicted. It was heart-breaking—risking my life on the streets, her being stressed and losing sleep trying to build a case, only to see them walk on technicalities. And we were always broke. Then, about five years ago, her folks died in a traffic accident and left us a modest house in Houston, which saved us the rent we were paying on an apartment in Dallas, so we moved. I got in with the Houston Police Department, she got a position with the district attorney's office. Her boss gave her a chance to shine and soon she was being courted by law firms all over the city... big money offers. By that time, I'd been promoted and was in charge of narcotics. It didn't take me long to see who a lot of those law firms were representing—and where the money was coming from."

He fell silent and Corrie shifted uncomfortably. "She wanted to start defending drug dealers instead of convicting them?"

"Trying to convict them," J.D. corrected dryly. "She was getting tired of it... and the money she was being offered was way more than she'd ever make in the D.A.'s office. We argued about it a lot," he said with a sigh that was heavy with regret. "It was as if she was fighting me personally. She said I could quit the police department and do something else... like that would make me forget everything I already knew. But I didn't want to do anything else. I wanted to make a difference... and I couldn't see how turning a blind eye to where the money was coming from was going to help me do that." He straightened up, the front legs of the chair punctuating his frustration as they struck the floor. He looked out the window, scanning the area with radar-quickness, before he stood up to make another circuit. Corrie said nothing until he came back. He didn't sit down, but leaned against the wall, his hands deep in his pockets, his mind deep in bitter memories.

"But she didn't actually take the job at the law firm?" she asked. J.D. shook his head.

"No. And maybe, somehow, I might have learned to live with that; at least, I knew what side she was really on. Then she realized that if she played her cards right, she could make as much money—maybe more—right where she was. Of course, I found her change of heart suspicious. I became really careful with the 'How was your day?' conversations at dinner. It was like I was living with the enemy and I didn't know what I was supposed to do. It didn't matter. During the last three years I spent building up a case to bring down a major cartel, she was working with that same cartel to blow the case and make me the fall guy.

"I figured it out... I don't think she ever knew I had. Then I went through hell, trying to decide what to do. Take her down with the cartel? Legally, that's what I was supposed to do. But could I do that to someone I vowed to love, honor, and cherish, even if she had already decided that I could be collateral damage? On the other hand, how could I let these criminals walk? The day I found her gone and our bank account cleaned out, she made it easy for me to make up my mind what to do. But in the end, it didn't matter... by that time, the decision had been made by someone else." He took a deep breath and turned away, moving toward the side door where he stood silently looking out into the night. Corrie stood and moved quietly up behind him.

"It wasn't your fault," she whispered. At first she didn't think he had heard her, but the tension that radiated from him told her that he had. He shook his head slowly and she went on, "You know you'd never have let her go in there if you thought...."

"It doesn't matter," he said, suddenly turning toward her, his eyes blazing and his voice harsh. She stepped back and he held his hands up. "Sorry," he said. "What I mean is, I should have known, Corrie. I knew the kind of people she was dealing with. Yeah, I know, SHE should have known better, too, but the money blinded her. I was the cop; I was the husband. It was MY job to protect her. I should have. I didn't."

His arms dropped to his sides and he stared at the floor. Corrie said nothing; there was nothing she could say that would make a difference. It occurred to her that there was a lot about J.D. that reminded her of Rick—his commitment to his job, his family, his values. That and a tendency to assume more responsibility than he should. It was no wonder she found herself attracted to him. She shook herself and J.D.'s eyes came into focus, the intensity in his gaze leaving no doubt about his determination. "I'm not making the same mistake again, Corrie," he said quietly.

Before she could say a word, headlights flashed in the front windows of the office, followed by the sound of tires squealing on the pavement and the roar of a car's engine headed straight for the main door of the office.

Chapter 22

J.D. and Corrie spun toward the front door. A vehicle—it appeared to be an SUV—had pulled into the campground, faster than the posted speed limit allowed, and seemed to be heading straight for the front of the building. Corrie gasped and J.D. grabbed her arm and pushed her toward the laundry room door as he ducked toward the TV room. Corrie paused with her hand on the door, her heart hammering wildly, as the SUV fishtailed to a stop just outside the front door. A door slammed and J.D. hissed, "Corrie! Get...."

Before he could finish, she heard Rick's voice as he pounded on the office door. "Wilder! Corrie!"

J.D. slipped out of the TV room and went to the door. "Sheriff?"

"Open up, Wilder! Where's Corrie?"

"I'm right here," she said, hurrying forward as J.D. unlocked the door and let Rick in. Rick's face was grim and his eyes fastened on Corrie. He didn't sigh with relief, but the emotion was quite plain in his eyes. J.D. shut the door behind him and locked it without being told.

"What's going on?" J.D. said and Rick turned to him.

"Anything?"

"Nothing," J.D. said.

"Well, something's going on," Corrie said. "I thought you were going to put a drive-through window in the front of the office! I've never seen you drive like that!"

Rick didn't answer; he shot J.D. a look and indicated with his head that J.D. should join him in making a quick circuit around the office. J.D. nodded and said nothing until they finished checking all the doors and windows and they met at the door of the TV room. Rick signaled Corrie to join them and she knew from the set of his jaw that whatever news he had to deliver in person was not good.

"What happened?" J.D. said, his voice low.

"I got the ballistics back on the gun found in the men's room," Rick said. "It's not the gun that was used to kill Marvin."

"What?" Corrie and J.D. blurted in unison. J.D.'s hand went to his side and he muttered a curse. It took Corrie a second to realize that he had instinctively reached for the firearm he wasn't carrying. Corrie turned to Rick.

"But how can that be? I mean, if the gun Myra found in the men's room wasn't Buster's...."

"It's Buster's," Rick said, nodding. "But it wasn't the gun that was used to shoot Marvin. In fact, the crime lab says it looks like that gun's never been fired."

Corrie was still shaking her head. "I don't get it... why did someone go to all that trouble to hide it if it wasn't the murder weapon?"

"To throw us off the trail of the real weapon," J.D. said, his jaw set just as grimly as Rick's. "Which means that whoever killed Marvin is not only still out there somewhere... they're still armed and dangerous!" He looked at Rick. "Still no leads?"

"I'm not sure," Rick said slowly. "They also found something in Buster's car... it might have a simple explanation...."

"What is it?" Corrie asked.

"They found a couple of blond hairs... long blond hairs. On the floor near the empty gun case."

"Blond hairs?" Corrie drew in a breath. "Buster's girlfriend has blond hair... long blond hair!"

"Yes, and because she is Buster's girlfriend, there is a perfectly reasonable explanation for those hairs to be in his car. She might not have known the gun was even there," Rick pointed out. "And then there is the matter of motive—none, as far as we know."

"Blond hair," J.D. murmured, his forehead furrowing. Corrie ignored him and addressed Rick.

"That's just it... we DON'T know," she said. "We don't even know how long Buster's known her. And as far as I'm concerned, she's the most likely person to have known that Buster had a gun and that he'd have it in his car." She could see that Rick agreed, but he wasn't about to commit to any opinion. He grunted but didn't nod.

"We'll have to question her. And Buster. We don't know how long she's had access to Buster's car and we don't know how long that gun's been missing. All along we've assumed that the gun disappeared from Buster's car the day Marvin was shot. If this woman...," He pulled out his notebook and flipped it open. "... Noreen Adler, has been dating Buster for a while, she might have found out about the gun some time ago and had a lot of other opportunities to take it. However...."

"She doesn't have a motive," Corrie finished. This time, Rick nodded.

"We'll have to see if there is some kind of connection with her and Marvin Landry. Not to mention trying to find the real murder weapon," he added.

"Blond hair."

Both their heads swiveled in the direction of J.D. His brow had cleared, but it was obvious he was still mulling over some thought. Rick cleared his throat.

"Wilder? Something you want to share with us?" he asked.

J.D. shook his head slowly, then his eyes came into focus. "What about your guests, Corrie? Any of them have long blond hair?" He looked from Corrie to Rick, including him in the question.

Corrie blinked as Rick began flipping through his notebook again. "Maybe. I haven't really noticed. Why?" J.D was nodding.

"The morning Landry was killed. Friday. There was a woman crossing the patio. She had long blond hair."

Rick's head jerked up. "When?" he said, his voice like a gun shot. J.D. gave him a tight smile.

"When you were here in the morning... you stopped in during your bike ride to check and see if Corrie had had any trouble with a certain guest."

Rick started jotting information. "Besides the long blond hair, what do remember about her?" He was in full investigative cop mode... Corrie knew she'd be questioned next and she began to rack her brain, trying to recall the woman J.D. had described.

J.D. shook his head. "It was a quick encounter, Sheriff. I mean, I was hanging around outside the laundry room door, trying to avoid being noticed, and suddenly, there she was. I almost ran right into her."

"Where was she coming from?"

"Not the laundry room. I was just in there. I assume the restrooms. And I have no idea where she was heading... I didn't stick around to find out," J.D. said, the color rising in his face. Corrie realized that J.D. had probably been listening to her and Rick's conversation... about him.

"Do you remember anything about her? Anything at all?" Rick pressed, his impatience tempered by his professional courtesy toward a fellow law enforcement officer.

"She was wearing biker clothes—Harley t-shirt and skin-tight bleached blue jeans. Too tight for her age."

"Which was?" Rick said, waving his hand in a "come on, come on" gesture. J.D. shrugged helplessly.

"Too old for hair that blond and clothes that tight."

"That's all you can tell me?" Rick said. The implied sentiment was "What kind of cop are you?" but J.D.'s face only turned redder.

Corrie bit back a smile; their mystery female guest must have taken a shine to J.D. and he was neither comfortable with it, nor seemed to want to elaborate on it in the sheriff's presence. Rick gave her a glance and she sobered. "Sound like a guest you recognize?" he asked her. She shook her head.

"The biker clothes sounds like most, if not all of them. The blond hair... well, it's hard to say. A lot of women on bikes wear their hair tied back under a bandana," Corrie said. She moved toward the desk and pulled out her guest register. She ran her finger down the list of guests that had checked in by Friday morning and shook her head. "At least half of my guests are listed as couples... but I don't remember any of the women in particular." She sat back and pushed the register across the counter and Rick picked it up. "What I do know," she went on, "is that none of the guests that have checked in since Thursday have checked out yet."

"That should make things easier," Rick said. He turned to J.D. "You haven't seen this woman again since Friday morning? You've hardly left the campground the whole time you've been here," he added in a cutting tone.

"I haven't seen her again. I'm positive of that."

"Maybe a visitor of one of your guests?" Rick asked Corrie.

"Then she should have signed in here in the office... especially if she brought in a vehicle. But if one of my guests picked her up and brought her here... well, the truth is, I'm not all that strict about policing visitors unless they end up staying overnight."

"Maybe you should put Buster in charge of checking on visitors," J.D. said with a humorless smile. Corrie rolled her eyes.

Rick tapped his notebook impatiently. "Okay, so now we've got a murder weapon that's missing and a possible suspect that may be missing as well. We're pretty much back to where we started," he said in disgust.

J.D. shifted restlessly. "It's after three in the morning, Sheriff," he said. "And we're all tired and have way too much information to process clearly. I suggest we call it a night and you," he said with pronounced emphasis, "get some much-needed rest. That goes for you, too, Miss Black," he added as he turned and gave Corrie a stern look. She raised her brows and looked at Rick.

He was staring at J.D. with an expression that hovered somewhere between "outraged at the audacity of the man" and "you're right"... with the first sentiment being the most predominant. "I suppose you're not including yourself in 'calling it a night', are you?" he asked.

"Sheriff, I'm supposedly on vacation," J.D. drawled. "So technically, I'm getting plenty of R-and-R, unlike you and Corrie who are working round the clock. I can stand to lose a little sleep. I'll keep an eye on things through the night. You get some rest so your brain can function at its best and get this case solved so I can go back to getting some sleep!"

Chapter 23

Corrie bit back a yawn and tried to focus on Father Eloy's homily which, ironically, happened to be on the subject of being watchful and awake. She shifted in her seat, mindful of the sympathetic glances from her pewmates who were all life-long friends and well aware of what she was going through... as aware as she was of J.D. standing at the back of the church by the doors with at least a dozen other men. With the exception of a couple dozen people, the population of Bonney—and Bonney County—was Catholic and "standing room only" was the norm for the eight a.m. Sunday Mass at San Ignacio, so he didn't look completely out of place... although the barely-beginning-to-fade bruise on his face, not quite hidden by his shades, and his black shirt, jeans and leather jacket probably invited a lot more curiosity about his newcomer status than normal.

Across the aisle, in his usual place in the last pew, Rick was sitting and probably being more successful at hiding his yawns than she was. He'd acknowledged her with a brief nod as he slipped in at the last minute. Since it was his habit to be at least ten minutes early for everything, she concluded that he had been watching the parishioners as they arrived, taking note of anyone he didn't know, and had a "briefing" with J.D. just before Mass started. Corrie would normally be either amused or annoyed by the attention if it weren't for the fact that, despite his usual polished attire of dress slacks, shirt, tie, and sport jacket, Rick looked worried and exhausted and that it was—and she hated to admit it—because of her.

She tried to concentrate on the rest of the Mass. The Pages and the Myers had assured her that everything would be all right, they would keep an eye on things and on each other, and that Rick had made sure to keep a deputy on patrol at all times. When Corrie had left the campground, she hadn't yet seen Betty Landry, nor had she seen Walter Dodson return, and that had a lot to do with her feeling of apprehension. To her annoyance, the nervousness she tried to keep under wraps kept showing up in small ways that J.D. homed in on immediately. The third time she dropped her keys, J.D. stepped in and offered to drive her to Mass in her father's old Ford pickup truck. "I don't think you'd be very comfortable on the back of my Harley... not dressed like that, anyway," he'd added, cocking an eyebrow in appreciation. Corrie's face had burned with embarrassment even as a thrill of pleasure spiraled down her back. Sunday morning was the one time she dispensed with her jeans and Black Horse Campground t-shirts and wore "squaw-girl clothes" as he father had jokingly called them. She even refrained from her customary braid and brushed her black hair into a silken cascade that fell to her waist, held away from her face with a silver-and-turquoise clip that had belonged to her mother. She was conscious of J.D.'s eyes fixed on her and she knew it wasn't merely out of a sense of duty.

After the final blessing, it took her a while to make her way out of the pew and down the aisle, fielding questions and expressions of concern and offers of help the whole way. She managed to disengage herself from her fellow parishioners, promising to call if she needed anything, then she took a deep breath as she made her way to the parking lot. Rick had managed to slip out just ahead of Father Eloy and he was engaged in what appeared to be a very serious conversation with J.D. and with Deputy Evans, who had arrived in full uniform and a patrol vehicle, just as the Mass was ending.

"Corrie!"

She turned as Myra hurried up, her dark eyes wide with agitation and her long black tresses coming loose from the beaded clip she wore to keep it neat. Myra and her eighty-something-year-old grandmother always sat in the front pew and Corrie wondered if Myra had slipped away while her grandmother finished her prayers— a ten-minute addition to the usual length of the Mass—to see her... or Dudley.

"What is it?" Corrie asked. She knew if she let Rick get too involved in his discussion with J.D. and Dudley, he'd turn into Sheriff Sutton and she would be hard-pressed to get any information from him about anything other than the weather.

Myra looked chagrined. "Would it be all right if I didn't get to work until about noon?" she asked. "Grandma suddenly decided that she wants me to take her to Roswell this morning to see her sister. I know you'll be short-handed since neither Buster nor Dee Dee are scheduled to work today, but I'll be sure to get the bathrooms done by one-thirty at the latest and I'll be glad to work later to make up the time for you."

"How's your grandmother supposed to get home? Are you going to drive all the way back up there tonight to get her?" Corrie asked, wondering what the chances were that she could actually convince either Buster or Dee Dee to give up their day off to cover Myra. But Myra was already shaking her head.

"She'll stay the night. She said that my great-aunt wants her to stay and my cousin will bring her home tomorrow. I can stay as late as you need me."

"It's all right," Corrie said, knowing that Myra was far more conscientious about her work than either Buster or Dee Dee. She noticed the young woman was looking past her at Dudley and, although Corrie's back was to the trio of law enforcement officers standing by her truck, she was certain Dudley was looking at Myra, too. She bit back a smile and wished Myra a safe trip, eager to get over to the pow-wow she was missing.

To her consternation, Dudley got in his cruiser and left even before Corrie reached them and Rick and J.D. had moved apart, as if trying to hide the fact that they had been talking behind her back. She hoped they knew that she expected to be fully briefed about any new developments, without her having to resort to asking—or begging—for information.

J.D. and Rick both decided to be obtuse. "Ready to go?" they both said. She stopped and folded her arms across her chest, giving them each a sharp look.

"I don't know... I guess I should ask you two, since it seems like I'm out of the loop."

Rick exchanged an amused glance with J.D. "Told you," the look clearly said. J.D. laughed. Corrie's temper flared and she forgot that she'd ever found either of them appealing in any way.

"I'm so glad you two find this funny!" she snapped. Her hair was blowing loose from the clip she wore and she swept it back from her face, which unfortunately let both men see the tears of anger in her eyes. Their amused looks vanished.

"Corrie," J.D. said before Rick could speak. "I know you think we're keeping you in the dark just because we're jerks. I'm not denying that maybe we ARE jerks," he said, giving her a smile that would normally have melted her heart. She refused to soften. He shot a look at Rick, as if he would give J.D. a clue as to how to deal with Corrie, but Rick's eyes remained fixed on Corrie and his face was unreadable. J.D. bit back a sigh. "Anyway, we're trying to protect you. As long as the person who killed Marvin is at large, everyone at the campground is in serious danger... and that means especially you." He paused as if waiting for Corrie to respond. She didn't. "It would make things easier if you would...."

"No, J.D.!" she snapped. She dropped her arms to her sides, clenched her hands into fists and stamped her foot. "I am NOT going to go 'someplace safe' until this is all over! The Black Horse is my home and those people are my friends and my guests! I am certainly not going to abandon them just so that you and Rick can play at being John Wayne without me getting in the way!" She held out her hand. "My truck keys, please."

"Corrie, I'm sorry," J.D. said, shooting a look at Rick and still getting nothing but a silent stare. "Look, forget that we—that I—said anything," he added. "I'll take you home."

"No, thank you," she said, anger clipping her words. She continued to stand with her hand out, and J.D. seemed prepared to hang on to her keys, then Rick made a short sound in his throat and inclined his head. J.D. got the message. He handed Corrie the truck keys.

She neither thanked him nor gave Rick so much as a glance. She brushed past them, got into her truck, and started the engine. As she pulled away, she looked back at the two men. J.D. looked hopelessly perplexed, but Rick was shaking his head and looking like he just might break into a whole smile.

"I'll give you a ride back to the campground," the sheriff said. J.D. nodded, his face burning with embarrassment and frustration. He was thankful that Sutton wasn't the type of man to rub "I told you so"s in anyone's face.

They got into the sheriff's personal vehicle, a dark blue Silverado, which, J.D. noted, was fully loaded and looked like it had just rolled off the assembly line, even though it was at least a couple of years old. Law enforcement must pay extremely well in Bonney County. J.D. wondered if Sutton only took his truck out of the garage on Sunday mornings.

The sheriff seemed to be reading his mind. "Being able to take my patrol vehicle home and back to work is one of the perks of the job," he said. J.D. nodded and the sheriff went on, "You can't blame her, Wilder, for being upset. You'd feel the same way if you were in her place."

"I suppose."

"I *know*," Sutton said with emphasis. "Corrie's not a coward, nor is she the type to sit back and wait for something to happen or someone to take care of things that she believes are her responsibility. But she's not reckless, either. Just incredibly stubborn and headstrong... always has been, always will be," he added dryly.

J.D. shot him a look. "Aren't you worried about her? You're the one who kept emphasizing to me how much danger she's in."

"I'm worried sick, Wilder," the sheriff said bluntly. "That's why I'm trying to keep an eye on her—either yours or mine or someone else I trust—but I know her well enough to meet her on her terms on this. I don't have the energy or time to waste trying to get her to agree to the conditions I'd like her to be protected under, so I do what I can and pray it's enough."

J.D. said nothing and they drove on in silence for a few minutes. A clear picture of Corrie walking toward them from the church came to mind—the breeze blowing her raven hair away from her face, her strong, graceful strides making the silver-and-turquoise earrings she wore dance and sparkle in the morning light. He suddenly wondered if the sheriff had given them to her... and why he should care.

The church was a twenty-minute drive from the Black Horse and J.D. debated broaching the subject on his mind or if doing so would simply mean he'd have a long walk back to the campground. He decided to throw caution to the wind. "So what's your story with her, Sheriff?"

He hadn't mumbled the question, but Sutton seemed to have suddenly gone deaf. When a full minute had passed without any reaction, much less an answer, he tried again. "Should I try to guess, or is it that big a secret?"

"Nothing to guess at," Sutton said, his voice neutral, his eyes fixed on the road ahead. "Corrie and I are friends. Have been for years."

"Years?"

"Since preschool. We practically grew up together."

J.D. stared at the sheriff. Unless he was imagining things, it seemed like the man's face had reddened slightly. He gave a short laugh. "Oh, I see. So she's like a sister to you... is that it?"

If Sheriff Rick Sutton had answered immediately in the affirmative, it might have laid J.D.'s curiosity to rest. But his hesitation, however slight, in responding gave J.D. more of an answer than Sutton probably intended to give. "She's just a really good friend, Wilder."

"You're crazy about her," J.D. said and he felt a sudden surge of anger and annoyance that he couldn't quite explain. Part of it had to do with the fact that he couldn't understand why Sutton didn't just come right out and say so... surely he couldn't be that insecure. But as much as he hated to admit it, J.D.'s feelings were mainly jealousy... purely, simply, and inexplicably.

Sutton's face had paled slightly, but his voice remained neutral. "She's a great person," he said. J.D. snorted.

"'A great person'? Right. I do believe I've lost all respect for you as a man. She's a hell of a woman, Sutton," J.D. said, turning and facing the sheriff, who still didn't look anywhere but straight through the windshield. "What are you waiting for?"

"Nothing to wait for," Sutton said, his irritation evident in his clipped words.

"Ah," J.D. said, nodding. "Now I understand. You've already bared your soul and declared your affection for the lady. And she shot you down and gave you the 'let's just be friends' line. Got it." He was trying hard to keep his elation from being too evident in his voice, but the way the sheriff's jaw tightened told him he wasn't being successful. "I'm sorry, man. I really am," he said, trying to sound at least halfway sincere.

Rick Sutton gave him a look that dropped the temperature in the truck by nearly twenty degrees. "Sure you are," he said, his voice gritty with an emotion that J.D. couldn't quite identify. The sheriff turned and looked back out the windshield. "And you're wrong, Wilder. Corrie never shot me down. I never gave her the chance."

J.D. shifted in his seat. "So what's the prob—?"

"I'm divorced!"

J.D. waited a few seconds, but only the hum of the tires on the pavement broke the silence. He cleared his throat. "So?"

Sutton threw him an incredulous look. "Have you already forgotten where we spent the last hour... you know, that place with the altar and the priest and all that?"

J.D. sucked in his breath. Of course. He had to have been dim not to realize it. Both Corrie and the sheriff were Catholic. There was no divorce and remarriage in the Catholic church... at least, that was what J.D. remembered. On his official personnel paperwork, his religious affiliation was listed as Catholic—only because that's what he was baptized as an infant and it seemed to be the easiest and most honest answer he could give. He hadn't practiced the faith since he was in junior high, never been much of a church-goer. Today had been the first time in years he'd set foot in a church, any church... even his marriage to Trish had been a courthouse one. He tried not to squirm. "I'm sorry," he muttered, not sure what else to say. Sutton didn't respond. "Hey," J.D. persisted. "Really, Sheriff, I'm sorry... I didn't know. Not that it's my business, I get that," he said quickly. "I was just...." He groped for some way to explain what he, himself, wasn't even sure he understood.

Sutton shrugged and cut him off. "So now you know... there's no competition from me, Wilder. If you want to try your luck with Corrie... I don't blame you and I certainly can't stop you. All I'm going to say is, you'd better treat her right. She's still the best friend I've ever had and I don't want her to get hurt."

"Hey, Sheriff," J.D. interrupted, heat searing his face. There was a hint of steel in the sheriff's words and J.D. knew it would be foolish for him to think that Sutton wouldn't care if J.D. did decide to "try his luck" with Corrie. "In case you forgot, I'm recently widowed—tragically widowed, I might add. I'm not exactly thinking... what you think I'm thinking."

This time, the sheriff did nod. "Understood," he said. Then he changed the subject. "You're still planning on staying at the campground tonight?"

J.D. welcomed the change. "Unless Corrie's got my tent and belongings in a pile at the gate, yes," he said. Sutton almost laughed out loud.

"She won't," he assured J.D. "Corrie doesn't hold grudges. Not for long, anyway," he added. "She'll be over it before you know it... as long as she knows you're taking her seriously." His expression grew even more sober than usual. "Dudley said several guests have checked out this morning... according to Jackie, there's at least a dozen more scheduled to leave today, and most of the rally guests will be gone by noon tomorrow. That doesn't give us much time to check up on everyone again. He's certain he didn't see a woman matching the description of the one you saw outside the laundry room Friday, but he asked the Pages and the Myers to keep an eye out and notify us if they do. I'm hoping you'll be around to identify her."

J.D. grimaced. "Well, Sheriff, I'll be here through tonight, but I'm sure you understand I need to get back to Houston in the next week... there's some unfinished business and a lot of unanswered questions I need to take care of."

Was it his imagination or did the sheriff seem to relax a bit? No matter what he said earlier about J.D. trying his luck with Corrie, the truth was he was happy to see the competition—whether he wanted to admit that's what he considered J.D. or not—eight hundred miles away from his "best friend". Whatever reason Rick Sutton had for marrying someone besides Corrie, it wasn't because he didn't care about her. Whether that had anything—or everything—to do with the fact that he was no longer married, mattered little to J.D. He was scheduled to leave on Monday, whether Marvin Landry's murder was solved or not. By this time next week, the Black Horse Campground, along with all of the people he met here, would be far away and the events that brought him to this place would be culminating in his making a decision about the direction in which his life would go. Right now, just like the identity of Marvin's murderer, all that was a mystery.

The only thing he was sure of was that after tomorrow, he'd never come back to Bonney County again.

Chapter 24

Corrie yanked the clip out of her hair, ignoring the sharp, painful tug, and immediately began to twist it into her customary braid. Her Sunday church outfit, which consisted of a calf-length broomstick skirt of midnight blue velour and crisp, white long-sleeved shirt, hung over the back of a chair in her bedroom, her tan dress boots kicked under it. She had hoped it would demonstrate to both Rick and J.D. that, in spite of everything, she was standing tall, strong and courageous, and not apt to fall apart like a fragile blossom in a rainstorm, while still being very much a woman. Apparently it only succeeded in inciting concern and reinforcing their proud, masculine determination to protect her like a piece of fine china.

She reached to take off her sterling silver earrings and paused. She didn't often wear jewelry, except on Sundays, and the earrings had been a gift from Billy the Christmas before he died. They were miniature dream catchers, with a silver feather dangling from the bottom of the hoop and a tiny chip of polished turquoise strung on the web-like strands. Dream catchers were traditionally hung over a child's bed to supposedly trap nightmares in the web until daylight made them disappear. Billy had never been one to put much stock in legends and old folk tales. But his life—and Corrie's—had by then begun to resemble a bad dream: the final round of chemo had failed to slow the cancer's relentless progress and done nothing but weaken Billy's already debilitated stamina. The doctors had informed them that there were no more options. Billy, ever the stoic, had contacted an old friend who lived on the reservation and made beautifully hand-crafted jewelry and commissioned the earrings. "When I am gone," he'd told his daughter on that last Christmas Eve together, "turn your face to the light and only remember the good and let the bad fade away, like nightmares caught in the web. Remember, your mother and I will always be with you, no matter what." Her fingertips closed over the small, silver dream catchers, squeezing them as if doing so would bring her parents hurrying into the room to reassure her that this was all just a bad dream and by morning it would just fade away.

She'd changed into her jeans and a lime-green Black Horse Campground t-shirt, and she stepped back and studied her reflection in the mirror. She nodded; confidence, capability and, most importantly, courage appeared to emanate from the woman who stared back at her... along with a healthy dose of "don't patronize me" and a dash of "outta my way, I'm busy". Yes, she was ready to get back to work and face J.D. and Rick again.

She kept the earrings on.

Renfro and Oliver had followed her up the stairs when she had arrived and had just settled into comfortably snoozing furballs when she finished putting her Sunday clothes away and headed back down the stairs to the campground office. Renfro opened one eye in a baleful glare and let out a long, drawn-out sigh. Oliver's eyes narrowed into slits and a deep growling "meow" sounded in his throat. Corrie smiled.

"It's all right, guys, don't get up," she said, pulling the door almost all the way shut. "You know where I'll be if you need me."

She emerged at the bottom of the stairs just as J.D. and Rick walked in the front door. She gave them a quick once-over. Rick looked so rock-solid, safe, and dependable in his jacket, tie, and dress slacks, and J.D. a complete contrast, dressed in black and looking cool, competent, and dangerous. Both extremely good-looking men—Shelli would say "hot"—both dedicated law enforcement officers, and both evidently quite worried about her. And both off limits. Rick by his own choice and J.D.... Corrie wasn't sure. She just knew that, much as she hated to admit it, she derived a great deal of comfort from having them in her corner... but the smart thing to do was to keep them both out of her heart.

She gave them a cool nod and made her way to the coffee-maker. They returned the nod and waited while she filled her cup and took a sip. She leaned against the courtesy table and raised a brow. "You're not waiting for me to get you a cup, are you?" she said as a greeting.

Jackie, who was sitting behind the counter, got to her feet awkwardly, remembering to use her cane this time. "I'd better go see what Jerry and the Myers are up to," she said with a false brightness that fooled no one. Corrie hadn't given her any explanations when she stormed in earlier after returning from Mass, but Jackie was sharp enough to interpret the fact that J.D. had left with Corrie to go to church and come back with Rick as a clear sign that both men had done something to tick Corrie off... and Jackie didn't want to stick around to find out what it was. She gave Corrie a look that said "we'll talk later" as she scooted out the side door. J.D. cleared his throat.

"I'm really glad she didn't leave that cane behind," he said. Corrie raised one brow at him and the smile he was starting faded before it fully erupted. He cleared his throat again. "Corrie, I'm sorry I offended you. I was only trying to look after you and keep you safe. It was just a suggestion. I'm not trying to muscle you out of your own home or imply that you can't take care of your own business."

She waited a full tick of the clock then shrugged. "Okay."

J.D. blinked; he stared at her for what seemed like a full minute, then he turned to Rick. "'Okay'?"

Rick held up both hands. "Told you," his posture seemed to say. He cleared his throat and addressed Corrie. "I need to go by the office and talk to the deputies that have been on duty. Dudley reported no suspicious strangers or activity."

Corrie nodded, ignoring J.D. "Walter Dodson's still not back," she said. "Doesn't that count as suspicious activity?"

"Technically not an 'activity'," Rick said with glimmer in his eyes that made Corrie want to laugh and throw her cup at him at the same time. "We've tried to check on his whereabouts, but we haven't had much luck. What we do know is that he checked himself and Betty into the Maison for last night and tonight, but he hasn't been back since yesterday evening."

Corrie nearly choked on her coffee. "The Maison Mont Blanc?" she sputtered, not sure she had heard Rick right.

"It's the only Maison I know of," he said dryly. "Dodson supposedly told the desk clerk that he wanted to have his mother stay somewhere where she didn't have to be reminded of what happened to Marvin every time she turned around."

No chance of that at the Maison, Corrie thought. Situated on the outskirts of Ruidoso, near the village of Alto, rooms there started at two-hundred-fifty dollars a night and, despite the establishment's French name, were decorated with pure Southwestern flavor, with original Peter Hurd, R.C. Gorman, and Georgia O'Keefe paintings, Nambe alloy and crystal, and world-renowned pottery, rugs, and artwork from nearly every Native American tribe in New Mexico. Not to mention it boasted of every imaginable comfort from Egyptian cotton sheets and in-room jacuzzis to complimentary room service coffee, tea, and croissants in the morning and gourmet meals prepared by a five-star chef. No, there was nothing at the Maison that would bring Marvin—much less the Black Horse Campground—to mind. She dragged her attention back to what Rick was saying.

"He paid for two nights in advance, but according to the clerk, no one has stayed in the room at all, and housekeeping has reported that the "Do Not Disturb" sign has been on the door since Dodson checked in. Seems strange to me that someone would pay that kind of money for a hotel room they're not using."

Or for one that they ARE using, Corrie thought. Maybe it was her father's frugality rearing its head, but she couldn't fathom paying that kind of money for what essentially amounted to a place to sleep. She didn't move in those kind of circles; none of her friends—well, maybe one of her friends—could afford the Maison Mont Blanc. She said, "Seems strange to me that someone who's recently had a large amount of money go missing could afford a place like the Maison."

"Noted," Rick said. "It's something we'd like to ask Dodson about... if we could find out where he is," he added.

J.D. cleared his throat and Corrie started slightly. She'd forgotten he was there, leaning silently against the counter, listening. "Are we positive he hasn't returned to the Landrys' RV?" he asked.

"I guess we couldn't be 'postive'," Rick said, shaking his head. "I mean, no one's seen him return...."

"No one has *reported* seeing him return," J.D. said. "Just as no one has seen—or reported seeing—Betty since Dodson brought her home from the hospital." He straightened up, hooking his thumbs into the belt loops of his jeans. Despite his all-black tough-guy biker regalia, at the moment he looked every inch a cop. "If I may suggest, Sheriff, it might be time to pay Mrs. Landry a friendly visit... just to make sure she's doing all right and to keep her apprised of the how the case is progressing."

"A courtesy call," Rick said, his half-smile showing a tinge of irony. "Nothing the least bit suspicious about that. I was planning on that after I go get changed."

"What, into your uniform?" Corrie broke in. She stared at Rick. "How is that supposed to be a 'friendly visit'? If the sheriff shows up at my door in full uniform, I'm certainly not going to feel it's just a neighborly social call!"

"You're kidding, right?" J.D. said as Rick raised a brow at Corrie. She felt her face burn and she shrugged, tugging at one of her earrings.

"That's different. The sheriff IS my friend. Betty's a guest who's had a terrible shock. And I'm not sure that Walter Dodson is completely innocent; I don't care how many witnesses saw him in town. Maybe he's got Betty scared and under his thumb. If the sheriff shows up officially, she's not going to say a word. Let me go talk to her. I have certain advantages over Rick showing up at her door expressing concern."

"And those advantages are?" Rick said as J.D. grinned. It occurred to Corrie that J.D. enjoyed seeing her riled up as long as it wasn't at him.

"Well, for one thing, I've known Betty since she and Marvin started coming to the Black Horse twenty years ago. I mean, known her as far as seeing her on a daily basis every summer. That's more than Rick has ever seen her," she said to J.D. He pursed his lips then nodded, conceding the point. She went on, "Besides, I think it will be easier for her to talk to another woman than it would be to a man... especially a man in a sheriff's uniform." This time she looked at Rick. "When this all first happened, don't you remember that she wanted me to stay with her while you questioned her? And she wanted me to get her clothes from the RV when she went to the hospital. I think she trusts me. If there's anything going on with her son, she might feel awkward discussing it with a law enforcement officer."

Rick sighed irritably. "If her son's not doing anything wrong...."

"Yes, I know, Rick," Corrie said, just as irritably. "But if she's afraid of him, then she won't say anything to you officially if she's worried that he might find out you stopped by to 'visit'," she said, hooking her fingers into quotation marks. Rick grunted in reluctant agreement and she went on. "However, if I stopped in just to chat, see how she's doing, maybe bring her some banana bread or something, then Walter Dodson shouldn't have any reason to suspect we're checking up on him. So," she said, clapping her hands together, "I'll just get Jackie to watch the shop and I'll go and... what?" she said, when both Rick and J.D. began shaking their heads.

"You're not going over there alone," Rick said and J.D. nodded in concurrence. Corrie stamped her foot impatiently.

"Did we not just have this conversation?" she asked in exasperation. "If one or both of you tags along with me, she's not going to be as open with me as if I went alone!"

"And if Walter Dodson IS over there and he thinks you're trying to get information from his mother about him, you might be in a lot of trouble." J.D. went over to the window and looked toward the Landrys' RV. It was a lazy Sunday morning and some of the campground tenants were just beginning to stir after their late night at the motorcycle rally. Check-out time was twelve noon and, before too long, the camp store would be filling up and getting busy with guests either getting ready to check out or making purchases for the next day of their stay. They didn't have much time to discuss their plans. J.D. looked back at Corrie over his shoulder. "I'm not going in with you. Mrs. Landry won't even see me. I'll just be nearby, close enough to hear what's going on and be there if you need me."

Corrie said nothing; she stole a look at Rick. He didn't seem particularly pleased that J.D. had volunteered himself for the task of keeping an eye on Corrie, but he was obviously on board with the idea. He was looking at her with an expression that said it was either their way or no way. She sighed. "Fine. Let me get Jackie over here and we'll...."

"Let ME go get changed and come back first," Rick interrupted.

"In the event that you'll need a law enforcement officer handy during this operation."

"This was just supposed to be a friendly social call," Corrie with a wry twist of her lips. "Now it's turned into a major sting operation."

"Only if there's anything to sting," J.D. said. He moved toward the door. "Guess I'd better go blend in with the rest of the guests... if I haven't already blown my cover by going to church and hobnobbing with the sheriff!"

"How are we supposed to let you know when we're ready to go pay Betty that friendly and totally un-suspicious social call?" Corrie asked as he opened the door. He paused and gave her a mysterious grin then winked.

"Don't worry... I'll know," he said and went out, the bell over the door echoing his cheerfulness.

Chapter 25

Corrie's plan to slip out to see Betty as soon as Rick left was thwarted by several guests converging on the camp store to buy early-Sunday morning breakfast supplies like milk, eggs, and bread, or to browse the souvenir selection before they got ready to leave, or to request change for the laundry room. Her ardent prayer that Jackie would have seen Rick leaving and return to help out or that Dana would show up to see if she could be of assistance went unanswered. She knew she shouldn't, but when a momentary lull came in business and the store was deserted once again, she took her chance.

She flipped the signs on the doors to read "Closed" but didn't lock them. She scooted over to the Landrys' RV, darting quick glances around to see if anyone was approaching, her heart racing so much that she was winded by the time she climbed up the steps to the door. As they had been for the last two days, the blinds and curtains were closed and the RV looked deserted. She hesitated, steeling herself against an onslaught of nerves, glanced around again, then cautiously leaned her ear against the door and listened. No voices. For a moment, Corrie was certain that she had wasted her time, that Betty wasn't here, that somehow she—and Jackie and Dana and

Rick's deputies—had missed seeing her leave. But as she hesitated, she heard footsteps moving inside the RV. Not heavy, not quick, but someone was obviously moving around inside. Her heart began pounding in double-time. Someone WAS there with Betty, someone ambulatory. She almost jumped off the steps to run back to the office, but forced herself to stay put. This was her chance, maybe her only chance to find out what was going on.

Before she could lose her nerve, she knocked on the door and started violently when Betty's voice, sharper than she'd ever heard it and closer than she expected, came through the door. "Yes? Who is it?"

It took her a second or two to find her voice. "Betty? It's Corrie. I was just...." She fumbled for another second. "Uh... I was just wondering how you were doing." She wondered fleetingly if she should have waited for Rick to get back, but it was too late now.

There was a long stretch of silence, then Betty's voice, more subdued and not as strong. "Oh, Corrie, dear... just a minute...."

Corrie waited. She heard movement inside the RV again, fading away, as if someone was hurrying toward the back bedrooms. Someone HAD to be with Betty. Why didn't they come to answer the door? The only reason could be that they didn't want to be discovered in the RV. Corrie heard another sound... Betty's wheelchair moving toward the door, then a slight scraping sound followed by a soft click and more scraping sounds.

Betty's voice came through the closed door suddenly and Corrie nearly backed off the top step. "Go ahead and open up, Corrie. It's unlocked." She hesitated for a second or two, then reached for the knob as gingerly as if it might be wired to a bomb and opened the door. Betty was framed in the screen door, sitting in her wheelchair, fully dressed, every hair neatly in place. Corrie blinked and realized that Betty had unlocked the outer door through the opening in the screen door that slid open and shut, but she hadn't unlocked the screen door. Despite Betty's usual gracious manners, it seemed that no invitation to enter was forthcoming, either. Did that prove there was someone else in the RV that she didn't want Corrie to see?

Betty was dressed impeccably, all the way from her neatly curled hair down to her nylon stockings and black shoes. Her dress, Corrie noted, had no buttons down the front; it either was a pull-over style or had a zipper or buttons down the back. Could she have dressed herself without help? Ten in the morning wasn't exceptionally early, and it was possible that Betty was a very early riser, but it seemed to Corrie that if Betty had been alone, she would have been dressed much more informally, in a house dress and slippers, maybe. But then again, perhaps Betty was planning on attending church services this morning, which meant she had to be expecting someone—her son probably—to arrive to pick her up....

"Yes, Corrie, is something wrong?" Betty said, breaking into Corrie's scrambled thoughts. Her voice wasn't as sharp as before, but there was an uncharacteristic hint of impatience in it. Corrie forced a smile.

"Oh, Betty, hi! It's so good to see you," she said, her voice sounding strangled to her ears. "I was... worried about you. I mean, I've hardly seen you since...." Her voice trailed away, partly from embarrassment at how phony her words sounded but also because she had absolutely nothing else to add.

"I'm fine, Corrie," Betty said. Her voice didn't seem as frail as it had before, and the words sounded a bit irritated to Corrie. "I've just been taking care of some paperwork and getting a few things in order. Of course, it's been difficult these last few days, but it must be done and there's no sense in putting it off."

She had made no move to unlock the screen door and it still didn't look like she was planning to ask Corrie in. She remained firmly rooted in the doorway, her wheelchair effectively blocking access into the RV. Despite her concern, Corrie couldn't bring herself to ask to be let in. "Yes, your son told me," she said, studying Betty's face closely. "I told him that I would be more than happy to help you with whatever you need to do."

Betty's cheeks turned a deeper shade of pink and she pressed her lips together before answering in her usual soft, hesitant voice. "Well, dear, I truly appreciate your concern and kind offer. But I'm managing quite well and... it's difficult enough without having other people around. Emotionally, I mean."

Betty didn't exactly look emotionally wrecked, but perhaps she was handling it far better than the average person. Corrie nodded, hoping that Betty wouldn't find her apparent acceptance of her refusal of help suspicious. "Well, I hope you'll let me know if you need anything—anything at all," she added, putting a slight amount of emphasis on the word "anything". She went on, "And if you would like us to fix a meal or two for you, or bring you something...."

"That won't be necessary," Betty said, her voice a bit sharper, more insistent. Was Corrie hitting a nerve, or just being a nuisance? She decided not to press any further.

"All right. I just thought I'd stop by and see how you're doing."

"Thank you, dear. Please make sure the door shuts completely when you leave."

And don't let it hit me on the way out, Corrie thought as she took the knob in hand and carefully shut it. She waited a moment, but not another sound came from within the RV, not even the sound of Betty locking the outer door. *She probably knows I'm out here and doesn't want to raise any questions.* With a sigh, she turned and headed back to the camp office.

Four people were waiting outside the doors to make some purchases or check out when she got back to the camp office. While tending to them, even more people arrived and Corrie was so busy that she hadn't even noticed Rosemary Westlake standing by the TV room door waiting for the crowd to dissipate. For once, Rosemary didn't have Bon-Bon in tow, and that was why Corrie hadn't received fair warning of her arrival, even though Rosemary was attired in a lime-green muumuu that probably could be seen from outer space and would have looked right at home at the annual Roswell UFO festival.

"Rosemary," she said, trying to make her surprise sound more like pleasure than alarm. The woman looked awful. She appeared to have used more than her usual amount of makeup and it wasn't hiding any of the lines of tension and—was it fear? "I haven't seen you in a couple of days," Corrie finished lamely.

Rosemary's lips moved in the direction of forming a smile but didn't quite pull it off. "Donald and I have been busy," she said. Her lip trembled and Corrie edged around the counter and went to her. Without a word, she guided the woman into a chair in the TV room, took a quick look around the store to see if they were alone, then joined her.

Rosemary nodded gratefully, then put a manicured hand to her ample chest and took a deep breath. "You know, don't you?" she said, making a supreme effort to keep her voice from breaking.

"Yes," Corrie said simply. There wasn't anything else she could say, so she waited. Rosemary took another deep breath and closed her eyes.

"I... I never thought it proper to talk about," she began, her face reddening. "It was... just a business for us, a good way to make money. I'm sure that's the way Marvin thought of it, too. I'm sure it was nothing more. I suppose I can't blame Betty for thinking the worst about it, but I assure you, Corrie, everything was legal and aboveboard and, furthermore, there was never anything— ANYthing—between Marvin Landry and myself."

"Of course not," Corrie said. The uncharitable thought that Dee Dee could take some lessons on acting from Rosemary flitted through Corrie's mind, but she banished it before she had too much time to dwell on it. She wished desperately that Rick or J.D. would walk back in, but Rosemary wasn't finished yet.

"Donald never wanted to be in this business... he insisted on keeping it quiet, just telling people we were involved in Internet sales. Which we were, but he wanted the exact nature of the business to be kept a secret. I did, too, actually... less competition that way," she added. "And when he felt we had done enough, had made enough, he just wanted to quit. But Marvin gave us a marvelous opportunity to sell out, make a little more money. Donald, as you heard, was rather opposed to that," she said and Corrie nodded, hoping her expression remained neutral even as she felt her ears prickle with embarrassment. She was thankful that Rosemary didn't seem to be intent on pursuing the topic of Corrie's eavesdropping any further. "But only because he didn't want Marvin to put it about what business we had been in and he was worried that Marvin might not make a success of it and blame us."

"But it was already a well-established business, wasn't it?" Corrie asked. "I mean, it wasn't a big risk, as if he were starting at entry-level."

"Oh, my, no, can you imagine?" Rosemary's hazel eyes widened and she tugged at the neckline of her lime-green muumuu. She shook her head. "It was just Marvin's personality... he could be a bit abrasive at times, you know," she said. "Donald was afraid he—

Marvin—would have trouble with the people under him... you know, try to tell them how to do business. Marvin considered himself quite business-savvy. But he wasn't. I knew all about his failed business ventures... that's really what led me to make the offer to him. I thought... I thought this would be an opportunity he might actually be able to succeed at. And now he's dead." She took a deep shuddering breath and touched a remarkably plain white handkerchief to her teary eyes.

Corrie wondered if Rosemary had merely come to unburden herself or if there was some other reason she was telling her all this. "Do you have any idea why he was murdered? I mean, did he ever say anything to you about feeling that he was in danger?" She realized she was going out on a very slender limb here, but she didn't want to waste a chance to find out something that might be important.

Rosemary shook her head and sniffed. "No, nothing like that. I knew he and his step-son didn't get along...."

"You knew about his step-son? I mean, knew about him before they came here this time?" Corrie interrupted. Rosemary gave her a curious glance.

"Well, yes, of course. They've been thorns in each other's sides for quite some time... it's only because of Betty that they tolerated each other. That and the fact that they lived with him for all these years... not in the same house, I mean, but in their RV on his property. Of course, Betty's son never traveled with them... the only reason he came this time was to try to dissuade Marvin from taking on this business venture."

"How do you know that?" Corrie asked, forgetting all about being a sympathetic listener. Walter Dodson actually KNEW what business the Westlakes were in? And he had come along specifically to dissuade Marvin from getting involved? It was ridiculous, but Corrie felt hurt; Betty had lied, Marvin had lied and now it seemed that even Walter Dodson had lied. Could she believe anything from anyone anymore? She forced herself to focus on what Rosemary was saying.

"Oh, Marvin was quite upset about it... he was really very enthused about taking on the business, but he was afraid that his step-son would put a stop to it. He—Marvin's step-son, what was his name? Oh, yes, Walter—kept insisting that it was too big a risk with what was left of Marvin's savings. He kept saying that Marvin should think of Betty. Well, he was, but that Walter didn't see it the same way. He got Betty all worked up against it... it was sad, because we really had been great friends at one time, but Marvin told me before they arrived that perhaps it would be best if I didn't approach Betty until he'd had a chance to make her see what a wonderful opportunity this was."

Corrie was grateful when Rosemary stopped talking; it gave her head a chance to stop spinning. "Why are you telling me all this, Rosemary?" she finally asked, realizing that she had a lot of information she had no idea what to do with.

"Oh," Rosemary sighed. "I'm not sure, Corrie. I mean, I felt you had a right to know what was going on in your own backyard, so to speak. I was concerned because the sheriff was asking questions and I didn't want you to think we were hiding anything... anything about Marvin's murder, that is," she added, having the grace to blush at the absurdity of the statement.

"Right," Corrie said shortly. "So you really have no idea why Marvin was murdered or who did it?"

"Well, really, the only person who had a motive, if I may be dramatic, was Walter Dodson."

"He wasn't here that morning," Corrie said absently, wondering for a brief moment if she should have shared that information, but figuring it was probably common knowledge.

"What do you mean?. Friday morning? Of course Walter Dodson was here."

"I know he was here in the morning," Corrie explained. "I mean later on, around lunchtime, when Marvin was killed."

"Oh," Rosemary said, her brow clearing. "I was going to say if you didn't believe me, find that extraordinarily dressed biker woman he was talking to Friday morning!"

Chapter 26

"Biker woman?" Corrie barked, sitting up straight. Rosemary nodded.

"Yes. Actually, I thought she might have been with that young man who showed up in the middle of the night, but surely he wouldn't have trouble finding a much more attractive woman much closer to his age."

"She was blond?" Corrie said, fighting to keep herself from bolting from her seat to the phone. What was keeping Rick anyway? And J.D.? Rosemary nodded, her eyes widening.

"Why, yes, she was blond—bleached blond. Of course, if she's a guest, you probably know who I'm talking about."

"Where did you see her talking to Walter Dodson?" Corrie asked. Rosemary stared at her. She probably thought that Corrie was an extremely insensitive and nosy person, but Rosemary's opinion of her character mattered very little to Corrie at the moment.

"By that tall fence around the pool... I was taking Bon-Bon to the dog yard and I noticed Betty's son talking to someone. It interested me," she said without apology, "because he'd been so anti-social with everyone else. I could hardly believe he was smiling at the woman!"

So Walter Dodson had had an accomplice. That's who that blond woman was... she came specifically to murder Marvin Landry on orders from Walter Dodson. Corrie felt her blood run cold and a shiver crept up her back. Rosemary wasn't supposed to have seen her, much less J.D. run into her, but the mysterious woman had done what she had set out to do—shoot Marvin, divert attention by taking Buster's gun and making it look like that was the murder weapon, and be gone. Long gone by now.

The bell in the shop rang and Renfro added to the alert with a "woof" from upstairs. Corrie jumped up and headed into the main store, hoping it was Rick and that she could persuade Rosemary to tell him what she had just told Corrie.

To her shock, she nearly cannoned into Dee Dee who was swiftly tip-toeing to the coat closet. She had her high-heeled shoes in hand, her jacket halfway off, and she was looking over her shoulder toward the front desk. She let out a shriek and dropped the shoes when Corrie spoke. "Dee Dee! What are you doing here?"

"Corrie!" Dee Dee gasped, staggering back a step and forcing a smile. It took Corrie a few seconds to assimilate her employee's new look. Dee Dee's previously blond hair was now a deep chestnut and her green contacts had been replaced with Elizabeth Taylor-violet ones. She looked strikingly beautiful, as usual, but Corrie had to wonder what on earth her description on her driver's license said. Dee Dee reached up and tugged on one of her silver hoop earrings. "Hey! How's it going?" she said brightly, then added in her pseudo-Texas drawl, "Oh, hi, Miz Westlake, how are you?"

To Corrie's dismay, Rosemary had followed her out of the TV room and was heading for the side door. "I'm fine, Dee Dee, thank you," Rosemary said, with a wave of her hand. "Corrie, I must be going. Donald and Bon-Bon will be wondering where I am."

"Rosemary, I...," Corrie began to follow her, but the woman was gone in a swirl of lime-green. Dee Dee cleared her throat and Corrie jumped; she'd forgotten Dee Dee was there and she turned to face her errant employee.

"Uh... how late am I?" Dee Dee inquired nervously as she stepped into her shoes and hung up her jacket. Corrie stared at her. Dee Dee usually didn't bother with apologies or explanations.

Corrie glanced at the white board behind the front counter where everyone's work schedule was written instead of at the clock.

"Actually, you're about thirty-six hours early," she said. "You had this weekend off...."

"I did?" Dee Dee said and her face paled under her perfectly applied makeup. "Are you sure?"

"Well, yes, I make up the schedules," Corrie said testily. It occurred to her that Dee Dee had probably been at some rendezvous that she had cut short because she thought she had to be at work. The young woman seemed to have no trouble keeping her social schedule straight. "In fact, you weren't supposed to be in until Tuesday."

"You mean, I have tomorrow off, too? Oh, wow," Dee Dee said her eyes brightening, then her cherry-red lips twisted in chagrin. "But Tuesday? Oh, Corrie, I can't work Tuesday. I have an appointment."

"What?" Corrie gritted her teeth. She made the work schedules up two weeks in advance, specifically so that her employees could set appointments and make personal plans around their scheduled hours at work... and let her know if they already had a commitment so she could work their schedule around it. Rarely did anyone, besides Dee Dee, deviate from the schedule once it was set... and Dee Dee did it often enough for all of the Black Horse Campground's employees. "What appointment?" Corrie said, heroically not throttling Dee Dee.

"I'm having a wax job Tuesday and I can't change it," Dee Dee said firmly. "I'm way overdue and it can't wait."

"Wax job?" Corrie repeated and then drew back when Dee Dee's eyes went as wide as saucers and her face flamed bright red then paled.

"_On my car_," Dee Dee said, her voice louder than necessary with pronounced emphasis on the word "car". "My CAR needs it badly... Oh, hi, Sheriff!" she cooed.

"Dee Dee," Rick said coming up behind Corrie. Corrie spun around and stared at Rick. How on earth had he gotten in without one of the bells or buzzers going off? He seemed to hear the question, because he nodded back toward the side door. "I caught the door from Rosemary Westlake just as she was leaving and I stopped to have a few words with her."

"Well, what brings the long arm of the law to our little campground?" Dee Dee drawled sidling up to Rick and almost—but not quite—elbowing Corrie out of the way. Corrie, already annoyed at the reference to "our little campground", figured Dee Dee was about ten words short of finding herself on Corrie's bad side permanently when Rick spoke.

"Official sheriff's department business," Rick said. He had changed into his uniform and didn't seem surprised at the change in Dee Dee's appearance, probably because he'd seen her at the sheriff's department since she last worked at the Black Horse. He also didn't seem to be particularly impressed, to Corrie's mean satisfaction. "And what brings you here? Working today?"

"Well, I thought I was supposed to," she said, leaning against the wall, one hand on her hip and her drawl becoming syrupy enough to pour over pancakes. The way she was smiling at Rick made Corrie feel invisible. That Rick seemed to be amused by Dee Dee's performance only added to Corrie's irritation. Dee Dee went on, "But it looks like I got my days mixed up and I'm actually not scheduled to work today, so maybe I'll just go get some lunch. Are you hungry?" she asked, her voice suddenly low and husky.

"Dee Dee," Corrie said before she could stop herself. "Since you've just informed me that you won't be able to make it in on Tuesday because your CAR," she stressed, "is being waxed, maybe you could just go ahead and work today... since you're already here," she added.

Dee Dee's smile wavered then became fixed. "Oh, sure, Corrie, if you like," she said, her voice lacking enthusiasm. She even forgot to drawl.

Corrie smiled back and tried to feel guilty over Dee Dee's discomfiture. She wasn't succeeding but she decided not to let that bother her. "Why don't you start in the TV room? We had some guests in there late yesterday evening playing cards and I'm sure it could use some straightening up."

"Sure. Okay," Dee Dee said, her voice flat. She gave Rick a weak smile and started to turn away when Corrie spoke up again.

"Oh, and would you be a doll and run the vacuum, too? They had snacks in there and I'm sure there are some crumbs on the floor...."

"Right," Dee Dee said shortly. She threw Rick a last, lingering glance, as if appealing to him to save her from the Cinderella-like drudgery to which Corrie, the wicked step-employer, was sentencing her. But Rick wasn't in the mood to play Prince Charming. His

expression hadn't changed but his fingers drummed on the counter—
a sure sign that the meter was running on his patience. He said
nothing until after Dee Dee had grabbed a dust rag from the storage
closet and disappeared into the TV room.

Corrie turned back to Rick and her smile faded at the sight of the
grim set of his jaw. She motioned him over to her desk where they
could talk without being taken by surprise by anyone. "What's going
on?"

"I'm assuming Rosemary Westlake already unburdened herself on
you and told you everything I know," he said, keeping his voice low.

"That the whole business enterprise was no secret to anyone... but
us?" she said and sighed.

"I know you feel betrayed and hurt," Rick said gently, sympathy
warm in his blue eyes. "But put yourself in Betty's place, Corrie. The
whole thing embarrassed her and Betty's never been the type to go
around crying about her problems—and that includes problems with
her marriage or with her son. She doesn't believe in airing her dirty
laundry for everyone to see... not even people she considers friends.
She's the epitome of refinement."

Corrie nodded; Rick was right, as usual. "I know what you mean,"
she said, more to herself than to Rick. "I went over to see her and...."

Just like that, Rick's eyes frosted over. "You were supposed to wait
for Wilder and me to be there!" he snapped, forgetting to keep his
voice down. Corrie frowned and held a finger to her lips, jerking her
head in the direction of the TV room to remind him that they weren't
alone.

"Oh, will you calm down?" she hissed. "It was no big deal. She
didn't even let me in the RV. Which is what seems strange to me,"
she went on, even as Rick glowered at her. "Rick, someone *is* there,
in the RV, with Betty. I'm almost positive of that."

"How do you know?" he asked, his glare still icy. "And if there is
someone in there, who is it? It's not Walter Dodson," he said,
reluctantly conceding that his interest in what Corrie discovered was
greater than his anger at her not having waited for him and J.D. to
provide backup for her.

She knew better than to gloat over this minor victory. "It has to be
that blond woman J.D. saw the morning Marvin was killed," Corrie
said. "Rosemary Westlake saw Walter Dodson talking to her that

morning." Quickly she filled Rick in on what she'd learned from her conversation with Rosemary. Rick frowned.

"If that woman is the same one Wilder saw that morning, why is she hanging around and staying in the Landrys' RV? And if she is staying in the Landrys' RV, how is it that no one has seen her in the last two days?"

"What I've been telling you all along, Rick," Corrie said in exasperation. "Betty is afraid... and this woman is working for Walter Dodson. She's the reason Dodson's alibi has been able to stand up— I'll bet she was the one who actually killed Marvin, on orders from Walter Dodson, and now that Betty is Marvin's sole beneficiary and heir, she's keeping Betty hostage until the dust settles and they manage to clean out the rest of Marvin's bank accounts. Who knows what will happen to Betty after that?"

Rick shook his head, but not in disagreement. He seemed to be trying to clear his head. "Corrie, it doesn't happen that fast. It could be weeks—months, even—before Marvin's affairs are settled. You really think this woman is going to hang around until then, just to make sure that Betty doesn't blow the whistle on them?"

"Maybe... if Walter Dodson offers her enough money. Or maybe she's even married to Walter Dodson, how about that?" she added excitedly. Rick groaned, shaking his head again. Even Corrie had to acknowledge that her theory was far-fetched, but she ignored his reaction. "Come on, Rick, it's worth considering, isn't it?"

"It's all speculation," Rick snapped. He glanced around the office, then lowered his voice. "We can't prove any of it... and even if it is true, we'd never get Betty to admit to any of it, no matter how much danger you think she's in."

"She can't be THAT proud, can she?" Corrie said. "I mean, I know she'd be embarrassed if anyone found out exactly how things were between her and Marvin, but surely she wouldn't be so ashamed of her son's behavior that she'd let him get away with murder!"

Rick said nothing, frustration silencing him as he put his hat on and squared his shoulders. "I think it's time the law made another official inquiry into Marvin's death... and it will take place inside the Landrys' RV. Whether Mrs. Landry considers herself presentable enough to accept a visit from the local sheriff or not," he added.

There was no stopping Rick once he had his mind made up.

Besides, he'd been gracious enough to let her try feeling Betty out on Corrie's terms, so she was in no position to argue with him. "No need to worry," Corrie said with a resigned wave of her hand. "She was dressed to the nines... for Betty, that is. You'd think she was on her way to a luncheon or church or something. That's why I think she's got someone in there helping her. It seems impossible to me that she's able to get herself dressed or groomed so early in the morning without some assistance."

"So now we have someone holding Betty hostage who also is willing to be her personal maid?" He shrugged and shook his head as he headed for the door. "After everything that's been going on these last few days, I'm ready to believe almost anything... even that!"

Chapter 27

Corrie sighed as Rick went out the door, the bell punctuating his determination to reach the bottom of this mystery. She wished she'd remembered to tell him to be careful but, she reminded herself, he *was* a law enforcement officer, used to dealing with dangerous individuals and quite capable of taking care of himself. He certainly didn't need her to tell him how to do his job.

Corrie turned as Dee Dee strolled out of the TV room. "The sheriff leave?" Dee Dee asked, glancing around. She seemed ready to leave as well. The dust rag, which looked as snowy-white as it had before she had picked it up, hung limply from her hand. Corrie didn't recall hearing the vacuum running in the TV room the whole time Dee Dee had been in there.

"You're done already?" she asked, ignoring Dee Dee's question. Dee Dee offered her a watery smile then chose to ignore Corrie's question.

"Unusual for him to stop by on a Sunday, isn't it?" she persisted, flicking the dust rag at a spotless display shelf. It was a poor attempt to look busy, let alone sound disinterested. Her acting skills were a bit rusty this morning.

"Not really," Corrie said, wondering if Dee Dee would believe her.

The truth was that Corrie usually only saw Rick at Mass on Sundays and at the evening steak cook-out. He never stopped by the campground during the day. But maybe if Dee Dee thought she was missing out on an opportunity to see the sheriff on the many Sundays she'd been scheduled to work and had called out, then maybe she'd be more conscientious about showing up.

Dee Dee pursed her lips and frowned. "He's still working on Marvin Landry's murder, isn't he?" Her brow cleared and she sighed, looking dreamily concerned. "He's so dedicated to his job, isn't he? So brave and... and dedicated," she finished lamely, obviously not having had time to work on her soliloquy.

"We should all learn a lesson from him about job dedication," Corrie said pointedly. Dee Dee blinked, her dreamy look vanishing and a sheepish smile tugging at her lips.

"Right," she said, dropping all pretense of working. "So, how are things going with the investigation?" she asked, the dust rag hanging limply at her side once again.

The question surprised Corrie more than Dee Dee's lack of industry annoyed her. "I'd think you'd know more about it than I would. Haven't you heard anything around the sheriff's department?" Maybe Dee Dee had missed a few days from that job as well, but it wasn't Corrie's place to ask. Dee Dee shrugged.

"Not much. I heard Betty hasn't been seen the last couple of days, since she got out of the hospital, but that's all. I'll bet she's just devastated."

Corrie thought about Betty's demeanor this morning. Betty had been distraught and upset when Marvin was killed, but this morning she'd mostly seemed agitated, as if her husband's murder was more of a nuisance than a tragedy. But then, perhaps that was just Betty's reaction to Corrie's offer of help—or fear that Corrie might discover who was hiding in the RV. "I'm sure she is," Corrie said dubiously, "but she's not the type to go around making a fuss. I can't believe she's managed so well on her own these last couple of days...."

"I can't imagine her son being much help to her," Dee Dee clucked, shaking her head so that her multiple hoop earrings swayed vigorously.

"Neither can I," Corrie said, absently fingering her own earrings, wondering if maybe Dee Dee knew more than Corrie did without even realizing it. "But I just saw Betty this morning and she was dressed so nicely... and even her hair was perfectly in place...."

"Oh, that's a wig," Dee Dee said, flicking at an invisible bit of lint on her blouse. Her off-hand comment caught Corrie completely off guard and for a moment she couldn't say a word.

"How do you know that?" she stammered. Dee Dee gave her a pitying smile and a shake of her head.

"Oh, honey," she drawled, crossing her arms and leaning against the wall. "This is Dee Dee you're talking to, remember? I've been working in the salon since I was a teenager. After all these years... not that it's that many," she amended quickly before Corrie decided to start tallying, "there's not much about any kind of beauty aid I don't know." She nodded. "It's a wig, all right. High quality, too. It's fooled everyone around here... for years, actually. Oh, yeah," she said, smiling at Corrie's stunned look. "I first noticed it about three years ago... she's just changed the style and color a little. Most women would have kept the color darker, you know, to look more youthful, but that would have been a dead giveaway that she was doing something to her hair. But I can tell it's not her real hair. It's almost TOO perfect."

Corrie slumped against the counter. "No wonder she looks so pulled together all the time... and I never suspected...."

"Well, that's probably why she got it... you know, it's so much easier just to pull it on than to spend time curling and setting her hair and fixing it up every day. Especially since she doesn't have anyone to help her. And I imagine," Dee Dee added, her voice dropping to a near whisper, "that Betty might not have that much hair of her own, either. Some women do lose their hair as much as men do... I've had female clients that were as bald as poor Marvin was. That would make it easier for her to get the wig on, too."

Yes, that was true, Corrie realized with a jolt. Perhaps there wasn't someone else in the Landrys' RV helping Betty... but that didn't mean that Betty wasn't being held hostage in some way. She should have guessed that a wig was the reason Betty seemed to be getting along so well on her own. And she wished there was some way to let Rick know right away....

"So, anyway, I was wondering," Dee Dee said briskly, folding the pristine dust rag, "the TV room doesn't look all that bad and you usually get a lot of people in there on Sunday afternoons, so it's really not worth the bother to run the vacuum if Myra's going to do it later on... I mean, it *was* supposed to be my day off anyway...."

For once Corrie didn't mind saying, "Go ahead and take the rest of the day off, Dee Dee. I'll see you Tuesday."

Dee Dee blinked in surprise, but didn't wait for Corrie to come to her senses. "Okay, Corrie, Tuesday, right, see you then!" she said, scurrying to the coat closet to get her jacket, apparently forgetting that she had already told Corrie that she had an important appointment scheduled for that day. Nevertheless, she darted out the door, calling, "Toodles! Till Tuesday!" over her shoulder. Corrie had no illusions that Dee Dee was going to show up on Tuesday but right now, she didn't care about that. An idea was forming in her mind, one she knew Rick would have a hard time believing, an idea she could scarcely believe herself.... Now all she had to do was get Jackie or Dana over here to watch the office and store....

She looked up with a start when Jackie and Dana came in the front door. Jackie gave an exasperated shake of her head. "You went ahead and let Dee Dee take the day off, didn't you?" she asked and Dana shook her head and clicked her tongue with disapproval.

"It was actually her day off anyway," Corrie said, straightening up and breathing a silent prayer of thanks. "Listen, can I ask you two to watch the shop for awhile?"

"I think we can manage," Jackie said, raising a brow and looking around the deserted store. "What's going on?" she asked, her eyes narrowing as Corrie began to make a hasty exit.

"Oh, uh, nothing, really," Corrie said, trying to think of a plausible reason for needing to take off for a while as she edged toward the side door. It occurred to her that most employers didn't feel the need to explain their actions to their employees, but Jackie asking was the same as if Billy were asking. "I need to talk to... uh, Rick about... something." She cringed inwardly at the look Jackie gave her—she probably thought it had something to do with Dee Dee being let off the hook—but decided to let her think whatever she wanted... she'd do damage control later.

"Hmm," Jackie said, giving Dana a glance. Dana smiled indulgently and headed for the storage closet where the cleaning supplies were kept. "Well, I suppose we can keep ourselves busy while you talk to... Rick about... something."

"I thought I saw him walking around to the patio, talking to that Mr. Wilder when we got here," Dana said over her shoulder, trying to sound disinterested—and failing.

Corrie felt her cheeks flame. "Thanks. I'll be back later and.... Thanks," she said again quickly as she slipped out the door

She made herself walk, not run, down the wheelchair ramp. She glanced around toward the patio, but saw no sign of Rick, nor of J.D. For a second she considered going to get J.D. for backup before she went to the Landrys' RV, but she didn't think he would approve of her barging in on Rick's questioning of Betty Landry.

She hurried across the gravel road and, on silent feet, she climbed the steps to the RV door and listened. She couldn't hear any voices and she frowned. Although the windows were shut, unless Rick was whispering, there was no reason she wouldn't be able to hear him through the door. She thought about knocking but swiftly discarded the idea. Either Rick had finished questioning Betty and left, not bothering to stop by the camp store and tell her, or else... he was in trouble. The thought of that chilled Corrie, and while she knew it would be prudent, she wasn't going to waste time going for help.

She reached for the doorknob. She had no idea if Betty had locked the door after her earlier visit or Rick's visit and she had no idea what her next move would be if it *was* locked. The thought that someone might see her and consider her stealthy behavior suspicious crossed her mind, but she decided that her best bet would be to try to act as natural as possible, as if Betty were expecting her to stop by and that she was welcome to let herself in.

She turned the knob and to her surprise it turned all the way. She held her breath and tugged gently. The door opened with only the slightest squeak of the hinges. The idea came to her that, if she was caught, she could say that she was passing by and had seen the door swinging freely—opened, of course, by the non-existent wind she would blame—and decided to see if Betty needed anything.

She glanced over her shoulder; no one seemed to be around, not even Rick or J.D. This next part could be tricky. Earlier, she had heard Betty slide the panel by the screen door handle open to reach through the door to unlock the main door. If the screen door was locked, maybe she could slide the panel over so she could reach in to unlock it. Or maybe her luck would hold and the screen door would be unlocked.... Her hand reached for the handle, pressed the button slowly and pushed. Locked. She felt perspiration break out along her back. She couldn't think of any reason why the door would be locked if Rick was still inside, unless.... She was going to have to try to slide the panel.

She looked over her shoulder again, then pressed her forehead against the screen and strained to see inside the RV. There were no lights on and the dimness made it hard to see, but Corrie wasn't about to call out to Betty to see if she was nearby. She took a deep breath and flattened her fingertips against the panel. She prayed it wouldn't stick or grate or screech when she tried to move it. At first it didn't move at all, and for a sickening moment, she thought it might be locked as well, but then it slid over a mere half-inch. It was all the room she needed to get her fingers into the gap and push it open.

She waited again; to her ears, the soft sounds of the panel moving resounded like a building collapsing, but there was still no movement within the RV, no voice demanding what she was doing. Emboldened, she reached through the opening and fumbled with the screen door lock, then pushed the door open.

She slipped inside and shut the door behind her, being careful not to let the latch click. Her heart thudded so hard in her chest she could hardly breathe, but she didn't have time to collect herself. She looked back toward the patio once more. No sign of either Rick or J.D. She was on her own.

She listened carefully, straining to make out any noises over the pounding of her heart, but she didn't hear a sound in the RV. She didn't stop to wonder why, but crept across the sitting room, through the tiny kitchen and dining area. Like Betty, everything was neat and not one thing seemed to be out of place, not even a coffee cup on the drainboard or in the sink. It looked as if no one was—or had been—in the RV at all. Had Betty somehow managed to leave without Corrie— or anyone else—seeing her?

She gathered her courage and licked her lips. "Betty?" she called softly, her voice barely a loud whisper. She cleared her throat and tried again. "Betty? Are you here? It's Corrie... listen, there's something I wanted to ask you...."

She paused, listened again. Not a sound came from anywhere in the RV and Corrie's confusion grew. She took a few more steps toward the bedroom and stopped outside the bathroom door. The last time she was in the Landrys' RV, Betty had been locked inside. She knew she'd look like an absolute idiot if it turned out that Betty was merely occupied in the bathroom, but still.... She raised her hand and tapped softly; in case Betty WAS inside, she didn't want to frighten her. "Betty?"

Not a sound. Corrie took a deep breath and reached in her pocket for one of the tissues she always carried before touching the door knob. She wasn't about to make the same mistake again.

The door was unlocked this time; she told herself that it was unlikely that she was about to encounter an unpleasant surprise when she opened the door, but she steeled herself nevertheless. She turned the knob and pulled the door open.

The bathroom was empty.

Her breath exploded out of her lungs. She had been certain she was going to find a body—either alive or dead—behind the door and the wave of relief that washed over her made her weak. She began to back out of the doorway when the cabinet under the sink caught her attention. Its door was slightly ajar, the only thing that was remotely out of place in the RV.

She didn't hesitate; she pulled the handle and peered inside and froze. Balled up in the back of the cabinet was a brightly-striped bathrobe. It matched Dana's description of the robe—"Joseph's coat", she called it—she had seen Marvin wearing the day he was murdered. Apparently no one had bothered to check the bathroom after the murder, since Betty had been in it the whole time. How long had the robe been here? She reached for it and, as she pulled it out, something fell out of it on to the floor.

Corrie stared at the object lying tangled on the tiles at her feet and as the realization of what it was struck her, she stood up and something hard struck the back of her head, sending her into painful darkness.

Chapter 28

"Sheriff, can I have a word with you?" J.D. asked as he stepped through the wooden gate leading to the patio area, intercepting Sutton as he came out the side door of the campground office.

The sheriff raised a brow as he looked at J.D. "Where've you been, Wilder? I thought you were supposed to be keeping an eye on Corrie while she paid Mrs. Landry a visit."

J.D. nodded, then jerked his head back toward the patio. Sutton followed without a question or hesitation. Whatever his opinion of J.D. might have been previously, he now regarded him as an equal and respected his status as a fellow law enforcement officer. J.D. wasn't sure how he felt about that; it would have suited him just fine to have remained an anonymous visitor, but right now he appreciated Sutton taking him seriously.

The sheriff glanced around once he was inside the gate and J.D. waved a hand at him. "It's all right, no one's around. There's something you need to see."

"You didn't answer my question," Sutton said as he followed J.D. across the patio and past the laundry room door. J.D. stopped and looked at the sheriff.

"I checked around the RV before Corrie had a chance to get over there, then I watched her from behind my tent. It wasn't a problem to keep an eye on her since she never went into the RV, and anyway, there's no one in there but Mrs. Landry."

The sheriff straightened up and his eyes narrowed. "No one?" he asked sharply.

"No one," J.D. reaffirmed with a nod. "The blinds don't reach all the way down to the window sills and from the ground you can't see inside. I borrowed a footstool from the laundry room and I was able to look through the slit between the bottom of the blinds and the sills. I looked in all the windows and all I saw was Mrs. Landry, sitting on the edge of her bed, looking through her dresser drawers. No one else is in there. Unless they were in the bathroom the whole time," he amended. "That's the only room without a window, but I listened at the vents. Nothing. Mrs. Landry is alone in there... why are you shaking your head?" he interrupted himself.

"Corrie said she heard someone walking around in the RV just before Mrs. Landry opened the door," the sheriff said, keeping his voice low.

"You're sure?"

"Corrie is," the sheriff said. "Maybe they *were* hiding in the bathroom." J.D. sucked in the corner of his mouth and grimaced.

"She have an idea who it might be? Couldn't be Walter Dodson; I mean, there's no reason for him to hide. He's got every right to be in that RV... unless there's some reason he doesn't want to be seen...." Sutton was shaking his head.

"She thinks it's that blond woman you ran into outside the laundry room the morning that Marvin Landry was murdered."

"She see her?"

"No," the sheriff said. "But Rosemary Westlake saw Walter Dodson talking to that same woman the morning Marvin was killed... just a few minutes before you saw her yourself," he added.

J.D.'s brows rose and he let out a low whistle. "Well, it's starting to make sense now, isn't it?"

"How do you figure?" the sheriff asked, pushing his hat back off his forehead.

J.D. jerked his head toward the side of the building. Sutton followed him. They waited a moment while they watched Dee Dee back her sports car out of one of the front parking spaces designated for guests. The sheriff grunted. "Looks like Dee Dee convinced Corrie to let her have her day off after all."

J.D. paused at the edge of the asphalt until the car had turned up the drive and out onto the highway, then he pointed at the flower bed that ran the length of the building from the front steps back to the patio. "It's been raining during the night or early morning for the last couple of days. It rained a little early Thursday morning and Thursday night," he said. "Corrie hasn't had Buster watering the flower beds since there's been some moisture each day, so the ground was only damp Friday morning... but it was damp enough for someone to leave footprints."

The sheriff moved closer then went down on one knee, careful not to disturb any possible evidence. Sure enough, three impressions, where someone cut across the bare flower bed from the patio to the asphalt, were clear in the nearly-dry ground. His head shot up and his gaze swept the parking area. "It's a straight line from here to where Buster's car was parked that day." He looked up at J.D. who nodded.

"And look at the size of those prints, Sheriff. They're fairly small and not very deep. No way Buster made those prints, nor any of the men I've seen around the campground. It had to be a woman." The sheriff nodded again. He seemed to be deep in thought and J.D. waited for him to say something.

He stood when the sheriff stood and fell in step with him as he followed the imagined path the footprints would have made. They stopped when they reached the parking area where Buster's car had been that day. Tire tracks criss-crossed the dirt parking area, some deeper than others, most overlapping. The marks of Buster's Pontiac's tires showed he was in the habit of parking in the same place every day. J.D. imagined there were tracks from sheriff's department vehicles and the other employees' cars as well. He could distinguish four different vehicle tracks. Partially obscured by the tire tracks were a few footprints. Some were clearly Buster's; they were deep and well-defined and obviously made by a large pair of work boots and, just like his tire tracks, they indicated a path followed repeatedly, to and from his car. But one footprint and part of another one that had been nearly obliterated by a tire track were identical to the ones in the flower bed.

The sheriff stared at the ground for several seconds, then turned and looked back toward the patio area, lost in concentration. A car pulled into the campground and drove slowly along the road toward the campsites. After a few seconds, J.D. heard a car door shut and still the sheriff didn't say anything. J.D. waited patiently. He knew Sutton was only doing what he, himself, had already done—following the movements of the person who made the prints, trying to get into their head, trying to see beyond what was physically in front of him. At long last he spoke. "Those aren't boot prints."

J.D. shook his head. "No, they're not. The outlines are very indistinct. Soft-soled shoes."

"Not the sort of thing a biker would be wearing?"

"I wouldn't think so. Most want to keep their feet protected while riding. Even the women wear sturdy footwear."

The sheriff frowned. "That doesn't fit with the rest of that blond woman's outfit. Of course," Sutton went on, "she might have changed into something more comfortable if she wasn't going to be riding for awhile. Or if she wasn't riding anywhere at all." His stony expression grew even more grim and he looked directly at J.D.

"You're thinking what I'm thinking; that outfit was to throw us off, direct our attention toward a group of people that had nothing at all to do with Marvin's murder," J.D. said. Sutton nodded.

"Corrie heard footsteps inside the Landrys' RV," he said. "She said they were fairly distinct, but not heavy, so whoever was walking around in there either wasn't a very big person or wasn't wearing heavy shoes... or else they were taking care to step lightly."

J.D. said, "I assume you were on the way to talk to Mrs. Landry again... and see if she has been harboring a dangerous individual in her RV. Any objection if I accompany you, Sheriff?"

Sutton shook his head. "I'd be much obliged if you'd watch my back, Wilder. I've got Deputy Fletcher, a rookie, patrolling the campground, and I'm going to put him on the front entrance while we talk to Mrs. Landry, but I don't want to wait for more backup." He stopped and gave J.D. a quick once over. "You're unarmed. You okay with that?"

"I'll have to be," J.D. replied with a shrug. "Despite the fact that Corrie managed to get the upper hand on me with a cane, I assure you I have had training in hand-to-hand combat and self-defense. I just didn't want to have to use my knowledge and skills on Corrie."

"Good thing, too," the sheriff said, his gaze telling J.D. that the payback on that would have been hell. "I'll get the word to Dudley to head over here with some help, but we're talking to Mrs. Landry right now." He keyed his handheld radio, gave instructions to both Bobby Fletcher, the deputy on patrol in the campground, and to Deputy Evans, then began walking, J.D. beside him.

They headed toward the camp office, the sheriff pausing by the front door. "Let's stop and let Corrie know what's going on," he said.

J.D. grinned. He wondered how the sheriff was going to keep Corrie from accompanying them to the Landrys' RV, especially since it seemed like her theory was about to be proved to be correct. He couldn't wait to watch what was going to happen next. "Lead on, Sheriff."

Chapter 29

J.D. followed Sutton into the office of the Black Horse campground and stopped in mid-stride to keep from running into him.

"Where's Corrie?" Sutton asked and J.D. edged around the sheriff's broad back immediately. Corrie's trusted co-workers, Jackie and Dana, stood at the counter, their greeting frozen on their lips. They stared back at the two men, their expressions blank.

"Why, Rick, I thought she was with you," Jackie said as she came around the counter. Her cane leaned against the wall, ignored as usual, but no one commented on it.

"Why would you think that?" J.D. said before the sheriff could respond. Jackie looked from one man to the other, her eyes growing wider.

"Well, because that's what Corrie told me," Jackie said. "She said she had to talk to you about something, Rick, and she went out the door. She seemed," she added with a self-conscious cough, "excited and, er, a bit flustered, like she didn't really want to tell me where she was going. Is something wrong, Rick... Sheriff?" she asked.

The sheriff had let out a word J.D. was certain he never would have used in the presence of a lady under other circumstances. "I told her I was going to check on Betty myself!" he snapped.

"Betty? Betty Landry?" Jackie said and exchanged a glance with Dana. Dana shook her head.

"Corrie never said a word about going to see Betty Landry," Dana said.

No, but she knew that's where the sheriff was going, J.D. thought. "How long ago did she...?"

"It doesn't matter!" Sutton growled. "Let's go!"

He strode out the side door, J.D. falling into step beside him. "You really think someone's in there with Mrs. Landry?"

"I've got a bad feeling, Wilder," the sheriff said, as they hurried down the wheelchair ramp. "I just hope to God I'm wrong...."

J.D. nodded. They crossed the gravel road to the Landrys' RV site and before they even reached the bottom of the steps, they saw that the door was ajar.

Sutton's hand went to his service automatic as his eyes met J.D.'s. J.D. had already backed up, soundlessly, against the RV and he gave Sutton a quick nod. He was ready.

The sheriff unholstered his gun as he moved up the steps, as silent as a shadow. He eased the door open. "Mrs. Landry?" he called. "It's Sheriff Sutton, Mrs. Landry. Are you in there? Are you all right?"

No answer. J.D. could sense the sheriff's tension even as his own muscles grew taut with preparedness. Sutton glanced back at him, then motioned with his head for J.D. to follow him.

Sutton pulled the outer door open and took hold of the screen door handle. He waited a moment, then with a swift movement, he swung the screen door open and stepped into the RV's living room, his gun drawn. "Sheriff's department!" he barked.

J.D. bounded up the stairs and edged into the room as Sutton slowly made his way down the hall, his gun aimed and ready. J.D. looked around quickly, noting the almost show-room condition of the tiny living area and kitchen/dining area, exactly the way he had last seen it a few days ago. He watched the sheriff as he made his way down the hallway, stopping to look in the tiny bathroom, then pausing outside the pocket door that opened into the bedroom. The door was pushed open about five inches; not a sound came from the room, nor anywhere else in the RV. Sutton glanced back over his shoulder at J.D. and J.D. responded with a quick nod as he stepped aside into the dining area, out of the line of any possible fire. The sheriff pushed the door open and slipped into the bedroom. J.D. watched as he disappeared into the room. It didn't take him long to check it out; he emerged, shaking his head and holstering his weapon. "Nothing," he said.

Before J.D. could answer, the squeal of tires on the gravel and asphalt road made them pause, then rush toward the RV's kitchen window. A car lurched out from behind the fence surrounding the patio and headed toward the entrance gate. It was the same vehicle, a maroon-colored, late-model sedan, they had seen earlier entering the campground while they were examining the footprints left by the mysterious woman.

"Go! Go!" Sutton hollered as J.D. moved toward the front door, the sheriff right behind him. They burst out the door, leaped down the RV's steps, and sprinted after the vehicle. The car roared, speeding up, flinging gravel and stones and leaving a thick cloud of dust in its wake. It nearly blinded J.D. and the sheriff, effectively slowing them down. The vehicle fishtailed past the front door of the campground office, narrowly missing Jerry and Red as they hurried out the door, heading toward the Landrys' RV, no doubt in response to a call from Jackie. The two men dodged out of the way as the car swerved, then straightened out, making a beeline for the entrance gate. The sheriff skidded to halt in the middle of the road and snatched his service automatic out of its holster. He took careful aim, then let out another expletive as he lowered his weapon. "Fletcher, watch out!"

Deputy Bobby Fletcher, with all the eagerness and bravado of a two-month rookie and the good judgment to match, stood in an impressive horse stance in the exact center of the entrance to the campground... too close to the target for the sheriff to risk firing. Deputy Fletcher had his gun out and aimed directly at the car which hurtled toward him. He wavered for a split second before good judgment carried the day over bravado and he dove out of the way, but by then it was too late for Sutton to take a shot. The sheriff turned to J.D.

"Did you see who was driving?"

"Walter Dodson," J.D. answered grimly. "And that sure as hell looked like Betty in the passenger seat!"

Sutton's face was almost completely white as he and J.D. turned and dashed toward the sheriff's Tahoe. The sheriff snatched the radio mike off the console and barked instructions at his deputies, along with the description of the car and the occupants, as he slid behind the wheel and gunned the engine, but J.D. barely heard what he said until he signed off and one word slipped out under his breath, the same word echoing over and over in J.D.'s mind:

"Corrie!"

Corrie's eyes opened a crack, wishing the headache would go away on its own and knowing that it wouldn't, that she'd have to get up and take an aspirin or ten, and really not wanting to get up while her head was pounding so badly... funny, this headache wasn't like her usual ones that started right in front in between her eyes, it was on the back of her head and her vision seemed blurred, dark... almost as if she'd hit her head....

Her eyes flew open and she tried to sit up. Her forehead came into contact with a hard surface barely a foot above her face. She tried to cry out, tried to grab her forehead, but her mouth was covered by a strip of duct tape and her hands were bound behind her back. Despite the pain in her head, her disorientation quickly turned to panic.

She shouldn't have tried to follow Rick to the Landrys' RV; that was easy to say now, but her concern for Rick had blotted out any thought of concern for her own safety. She should have gone to look for J.D., or even Red or Jerry, but all she could think was that Rick might have gone blindly into an ambush and she had to warn him.

Well, she had been right... only it wasn't Rick that was ambushed.

She groaned and tried to work her hands free. She twisted her wrists around, feeling for a knot, and her heart sank when she realized that duct tape was indeed effective for many uses—including binding and gagging someone. Apparently her assailant, or assailants, had used whatever was readily available. The tape was tight and all the tugging and twisting caused it to rub the skin on her wrists raw. She felt sick to her stomach, partly from the speed at which the car was traveling, but mostly from the realization that she had been a complete and total fool.

Even if she had been right about Marvin's killer.

But knowing she was right wouldn't do her any good if she were dead. It was a consolation that they hadn't shot her, right there in the RV, but Walter Dodson and his accomplice, the mystery woman, weren't taking any chances... they were going to try to get away with murder one more time.

Not if Corrie could help it.

She forced herself to swallow her panic and concentrate on breathing normally through her nose. She tried to figure how long she'd been unconscious, tried to guess from the twists and turns in the road where they were heading. But the car lurched back and forth, changing lanes, slowing down then speeding up, confusing her and making her violently carsick. She lay back and closed her eyes, fighting back the queasiness in her stomach and knowing that her best bet would be to wait for the car to stop, for her attackers to open the trunk, and then....

Pray that Rick or J.D. would show up.

Tears clogged her throat and a muffled whimper leaked out from under the tape on her lips. She blinked her tears away and tried to swallow her fear along with her nausea. She had to think. She knew that whenever the car did stop and Dodson came to open the trunk, she wouldn't have much time to act before he and his partner took action to keep her from telling anyone—especially Rick—what she had learned about Marvin Landry's murder.

She focused her energy on trying to unwrap the tape from around her wrists. She ignored the stinging pain of her raw skin, knowing that if the car came to a stop and she was still tied up, it wouldn't be long before she wouldn't be feeling anything at all.

Chapter 30

J.D. hung on grimly as the sheriff's Tahoe roared out onto the highway and Sutton floored it. The tires screeched as they spun, nearly drowning out the sound of the siren. "You're sure they went this way?" he shouted, noting that they were heading east on Highway 70. Sutton nodded.

"They wouldn't head west... the highway goes straight through Bonney and Ruidoso... too much traffic and no place to turn off and hide. If they head east, there's a half-dozen side roads they could take and miles of highway to speed on." J.D. nodded. He kept his eyes trained on the highway ahead, his mind racing to what lay before them.

Before long, he caught a glimpse of a maroon-colored vehicle moving at a high rate of speed along the curving highway. It was just a speck, but no one would drive like that on a winding two-lane highway on a Sunday. "That's it," he said tersely.

"Damn right," Sutton muttered, keying the mike. The Tahoe screamed its way past the 100 mph mark on the speedometer. The sedan slowed as it climbed a slight, curving incline that wound around to the left but before the sheriff could report the car's location to his deputies, the driver of the sedan suddenly jerked the car to the left. A yellow diamond-shaped sign at the crest of the hill indicated a side road to the left with a green sign underneath it, pointing toward the communities of Tunstall and Garrett, which was apparently where the driver of the sedan was heading. The vehicle seemed to skid in slow motion, pivoting on the front wheels and looking as if it were going to make a complete one-hundred-eighty degree turn and head right back at the sheriff's vehicle. The car shot across the left lane in a cloud of blue smoke from the tires, right across the path of an on-coming eighteen-wheeler.

The trucker, blinded by the hillside on the curve and shocked by the sudden appearance of the car cutting right in front of his grill, slammed on his brakes and swerved, first to the left, then to the right, trying to avoid the sedan. He only succeeded in locking his brakes and causing his rig to skid in seemingly slow motion right toward the sheriff's Tahoe.

"Oh, God!" Sutton dropped the mike and grabbed the steering wheel with both hands as he stood on the brake and yanked the wheel hard to the left. J.D. felt his stomach spin as he grabbed the dashboard with both hands and the seat belt locked.

The rear end of the sheriff's SUV slid toward the trailer of the rig as it swung around into the eastbound lanes of the highway. The front of the truck clipped the guardrail on the opposite side of the highway, ripping the posts out of the ground and curling the rail into a corkscrew, as the front tires slipped into the ditch and brought the cab of the truck to a dead stop... but not the trailer. As the truck and trailer loomed above them, tires and brakes burning, Sutton floored the gas pedal. J.D. gritted his teeth, noticing that he, too, was standing on an imaginary gas pedal on the passenger's side, and the Tahoe gained traction and shot across the westbound lane and into a pull-off on the opposite side of the road, not twenty feet from the stalled cab.

The Tahoe came to a screeching halt barely six inches from the hillside and both J.D. and the sheriff scrabbled to unfasten their seatbelts. J.D. bolted from the Tahoe and ran up to the cab of the truck as Sutton retrieved the mike and called in the accident. "Are you hurt?" J.D. shouted to the driver as he jumped up onto the steps of the cab and looked in the open window.

The driver's face was white and covered with a fine sheen of sweat, his eyes bulging like bowling balls, and he managed a shake of his head. J.D. felt a twinge of sympathy; the driver was probably fine physically, but his mental state was another question, and J.D. didn't have time to dwell on it. "Stay put! An ambulance is on the way!" he said and he jumped off the step and ran back to help the sheriff set up emergency flares.

Before they were finished, the first of several state troopers showed up and Sutton grabbed J.D.'s sleeve. "They've got this now. Let's go!"

J.D. didn't question him; accident details could wait and law enforcement protocol could go to hell for all he or the sheriff cared. Walter Dodson had a tremendous lead on them. They ran back to the Tahoe and jumped in. The sheriff backed out of the pull-off and swung west, back toward the campground, as J.D. buckled his belt. "Where are you going? Dodson went the other way!"

"That road Dodson took has no turn-offs. It cuts through public and private land for about twenty miles and winds like a snake," Sutton said. "I know the land owner... he won't mind if we take a detour."

"Cross country?" J.D. said as the sheriff took an unmarked turn-off to the right. Not thirty feet from the highway was a gate which stood wide open across a gravel road. The sheriff barely slowed down as he gunned the Tahoe through the gate. J.D. caught a glimpse of the name on the gateposts as they blazed through, but was sure he was mistaken.

"There's a cattle trail and several dirt roads, in fairly good condition, all through the property," Sutton was saying. "The road Dodson took goes through the towns of Tunstall and Garrett and he'll have to slow down or risk losing control on a hairpin turn." J.D. nodded, groping for a handhold in the Tahoe as the SUV jounced up and down the gravel road. A glance at the speedometer told him that Sutton was pushing eighty and apparently the sheriff had no qualms about going faster. "There's a place I can cut him off, if I can get there before him... and if I don't, Dudley's got the road blocked where it meets another county road."

J.D. didn't bother to nod again; the motion of the Tahoe did it for him. He gritted his teeth and tried to calculate how long it had been since Dodson's sedan had taken that left turn, but he couldn't concentrate. His mind kept returning to the one thought that he knew was driving the sheriff to catch Dodson, with or without the help of his deputies or any other law enforcement agency.

Corrie.

Corrie's concentration on freeing her wrists was interrupted by the sudden sideways lurching of the car, punctuated by squealing tires and screeching brakes. She gasped as she slid violently first one way, then the other, slamming into the sides of the trunk like a pinball. The smell of burnt rubber filled the small dark area and, for one sickening moment, she envisioned the car flipping over or crashing into another vehicle or into a ditch and bursting into flames with her trapped in the trunk. Despite the high-speed swerving, she managed to jam her knees against the trunk lid and braced herself to keep from being tossed around. For several moments, the car sped along, barely slackening its pace, and Corrie relaxed her stiffened knees. Suddenly there was a loud bang, then she was flung forward, slamming against the back of the trunk. She tried to scream as the car pitched forward, then it seemed to stumble several times before it came to a sudden stop.

She didn't move, barely dared to breathe. She heard voices but no distinct words, then car doors slamming. She could hardly believe what happened and the thought both energized and terrified her.

They had a flat tire.

She rolled over, wincing at the pain in her bound wrists, and scrambled up onto her knees into a crouch, wondering what her next move should be. She knew that if the car had gotten a flat, the logical next move would be for her captors to change the tire.

Which meant they'd have to open the trunk.

Frantically, she dropped to her side and scrabbled around in the darkness, feeling for something, anything, she could use as a weapon. Her hand brushed against a slender metal object. A lug wrench? Crowbar? Did it matter? She managed to grasp it in her rapidly numbing hands, not sure if it was going to be of any use to her with her hands behind her back, and debated whether it would be best for her to be right at the front where the opening was, maybe surprise Walter Dodson when he opened the trunk lid, or whether she should scoot back, maybe buy herself some time.

She crept back until she felt the rear wall of the trunk against her back and, to her surprise, it moved. She pressed her shoulder against it. Her heart began to pound in double-time as a crack of daylight appeared all around the edges of the seat back. She hesitated. Should she try to push through the seat? What if she were seen? Gripping the lug wrench tightly, she slowly leaned against the seat, pushing it out until she could see the blue sky through the car windows.

And she could hear voices.

Walter Dodson was saying, "There's no way we'll get away now... not with both front tires blown out!"

Corrie nearly sobbed with relief. Both tires blown out! The spare tire wouldn't be much use to Walter Dodson and his accomplice.

"Shut up and let me think!" a woman's irritated voice snapped back at him, jolting Corrie. She'd known Walter Dodson's accomplice was that mysterious blond woman, but this woman sounded like....

"Well, do your thinking sitting down before the sheriff catches up to us and sees you parading around out here! I can't believe we didn't bring your wheelchair!"

Corrie froze. Betty? So great was her shock that she didn't hear the heavy footsteps approaching the trunk. The latch popped and the lid flew open and Walter Dodson stood glaring down at her. Betty stood beside him, without a trace of infirmity, her usually gentle face grim and a large gun in her hands, aimed directly at Corrie.

Chapter 31

Corrie blinked from the sudden onslaught of sunlight and cringed back, hoping for one crazy moment that this was all a nightmare and she was going to wake up any minute.

"Get her out of there," Betty snarled at Walter. He flashed his mother a look of pure malevolence before he reached into the trunk and grabbed Corrie's upper arm. He yanked her up out of the trunk, ignoring her muffled cry of pain, and unceremoniously dumped her on the ground. She tried to scramble to her feet, but Betty moved to stand over her and the muzzle of the gun, just inches from her face, effectively stopped Corrie from making another move.

"If I didn't think we still had a chance to get out of this mess, I'd finish you off right this second," Betty snapped. Walter Dodson shot her an incredulous look.

"What chance?" he barked, shaking his head. "We've got two flat tires and a hostage and the sheriff has us surrounded! You might as well pull the trigger!"

"Don't be an idiot," Betty hissed at him and Corrie was thankful that it was Betty holding the gun and not her son. "The sound of the shot will carry. All we have to do is keep her quiet until after the sheriff rescues us...."

"WHAT??"

"... and then we'll just let nature take its course."

"The sheriff isn't coming to rescue us, Ma! He's coming to arrest us!" Dodson cried, looking around frantically. Betty gave him a withering look.

"If he finds her with us, then, yes, he'll arrest us!" Betty snapped. "But if he finds us out here, alone, with us stranded in a car with blown out tires, he'll rescue us."

"And how do we explain...?"

"Your blond 'mystery woman'," Betty said, nodding. "SHE'S the one who forced us to drive out here, then she took Corrie and made her getaway. She had an accomplice waiting for her out here...."

"Are you nuts? No one's going to believe that! Especially not the sheriff!"

Corrie was inclined to agree, but as long as Betty was holding the gun on her, she wasn't going to argue... even if she could. She tightened her grip on the lug wrench; so far, they hadn't seemed to notice she had it. If only she had some idea on how to use it....

"Hold this and keep it aimed at her," Betty said, handing the gun to Walter. She stepped briskly around Corrie, reached down and yanked the lug wrench out of her hands. Corrie winced as Betty chuckled and slapped it into the palm of her hand.

"You're so gullible, Corrie... so quick to believe that I was just a helpless old lady, content to sit around and let my sorry, worthless dreamer of a husband run the whole show and milk me dry, trying to prove he was so smart and savvy. Well, not with my money... not anymore. I've still got a lot of living to do and Marvin's not around to waste another penny on another worthless scheme. I'm collecting my pay on all the 'business loans' he took from me... and it's too bad you were even nosier than you were gullible. I guess you know I won't be coming to the Black Horse anymore... not now that I can afford luxury hotels. Besides, I doubt the Black Horse will survive if you don't."

Corrie tried to scream as Betty swung the lug wrench in a backhand that connected with Corrie's temple and once again she felt darkness descend. She struggled to hold on to consciousness, but when she felt Walter Dodson grab her shoulders and begin dragging her, she let herself go limp.

"Over in that arroyo... take this knife, put it in her, then push her off over the edge. If that doesn't kill her right away, she'll be dead before they find her."

She didn't hear Walter Dodson's response; she only knew that if she let herself black out, she'd never see daylight again.

"There they are!" J.D. cried as the sheriff's Tahoe crested a hill, the tires barely touching the ground. The maroon sedan sat in the middle of the two-lane road, listing forward on the two flat front tires, and J.D. breathed a prayer of thanks—he hadn't been as confident as the sheriff that they'd be able to catch up to their quarry.

Both front doors were open and they could see a man pacing back and forth in front of the car. Walter Dodson. They covered the quarter-mile between them and the fugitives in less than five seconds and skidded to a stop in a cloud of dust in front of the car—not that there was any danger of the vehicle going anywhere. Dodson held his hands up as Sutton jumped out of the SUV, his gun drawn and aimed at Dodson.

"Where's Corrie?" Sutton asked, his voice not as unwavering as his aim. Walter Dodson shook his head, his hands still up, and he looked at Betty Landry who was seated in the front passenger seat, wringing her hands.

"Oh, Sheriff, I'm so thankful you're here!" Betty quavered in a plaintive voice. "That horrible woman...."

"Where is Corrie?" Sutton repeated, his voice becoming dangerously unsteady, as he approached Walter Dodson and shoved him toward the sedan's hood. "Hands on the car, feet apart," he snapped, then glanced at J.D. and motioned for him to do the honors. J.D. patted Dodson down none too gently. Whether it was proper procedure or not, J.D. didn't care; he just knew that someone had better answer Sutton's question before the sheriff's—and his—patience ran out.

"She took her... that woman took Corrie," Betty cried, her voice shaking. J.D.'s eyes met the sheriff's and he could see his skepticism mirrored in them.

"How?" Sutton asked as he tossed his cuffs to J.D. and J.D. secured Dodson's wrists behind his back. Dodson finally spoke.

"Some guy in a Jeep was waiting for her out here.... They took

Corrie and took off," he said, his voice sounding defeated.

"Really?" Sutton said. "Which way did they go?"

"Cross country. That way," Dodson said, jerking his head in the direction that led towards hills and rocky outcroppings.

"Well, then they won't get far," Sutton said, lowering his gun. "That arroyo," he said, nodding toward the ditch that ran twenty yards behind them and zig-zagged into the distance, "loops around across the road and cuts in front of those hills. If your tires hadn't blown, you'd have reached the bridge about a mile down and then your friend would have had miles of open country to travel on in any direction."

J.D. had moved to the shoulder of the road and scuffed the dirt with the toe of his boot, noting the dust that rose up from that minor disturbance, and glanced around. There were no tire tracks, nor any other indication that a vehicle had gone off the road to travel cross-country, and no tell-tale cloud of dust that would have signaled the movement of a vehicle. He exchanged a glance with the sheriff, but neither of them commented on it. "Who was the guy in the Jeep?" J.D. asked.

"We don't know," Betty said, wringing her hands. "We have no idea who he was or who that awful woman was!"

"Mrs. Landry," Sutton interrupted, "are you aware that your son was seen talking to that woman just before your husband was killed?"

Betty paused with her mouth open, then she sat up stiffly. "Why, Sheriff, just what are you suggesting?" she said in a most affronted manner.

"Ma...," Walter Dodson said and the sheriff pulled out his note pad and perused his notes.

"I have a witness who saw Mr. Dodson talking to this woman on Friday morning."

Walter Dodson's face had paled and he kept licking his lips, his glance darting between Betty Landry and the sheriff. J.D. wondered how much longer he'd be able to keep whatever it was he wanted to say under sealed lips.

"Well, that woman was bothering Walter at the campground. She kept hanging around him, trying to get him interested in her, no doubt...."

"Ma!" Dodson said sharply, with a shake of his head. The sheriff glanced up from his notes as Betty threw her son a glare. The sheriff noticed, but pretended he was too involved in his notes to comment.

"How do you know this... that this woman was 'bothering' your son?"

"How? Well, Walter told me, of course!" Mrs. Landry sputtered.

"When?" The word shot out simultaneously from both J.D. and sheriff. Betty Landry drew back slightly.

"'When?' Well, later... later that morning, I'm sure...."

"Ma!" Now Dodson's voice had taken on a tone somewhere between a plea and a threat, but Bettty ignored him.

"Now, Walter, you mustn't be embarrassed. I know it's humiliating for a gentleman to be pursued by a woman who can't take 'no' for an answer, but you can't let your sense of chivalry keep you from telling the truth."

"Agreed, Dodson," the sheriff said, shutting his notebook. "Is there something else you want to tell us?"

J.D. leaned forward as Dodson's head jerked up. He looked at J.D. first, then at the sheriff, then his head began to bob, almost too eagerly.

"Walter!" Betty's sharp voice cracked like a whip. It even made Dodson flinch. The sheriff took hold of Dodson's upper arm and Dodson didn't resist as they began to move toward the Tahoe. Betty hitched herself forward in the passenger seat of the sedan and implored, "Sheriff, please, don't arrest my son! I'm sure if I can talk with him, this will all be sorted out."

Sutton shook his head. "Sorry, Mrs. Landry, we're dealing with a dangerous criminal... one who's taken the life of a close family member in cold blood. I think it's in everyone's best interest that we keep your son away from you."

"NO!" Betty cried. "No, please! Sheriff, please, let me talk to my son!"

The sheriff ignored her and kept walking. J.D. cleared his throat. "Mrs. Landry... ma'am?" he said. "The sheriff will call for a deputy to bring a car and we'll get you back into town. I'll just get your wheelchair for you...." He drew back when he saw the expression on the old woman's face. It was a look of such fury that J.D. didn't think was possible, but in a flash it was gone and Betty Landry's face seemed to crumple.

"Very well," she said, her voice a mere raspy whisper. "It's in the trunk." He hesitated for a second before reaching across her to press the button on the keyring dangling from the key in the ignition switch to pop the trunk lid. Betty Landry slumped down in the seat as if every ounce of strength had drained out of her and, after J.D. withdrew from the car's interior, fumbled on the floor of the front seat for her handbag. J.D. almost considered offering to get the purse for her, but decided that the poor woman needed a moment to collect herself. He turned to open the trunk of the sedan.

Corrie stifled a groan, hoping that her ragged gasps weren't as loud as they sounded to her own ears. She looked up the steep incline of the arroyo, then turned her head and looked down the sheer drop beside her. Thanks to the cluster of rocks that had fallen down the slope at some time in the past, there was a convenient barricade between her and a deadly forty-foot drop. She drew a deep shuddering breath.

The last thing she remembered was Walter Dodson bending over her and whispering, "I'm sorry, Corrie... you didn't deserve this," before using the knife to rip through the tape on her wrists, then push her down the incline. The shock nearly drove her sense of self-preservation out of her, but she managed to gather her wits in time to scrabble frantically for a way to slow her tumble down the arroyo and find a handhold somewhere... anywhere. It was nothing short of a miracle that the rocks stopped her.

She brought her shaking hands to her face and pried the corner of the tape up and away from her mouth. Steeling herself, she yanked the tape off her lips, fighting back a yelp of pain. She allowed herself a second or two to lick her lips, primarily to make sure she hadn't ripped them off with the tape, before she attempted to sit up.

The world began spinning and she leaned back on her elbow, trying to find her focus. She reached up and winced as her fingertips made contact with the throbbing lump on her temple. She felt a stickiness, but didn't look. It was enough to know that Betty hadn't shattered her skull with her backhand and that Walter Dodson had been kind enough not to follow his mother's orders to stick the knife into her. She took another deep breath and the pounding in her head subsided and she could hear voices. Walter and Betty and... Rick! And J.D.!

This time she sat bolt upright, fighting off the dizziness and blurred vision. She heard Betty's piteous voice: "... that woman took Corrie...," and her weakness and pain disappeared as fury surged through her. She opened her mouth to yell a warning, but stopped when she realized that her voice—or what was left of it—probably wouldn't carry the thirty or so feet up to the edge of the arroyo and that Betty Landry had the element of surprise on her side... along with a gun.

She tried to stand up, but her numb feet and legs wouldn't allow her to do more than crawl on her hands and knees. Gritting her teeth, she managed to drag herself up the steep, red-dirt incline, grabbing at rocks, grass clumps, anything that gave her any kind of handhold, feeling as if she were sliding back a foot for every inch she managed to climb. Powdery red dirt sifted down on her, stinging her eyes and clogging her nose and throat. After what seemed like an eternity, she reached the top of the arroyo and cautiously peered over the edge.

The sedan sat where it had stopped, twenty yards from the arroyo, with Rick's Tahoe parked at an angle in front of it. Both front doors of the sedan were wide open, the driver's side door facing Corrie, and she could see Betty sitting in the passenger seat, turned so that her back was to Corrie. Corrie sucked in her breath. Rick was walking Walter Dodson, in handcuffs, toward the Tahoe, his back to Betty Landry. J.D. was standing at the trunk, apparently getting ready to open it, his attention diverted away from Betty. Corrie saw Betty reach into her handbag and withdraw the gun.

The gun she had used to kill her husband.

Corrie went cold. Her lips moved, but not a sound came from them. She pushed herself up, her legs shaking so badly she sank to her knees again and, as she put her hands out to steady herself, she felt a baseball-sized rock under her palm and her fingers closed around it....

Chapter 32

J.D. shook his head. Something didn't feel right about this whole thing... the main thing being that it appeared that he and the sheriff had apprehended Marvin Landry's murderer, but Corrie was still missing. He knew that Sutton would be questioning Dodson very closely about what exactly happened to Corrie after they left the campground—he was positive the mysterious blond woman, whatever her role may have been in Marvin's murder, was nowhere in the vicinity—and hoped that they weren't too late. He grabbed the edge of the trunk lid and pulled it up.

He blinked, then stared for a second or two. There was no wheelchair in the trunk of the car. He started to turn away to see if he'd missed it in the back seat when he noticed two things. The back wall of the trunk—the back of the car's rear seats—was pushed out of place. And a glint of shiny metal on the floor of the trunk caught his eye, a thin circle of silver with a speck of turquoise. He picked it up and his eyes widened.

Corrie's earring.

He wheeled around, once again reaching for and cursing the weapon he didn't have. Betty Landry was on her feet, her back to J.D. and her arms fully extended, steadying the gun aimed directly at the sheriff's back.

"*Sutton!*"

J.D. launched himself at Betty Landry. She half-turned her head, a tight cold smile on her lips as if telling J.D. he was too late. With sickening clarity, he saw her finger tighten on the trigger.

Then a baseball-sized rock arced over the roof of the sedan, like a meteorite heading for earth, and connected squarely with the top of Betty's head.

Betty's arm jerked up as her finger squeezed the trigger. Dimly, J.D. saw the sheriff shove Walter Dodson to the ground as he dropped, drew his automatic, and spun back toward the car. Then J.D. saw nothing as he connected with Betty Landry. He grabbed the gun in her still-upraised hand as they hit the ground and rolled. In a flash, J.D. was on his feet, the gun aimed at Betty Landry, but Betty Landry wasn't moving. A soft moan escaped her lips before she lay still, unconscious.

J.D. looked over at the sheriff. "You okay?" he yelled. Sutton nodded as he got to his feet, his gun still drawn and aimed at the inert form at J.D.'s feet.

"What the hell happened?" he barked.

"Rick."

J.D. and the sheriff spun in the direction of the faint, raspy voice. J.D.'s eyes widened in disbelief as the apparition covered in red dust stumbled toward them, hands outstretched.

"Corrie?" J.D.'s and the sheriff's eyes met, then Sutton holstered his weapon and ran toward her.

"Rick...." She stopped, swayed on her feet, then toppled forward. The sheriff caught her in his arms before she hit the ground. He dropped to his knees, cradling her as her body went limp and J.D. saw the sheriff's hand gently brush her hair from her face.

"Wilder!" Sutton shouted. "We need an ambulance!"

Before J.D. could respond, he heard the shriek of sirens, then saw the cloud of dust stirred up by Deputy Dudley Evans and the entourage of sheriff's department and emergency vehicles he was leading up the red-dirt road. He stepped around to Betty Landry's side and felt for a pulse. He grimaced as he looked up, first at Walter Dodson, then at the sheriff. Dodson was sitting up, his wrists still locked behind him, looking dazed and shaking his head. He could wait. J.D. said, "Sheriff, how's Corrie?"

"Bruised, dehydrated, and shaken up. Other than that, she's fine!" Sutton snapped. J.D. straightened up.

"Then Mrs. Landry gets dibs on the ambulance... if it's not too late," he said.

Chapter 33

Corrie grimaced, opening her eyes the merest slit and fighting back the stinging tears that flooded her vision. Everything was too bright, too white, then a soothing familiar voice she hadn't heard in days said, "I think she's coming around." Shelli!

That triggered a jack-in-the-box reaction where she sat bolt upright only to feel a sharp pain on the left side of her head followed by gut-wrenching dizziness. Strong, comforting arms encircled her shoulders and Jackie's soft, motherly voice crooned, "Now, now, Corrie, honey, it's all right, you're all right, just lay back down...."

She did, only because sitting up felt lousy. The pain in her left temple settled into a rhythmic thumping and she waited a few moments for it to subside. She managed to open her eyes and, this time, the white light didn't blind her so much. She was in the emergency room. Jackie's face, lined with worry, swam into focus. "There, now, honey, everything's all right, you're going to be fine." Corrie frowned. Had she only dreamed she heard Shelli's voice? Then her friend's sweet, freckled face appeared over Jackie's shoulder.

"Hey, girlfriend," Shelli said softly, her hazel eyes brimming with tears.

"Shell? When did you get back? Where are Rick and J.D.?" Corrie managed to stammer. Her voice sounded, to her own ears, a whisper so faint that she was surprised Jackie heard it. Jackie reached for a cup of water and held it Corrie's lips. Corrie thought nothing in the world would ever taste or feel so good as that water again. She cleared her throat. "Jackie, what's going on?"

Jackie set the cup back on the tray and adjusted the hospital bed until Corrie was semi-upright before she spoke. "Shelli walked in to the camp office about five minutes after Rick and J.D. went after you... and they are both fine," she said crisply, smoothing back her silver-gray ponytail. "Both are worried sick about you and bothering the doctors and nurses to no end... along with Jerry, Red and Dana. Rick's been insisting—make that demanding—that he has the right to be here to question you as soon as you wake up, regardless of what the doctor says, since you're the victim in a kidnapping and material witness in a murder investigation, but now he's tied up answering questions from the state police and some of the county officials... and it hasn't done a thing for his patience. He left word to call him as soon as you woke up, then Dr. White threw everyone but me and Shelli out and told them that there'd be plenty of time to question you when you got your head together."

Corrie touched the bandages on the side of her head and wondered how long it would be before she felt her head was back together. "Betty... Betty Landry... what happened to her? And Walter Dodson? I mean...." Her voice trailed away but Jackie nodded with understanding.

"Walter Dodson is in custody until they figure out what role he had to play in Marvin's death. Betty... well, Betty won't be standing trial for murdering Marvin... at least, not in this life." Corrie's stomach lurched.

"You mean, that rock...? She's...."

"Try not to think about," Shelli said, taking Corrie's hand and squeezing it gently. Corrie managed a nod, but her vision blurred with tears. Shelli exchanged a glance with Jackie and the older woman nodded.

"I'll go tell the doctor you're awake.... and I'll hold everyone off until you feel up to having more visitors."

"Thanks, Jackie," Corrie said, choking on the words. Jackie bent to give her a hug then turned and limped out of the room. Shelli pulled up the chair Jackie had vacated and sat in it.

"It's not your fault, Corrie... you only did what you had to do. Rick could be dead right now if you hadn't...."

"I know," Corrie interrupted, wiping her tears and sniffling. She took a deep breath. "I know, Shell. But I only wanted to stop Betty. I never thought that... THAT would happen."

"If you'd had a gun in your hands," Shelli said, emphatically, "and the only way to stop Betty was to pull the trigger, you'd have pulled the trigger, right?" Corrie shivered, managing only the tiniest of nods. "You did what you had to do," Shelli repeated.

"I know," Corrie said and sighed. Knowing it was true didn't make her feel any less lousy about it. Shelli leaned forward.

"Seriously, Corrie, are you okay? Physically, I mean? I'm still freaking out... I had no idea what was going on and when Jackie told me...." Her voice trailed off and she shook her head. "I wish I hadn't gone out of town this weekend," she said.

"Only because you hate to miss out on any excitement," Corrie quipped, trying to erase the lines of concern in her friend's face. "It was supposed to be dull and boring while you were gone... and I wish it had been!"

"Me, too," Shelli said. "Of course, I'm not the only one who's probably going to go gray over this little escapade. You've got that poor man pacing the floor with worry out there!"

"Rick's a born worrier," Corrie murmured as she leaned back against the pillows. "He's got a highly over-developed sense of responsibility. Comes with that sheriff's badge he wears. You know that," she added as she closed her eyes.

"Yeah," Shelli drawled. "But I wasn't talking about Rick."

Corrie's eyes flew open and she sat up, unmindful of the flash of pain that shot through her head. "What?"

Before Shelli could say a word, there was a soft tap on the wall by the open door. J.D. stood in the doorway, his steel-gray eyes fixed on Corrie. "Mind if I come in?"

"No, not at all," Corrie stammered. She fumbled with the button to raise the head of the bed, then tried to brush her hair back from her face and almost succeeded in getting the cord tangled around her neck. She caught Shelli's bemused expression as her friend helped save her from strangling herself. "J.D. Wilder, this is my best friend,

Shelli Davenport."

He nodded, his gaze only leaving Corrie's for a split second to acknowledge Shelli, then he turned his attention back to Corrie. "Jackie said you were doing better," he said.

"Better than what, I'm not sure," Corrie muttered. "But I'm alive and conscious... which is better than the alternative."

J.D. had moved to the end of the hospital bed and rested both hands on the footboard. His eyes had never left her face and she felt herself grow warm. "We were worried sick about you." His cool, confident demeanor had vanished and nothing but raw, aching worry and relief were evident in his eyes and face.

"Same goes both ways," Corrie said, meeting his gaze despite her discomfiture.

Shelli cleared her throat in a theatrical manner. "Let me see if I can't find out where Jackie went," she said as she backed toward the door. Behind J.D.'s back she gave him an appraising look up and down, then gave Corrie an approving glance and two thumbs up before slipping out the door.

"Why don't you sit down, J.D.?" she said, indicating the chair Shelli had been sitting in. He did, his eyes never leaving her face. She tried to think of something humorous to say, anything to alleviate the tension emanating from him, but nothing came to mind. She tried to smile. "I don't know what to say, J.D.... except thank you."

He raised a brow. "For what? Being too late to save you from Betty Landry?"

"You weren't too late," Corrie argued. "We wouldn't be having this conversation if you had been."

"You should have never been out of my sight," J.D. said, shaking his head and leaning forward, his elbows on his knees and his hands clasped together in front of him. "I'm just thankful that Walter Dodson wasn't as cold-blooded as his mother. And don't you dare feel bad for taking her out," he added, his gaze turning to steel. "I only wish I had figured it all out before she had the chance to hurt you."

"Yeah, well," Corrie said with a shrug, trying to lighten the mood and shake off a chill at the same time. "I'm sure we all feel that way. I can't believe I'm going to say this, but I should have listened to Rick."

"Damn straight, Maria Inez Corazon Black Horse!" Rick bellowed as he strode into the room and made a beeline for Corrie's bed.

"Oh, boy," Corrie muttered, tugging the blanket up to her chin as if she wanted to hide under it. She was glad that she was the only patient in the ER at the moment or else heart monitors would have been blaring like sirens. J.D. leaned back in his chair and folded his arms across his chest, shooting a quizzical glance at her. Rick stopped at the foot of the bed, his eyes blazing, and gripped the footboard so tightly it seemed it would snap off in his hands. Corrie forced a smile. "Hi, Rick!" she said.

"Don't 'Hi, Rick' me! The doctor said it was a good thing you had a hard head or that lug wrench would have shattered it! It's that hard head that got you into this in the first place!" Rick snapped.

"It's good to see you alive and well, too, Sheriff!" she said, sitting up and forgetting the pain and dizziness. "No need to thank me for helping you out!"

"Thank you? For helping out? You nearly got yourself killed for ignoring, once again, an order I specifically gave you!"

"Yeah, well, first off, Sheriff, I don't work for you and I don't take orders from you! Second, if it weren't for my hard head ignoring your hard-headed orders, you'd have never suspected Betty Landry being the one behind Marvin's murder, and you and J.D. and Walter Dodson would all be dead!" Corrie fired back.

Rick straightened up as if he'd been slapped and his face went crimson. That he seemed to be at a total loss for words surprised Corrie and she didn't know what else to say, either. J.D. cleared his throat and stood up. "I'll be back," he said, not bothering to come up with an excuse to offer and he strolled out of the room, intercepting Shelli and Jackie who had come rushing back at the sound of Corrie's and Rick's shouts and steering them back down the hallway.

Rick bit his lip and looked away for a moment. Corrie could see the muscles in his throat working. Finally he looked back at her, his eyes glassy. "I thought you were dead," he said hoarsely.

Corrie swallowed hard, but the lump in her throat refused to budge. She knew that would be the closest to an apology that he could manage. Rick's image blurred. "I know," she stammered. "I thought I was, too. But I'm okay." It seemed like a ridiculous thing to say, but nothing else came to mind and the last thing she wanted to do was start bawling in front of Rick. He took a deep breath and let go of the footboard and wiped his hands over his face.

"Yeah," he said shortly. "I see that. And while I do appreciate your mad fielding skills, you should have stayed away from the Landry's RV!"

"You had no idea it was Betty who killed Marvin... not until she tried to kill you," Corrie argued. Rick gave her a stony look.

"The same could be said for you."

Corrie took a deep breath. "I should have known... when Dee Dee said that Betty wore a wig... I should have figured it out that there was no blond woman... it was Betty all along... it wasn't until I found that wig under the bathroom sink along with that bathrobe...." She looked at Rick. "You'd have figured it out right away... you and J.D. The professionals."

Rick had moved to the side of the bed and sat in the chair beside it. He looked haggard and exhausted. He removed his hat and held it in his hands, studying it intently. "Maybe, maybe not," he said at last. "Too many people had seen that blond woman... too many people believed Betty was infirm... hell, even Marvin, her own husband, believed she was wheelchair-bound. Only Walter Dodson knew the truth... but Betty had him under her thumb. I suspected that Betty knew a lot more about her husband's death than she was letting on, but I never dreamed that she actually pulled the trigger." He sighed and sat back, shaking his head.

Corrie pulled the blanket up to her shoulders, but this time to try to fight off a chill that had little to do with the room's temperature. "So she did it all... she heard about Buster's gun and took it to throw everyone off... she shot Marvin then she took off her wig and put on Marvin's robe and walked on her own two feet to the men's room to hide it... and then she locked herself in the bathroom.... And all along, I felt sorry for her, I trusted her...." Corrie's voice trailed away and Rick leaned forward.

"She fooled us all, Corrie, not just you."

"I thought she was my friend!" Corrie said, her voice shaking as a single tear slid down her nose and she impatiently brushed it away.

Rick handed her his handkerchief and waited a moment while she regained control. "She took advantage of your friendship," he said. "She knew that at the Black Horse there were people who would vouch for her and believe anything she said. She probably never gave it a thought that Dee Dee might suspect she was wearing a wig."

"I can't believe Dee Dee could tell it wasn't Betty's real hair. I'd have never suspected it," Corrie said and Rick shrugged.

"Dee Dee's an expert. Besides, she wears a wig, too," Rick said matter-of-factly and Corrie threw him a stunned glance.

"*Dee Dee* wears a wig? How on earth do you know that?" she blurted and was immediately sorry she asked. The thought occurred to her that there was only one way for Rick to know that bit of information, but that was something Corrie didn't want to think about. He shook his head and gave her a mildly amused but reproving glance.

"Corrie, no woman, especially one that knows as much about hair care as Dee Dee does, would subject her crowning glory to that amount of coloring, perming, and straightening. She's got more wigs than she has colored contacts."

"Oh," Corrie said, feeling her face prickle with heat. She felt foolish for not having thought of that herself, but then again she didn't even wear lipstick, much less bothered with the finer points of women's beauty aids. "I guess Betty Landry figured no one here would ever have a reason to doubt anything she said or did."

"The fact that Marvin was contemplating this business venture with the Westlakes just helped her make up her mind to wait till they got here to make her move," Rick said. "If she couldn't blame Marvin's murder on a passing burglar, she could muddy the water by implicating the Westlakes... and then getting Buster involved by taking his gun only added to the confusion." He shook his head. "I wonder if Marvin wasn't starting to suspect his life was in danger... if that was why he asked Buster about buying a gun. I guess we'll never know."

Before Corrie could respond, they heard throats clearing and they looked up. J.D. and Shelli stood in the doorway, holding steaming Styrofoam cups in their hands. "Nothing like a shot of caffeine to make everything better," Shelli said, making her way to the bedside. She handed Rick the larger of the two cups she held. "Sorry it's black, Sheriff, but Corrie says you'd rather drink it that way than with powdered creamer."

"She's right. And welcome back," Rick said, taking the cup and hug from Shelli. Shelli's eyes widened and she looked at Corrie.

"Did you hear that? Rick said you were right about something! You should mark this day on the calendar. And you have witnesses!"

"I'm not THAT bad," Rick protested as he took a sip of the coffee, then grimaced. Shelli gave him a reproving glare.

"Yeah, see if I vote for you in the next election, Sheriff. I can't leave town for four days without you letting my best friend in the whole world get kidnapped and almost killed by a dangerous criminal!" Shelli said, giving Rick a slap on the arm as he lifted the cup to his mouth. Corrie bit back a smile as he held the cup away from his uniform and shook his head at Shelli. She wondered if he'd had a chance to change into a fresh uniform after all the excitement or if he'd somehow managed to keep the one he was wearing spotless through it all. She glanced at J.D. He was watching her with a bemused expression on his face.

"Sorry, no piñon coffee for you. Dr. White let me bring you something other than water... sort of," he amended, handing her a small cup that held tea so weak it was barely discernible from the water she had been drinking earlier. She took a sip and made a face.

"Thanks, but dying of thirst suddenly holds a lot of appeal," she said, handing the cup back. J.D.'s grin widened. He turned to Rick.

"Deputy Evans just stopped by. He said Dodson's suffering from diarrhea of the mouth and is telling everything he can to keep himself out of prison. Dodson claims that Betty planted the idea in Marvin's head about getting a gun for protection... and that she hinted that it was from Dodson that he needed protection. She encouraged him to ask around about a gun... that was supposedly to make people think that Marvin had some kind of enemy after him. She hit pay dirt with his first attempt."

They were all silent for a while, then Corrie spoke. "It's beginning to sound like maybe Betty was the one who had Marvin under her thumb."

J.D. shrugged. "I think Marvin may have been suffering from guilt once he thought Betty became wheelchair-bound. And I think he genuinely believed he was going to be able to make it all up to her when this business venture succeeded. But by then it was too late... Betty had had enough and she was going to follow through on getting rid of Marvin and living life on her own terms. She already had the gun... Dodson had been pressured into purchasing it before they ever arrived and who knows what she promised—or threatened—to get him to go along with her plans."

Corrie shook her head to clear it; she felt dizzy but it wasn't entirely from her injuries. "All this time I was thinking she was a sweet, helpless old lady... I'm almost starting to feel glad that I hit her with that rock!"

"I'm still impressed by that," J.D. said, eyeing Corrie with respect and admiration. Rick grunted.

"I told you that fielding was her strong suit," he said. "She's got a hell of an arm on her, Wilder." J.D. looked puzzled and Shelli laughed.

"The sheriff's department and the volunteer fire department have a softball team—Guns 'n' Hoses," Shelli explained to J.D. "However, because they don't have enough players...."

"Half the sheriff's department IS the fire department," Rick explained dryly.

"They recruited some players from Bonney County citizens— Corrie plays center field," Shelli stated proudly.

"Yeah, and half the team has to pinch hit for me," Corrie muttered, feeling her face redden as J.D. threw her an incredulous look.

"I find that hard to believe," he said. "You nearly knocked ME out of the park!"

"The pitchers refuse to get that close to me to throw the ball," Corrie said and J.D. laughed out loud.

"They should let you use a cane!" His smile faded slightly. "Maybe we shouldn't be laughing, but there's no reason for you to feel bad about what happened to Betty Landry. You did what you had to do to stop her."

"You might have done her a favor," Rick interjected and Corrie threw him a startled glance. He nodded. "I doubt she would have held up through the trial and all that... she needed psychiatric help besides imprisonment. Either way, she'd have considered it the same, being committed to a hospital or to prison, without a chance to live life the way she always wanted to, and I don't think she would have lasted long in either."

"Let's not talk about it anymore," Corrie implored. Rick seemed about to say something when Dudley Evans poked his head around the door frame.

"Sheriff," he said somberly, "there's someone here to see you."

"Tell them I'm busy and to make an appointment," Rick said. For once, Dudley stood rooted to the spot instead of responding with a prompt "Yes, sir".

"It's, uh, important," he said. Rick looked at him sharply.

"So is this, Deputy Evans. Tell them I will get back to them when I can," Rick said, but Dudley shook his head and cleared his throat.

"Um... someone heard about an incident on their land... they heard you were here at the hospital... she, uh, wants to verify the truth of what she heard...." Dudley's voice trailed off and he gave Rick a wide-eyed look, mouthed two words in an exaggerated manner, and tilted his head back down the hallway.

Rick rolled his eyes and muttered something under his breath. "I'll be right there," he said and Dudley nodded, visibly relieved, inclined his head and tipped his hat to Corrie, then scooted away. Rick turned and left the room without making eye contact with anyone.

"I'll go see if Dr. White's going to let your fan club in to see you," Shelli said, edging around J.D. and slipping out of the room after Rick. Silence descended as J.D. leaned against the wall, his eyes fixed on Corrie.

"What was that all about?" J.D. asked. He nodded toward the door. "I didn't quite catch what Deputy Evans was trying to tell the sheriff... it almost looked like he said 'your mother'—"

"He did," Corrie sighed with a shake of her head. "Rick's mother heard about the ruckus out on their property and wants to know what's going on."

J.D. let out a low whistle. "So I didn't just imagine the name I saw on the gate when the sheriff took that shortcut. No wonder he knew he'd be able to cut off Walter and Betty by going cross-country!" He looked at Corrie pointedly. "The sheriff and his family are quite well-off, aren't they?"

"Yes, but Rick doesn't like to talk about it," Corrie said. "He loves his job and he's good at it and he didn't get it because he 'bought' the election. Rick is fair and honest and doesn't use his position to his own benefit and...."

"Whoa," J.D. said, holding his hands up as he pushed away from the wall and came to her bedside. "You don't have to convince me. The fact that I had to learn from someone other than the sheriff that he doesn't have to work for a living impresses me."

"He's not trying to impress anyone. He really does love his job," Corrie said, feeling the heat rise in her face under J.D.'s direct gaze.

"I know that," J.D. said softly. "Maybe more than you know, Corrie." He cleared his throat. "So, I guess we've learned a lot from this little adventure... especially about each other," he added with a glimmer in his eye.

Corrie was positive her face was literally glowing red. "Yeah, I'll bet," she muttered. "I'm sure my real name isn't one you've heard very often!"

"What, 'Maria'?" J.D.'s eyes opened wide. "Are you kidding? I'm from Texas... I think every other woman I've ever met has the name 'Maria'!"

"You know exactly what I'm talking about, Jesse Dean Wilder!" Corrie shot back.

J.D. chuckled. "'Corazon'... it means 'heart', right?" Corrie nodded, not willing to make eye contact. "I think it suits you quite well,... Corrie."

She looked up at him and saw that the glimmer in his silver eyes had turned to a warm glow. "Thanks," she said simply. He seemed to be about to speak again when Shelli bustled into the room.

"Good news!" she crowed, waving a piece of paper over her head. "Dr. White says you can leave if you promise to take it easy and not try to catch any dangerous criminals or get hit over the head with heavy metal objects. Looks like you'll have to find yourself some new hobbies," she added with a sly grin and a glance at J.D.

Corrie caught a glimpse of J.D.'s blush—which she was sure mirrored her own—as she snatched the paper out of her friend's hand. "Did he say anything about throttling smart-aleck best friends?" she asked through gritted teeth. Shelli laughed.

"Only first thing in the morning, on an empty stomach... and with a full glass of water," she said, then planted her hands on her hips. "He wanted to keep you overnight for observation, but Jackie and I convinced him that that would only stress you out more... so we had to promise to do just about everything but sleep, breathe, and digest food for you in order to get you released. So don't kick up a fuss when they come in to disconnect you from all this equipment or all bets are off!" she warned, wagging a finger in Corrie's face.

Corrie sighed. "All right," she said. "Just as long as I get to go home. I'm in desperate need of a shower. And don't you dare tell me that's not allowed!" she growled. "Not in the condition I'm in!"

Shelli grimaced as Corrie held out a lock of her red-crusted raven hair. "Agreed," she said. "Jackie and I will figure something out. And as for making you take it easy for a while," she went on, giving J.D. a speculative look, "we may have to recruit an army to keep you in line."

Neither J.D. nor Corrie made eye contact with each other or with Shelli. "Let's get going," Corrie muttered.

Chapter 34

It took Córrie every ounce of will power to get out of bed Monday morning. She had thought a hot shower, a couple of ibuprofens, and good night's sleep would help her feel one-hundred-percent better, but it was apparent that all the bruises, aches, and pains had also gotten a good night's rest and attacked her with a vengeance. Though it was tempting to take everyone's advice and spend the day recuperating, Corrie forced herself up and into action.

She almost changed her mind when she caught sight of herself in the mirror. The bandage on her left temple only covered the broken skin where the lug wrench had hit her... she would need a ski mask to cover the spectrum of color that extended across her forehead and eyes and down her cheek. She shuddered and looked away. The realization that she was extremely lucky to be alive hit her with a force harder than Betty Landry's backhand.

She shrugged off the chill that ran down her back and followed her usual morning routine, albeit a little slower than usual. Even walking down the stairs required gritting her teeth and swallowing little yelps of pain as her sore limbs navigated each step. Renfro, in an unusual display of energy, expressed his concern by following her down the steps, murmuring whiny growls the entire way and occasionally bumping into the backs of her legs, forcing her to grab both rails in order not to finish what Betty Landry started. Oliver contributed by doing figure-eights around her ankles on every step and meowing pitifully. It took her nearly three times as long to make it down to the first floor than it normally did and the dog and cat, feeling that they had done everything they could to make their owner's descent to the camp store as safe as possible, immediately took to their customary haven behind the counter and curled up to resume their sleep.

Corrie took a deep breath at the bottom of the stairs. The unhappy thought that she would, eventually, have to climb back up to her living quarters came to her, but she decided she'd worry about that later. Right now, she was thankful that one of her wonderful friends had taken the trouble to set up her auto-start coffee maker with piñon coffee.

"What are you doing up?" Jackie said, nearly sending Corrie through the wall with shock. Corrie's shriek was mostly from the pain that shot through her body as she jumped, not so much from being startled. She spun around, her heart hammering in her chest, and glared at Jackie who was standing in the TV room doorway, leaning on her cane and looking bemused.

"What are you doing here?" Corrie's voice was more of a croak than a growl. She put out a hand to steady herself against the wall and accepted the coffee cup Jackie held out to her with a disapproving cluck and a shake of her head.

"I came in to open up... you shouldn't even be out of bed," Jackie said. "You have plenty of help to run this place until you feel better."

"I'm fine," Corrie said, willing her hands to stop trembling as she brought the coffee to her lips. "I can't just lie around and let everyone else take care of everything."

"You could... but you won't," Jackie said dryly. "Maybe if you consider what your appearance might do to some of your guests, you might think about keeping a low profile for a day or two."

"I didn't think about that," Corrie said with a grimace. Seeing herself had been bad enough; she didn't want to think about the looks of horror and sympathy she might get from her guests, nor how her looks might discourage repeat business. "Maybe I should stay upstairs and do paperwork."

Before Jackie could agree, there was a knock at the side door, which made Corrie jump again and nearly drop her coffee. The sign clearly stated that the office and store opened at seven in the morning, but someone had apparently seen the light on and decided to try their luck. Corrie's annoyance had more to do with her jumpiness than with an early customer but she shrugged off the chill that ran down her back and went to the door to politely explain her business hours to the persistent guest.

To her surprise, J.D. Wilder stood at the door. "J.D.," she said, forgetting her annoyance as she opened the door and moved back to let him in. "What are you doing up so early?"

He didn't answer right away as he stepped through the door. Except for the fading bruise she had inflicted on his temple, he looked exactly like he did the day she had met him, in his sleeveless black t-shirt and jeans... was that only four days ago? Freshly showered, his still-damp black hair slicked back into a ponytail, his steel-gray eyes bored into hers as if searching for something but he didn't smile. Corrie felt her cheeks warm up and she took a deep breath, inhaling the scent of his aftershave and feeling herself grow a little light-headed. She was pretty sure the feeling had nothing to do with the knot on her own head and she tried to think of something else to say.

"How are you doing, Corrie?" he asked, his voice soft, belying his tough-looking exterior. Self-consciously, Corrie touched the bandage and shrugged.

"Not bad," she said. "I came down to get things going for the day, but Jackie beat me to it." She glanced at Jackie who, to her surprise, was heading for the front door.

"I forgot something at my place... and I want to see if Jerry's gotten up yet. I'll be back," Jackie said over her shoulder as she scooted out the door. Corrie stared after her, only because she was embarrassed to let J.D. see the high color in her face that had nothing to do with her bruises.

J.D. cleared his throat. "I know you're not open yet, but I was hoping for a chance to see you alone for a few minutes. There's something I want to talk to you about before I check out."

That made Corrie turn around quickly. She'd forgotten that J.D. had made it clear the other day that he was only staying through the weekend... that he had a lot of things he needed to take care of back in Houston. A lot had happened in the last few days that made her forget he was leaving. Or maybe, if truth be told, she really hadn't wanted to think about it.

"Check out time isn't until noon, you know," she said, trying to keep her voice light even though her heart was hammering painfully. "Or were you thinking about slipping out the way you slipped in?"

He chuckled and ran a hand over his hair. "I won't do that again," he said. "And as for leaving early, I'm catching the first airport shuttle out of Ruidoso down to El Paso."

"Airport shuttle? You're flying back to Houston?" Corrie asked. J.D. nodded.

"I need to get back there fast... there's a lot of things that need to get taken care of quickly."

"What about your Harley?"

"Well, that's what I wanted to talk to you about," he said, leaning against the wall with his arms folded across his chest. "I noticed you have some storage sheds over by the employee parking lot. Is there room in there to store my Harley and, if so, would you be willing to do so for a few weeks?"

"You want to store your bike here? Does that mean...?" Corrie broke off, feeling her face heat up again as J.D. nodded.

"As soon as I finish up in Houston, I want to come back and finish up my vacation. I wanted to see if you could hold my camping site for me, if I pay for it in advance. I'm not sure how long I'll be gone. It might be a couple of weeks, might be longer than a month. I want to pay for the next four weeks and whatever you want to charge me for storing the bike in your shed." Corrie snapped her fingers.

"Was that you by the shed the night Rick and I went to talk to Buster? I thought someone was hanging around there, but then I thought I was imagining things. You were checking to see if we had room for your Harley in there?" she asked. To her amazement, J.D. blushed and looked away for a second.

"That was partly the reason I was there.... No, that's not true," he said with a sigh as he turned back to face her. "At that time, I had no concrete plans to come back. But I had just scared you half to death by walking in on you and then I saw you and the sheriff going to talk to Buster and I... decided to be nosy. I didn't know if Marvin Landry's death had anything to do with my situation and I wanted to find out what was going on."

"Oh," Corrie said. She felt a twinge of disappointment that J.D. had only been interested in finding out more about Marvin's death... but why did that make him look embarrassed? "I guess the only thing we haven't figured out is how that laundry room door got propped open that night," she said. J.D. cleared his throat and his face grew a few more degrees redder.

"Speaking of nosy," he said, "I overheard your friend, Dana, in the waiting room yesterday, saying something to Jackie about dying to find out what was going on...."

"Weren't we all?" Corrie interrupted but J.D. held up a hand.

"...What was going on with you and me... and the sheriff," he finished. Corrie's mouth dropped open and she was positive she matched J.D.'s own shade of crimson. "I gathered from Jackie's rather sharp response that there was nothing to find out and it wasn't any of their business anyway. However, Dana let slip that she had tried to find a way to slip into the camp store without triggering the buzzer... I didn't realize at the time that that's why you were so alarmed to see me in the store that night."

"Dana had rigged that pen to keep the door from buzzing," Corrie said, shaking her head and trying not to make eye contact with J.D. "I remember that she was in and out of the laundry room quite a bit that afternoon... and we were so busy and preoccupied with Marvin's murder that I hadn't even noticed that the laundry room door hadn't buzzed all day." J.D. nodded and Corrie sighed. "Rick's going to kick himself for not even considering there was some innocent explanation for that."

"Why should he?" J.D. said, raising a brow. "He had every reason to be concerned, Corrie. I would have done the same, considering everything that was going on at the time. He was afraid you might be the murderer's next victim... and you almost were."

Corrie folded her arms across her chest. She took a sip of her coffee, but it had cooled off to the point that it did nothing to help warm her up. She nodded toward the courtesy table. "Why don't you come in and have a cup of coffee before you go, J.D.? It'll be a while before you get any piñon coffee where you're going."

He grinned. "All right. And let me settle up with you about my campsite and bike storage." Before she could respond, there was a knock on the front door.

"Jackie must have left her key...," she began, then saw, to her surprise, that Rick was standing outside the door. That he was an hour earlier than his usual time stunned her almost as much as the scowl that marred his face as she let him in. "You're awful early this morning, Sheriff," she said.

"What are you doing up and around? I thought Jackie and Dana were taking over for you for the next few days," he said as he removed his hat. He glanced at J.D. and gave him a cool nod. "You're up early, too, Wilder."

"I'm checking out. Thought I'd beat the crowd and have a minute or two to talk to Corrie before I left," J.D. said. Rick's face had brightened when J.D. mentioned checking out, then his scowl returned just as quickly when he added the part about wanting to see Corrie. Corrie inserted herself between the two men, holding out their respective cups of coffee and cleared her throat.

"What brings you by so early this morning?" she asked Rick as he accepted his cup.

"I was going to talk to Jerry and Red about making arrangements to remove the Landrys' RV from your property. But I didn't want to have to bother you about it; you've been through enough as it is already."

Corrie bristled, preparing to let fly a scathing diatribe about how she had a right to know what was going on with her own home and property, regardless of what she had been through. J.D. cleared his throat and caught Corrie's eye and gave her a slight shake of his head. And for some reason, that didn't annoy her as much as she thought it should. She sighed in resignation. "It's not a bother, Rick. But thanks for your consideration."

Rick froze with the coffee cup halfway to his mouth and stared at her. He shot a glance at J.D. who simply shrugged. Rick nodded with uncertainty.

"Well, anyway, it was good to meet you, Wilder, and I appreciate the help you've been over the last few days. Hope you'll think about visiting Bonney County again... under less suspicious circumstances."

It was a strictly cordial formality and both J.D. and Corrie knew it. But J.D.'s silver eyes glimmered and he said with great solemnity,

"Thanks very much, Sheriff. Think I'll take you up on that invitation."
He turned to Corrie. "How about I reserve my campsite for a few
weeks until I get my affairs in Houston settled and then I'll be back to
finish my vacation. Would that work for you, Miss Black?"

It took every ounce of willpower for Corrie not to burst out
laughing at the look on Rick's face and the playful gleam in J.D.'s
eyes. "Let me get the paperwork ready for you, Mr. Wilder," she said.
"And thank you for making the Black Horse Campground your choice
for a relaxing weekend getaway!"

About the Author

Amy Bennett graduated from Father Yermo High School in 1985 (a Catholic all-girls high school) where she was encouraged by an English teacher, Pat Hollis, to pursue creative writing. She attended the University of Texas at El Paso for a couple years, married husband, Paul Bennett, in 1988 and moved to Alamogordo, NM where she attended New Mexico State University-Alamogordo for another two years, with the intention of earning a degree in elementary education. After her son was born in 1994, she stayed at home for two years (after having worked as a cake decorator, a clerk for a medical supply company, and retail sales clerk for her in-laws' religious gift shop) where she began to study the craft of writing fiction and started the first of several attempts to write a novel. When she first heard of National Novel Writing Month in 2004, it took her a year to work up the courage to register. She "won" NaNoWriMo in 2005 and discovered that she could finish what she started and began writing in earnest.

The Black Horse Campground series started as a NaNoWriMo project in 2009 and when Bennett finally finished it in 2011, she already had two more books in the series in the works! Currently, she works at Wal-Mart of Ruidoso Downs (not too far from her fictional Bonney County) as a cake decorator and at Noisy Water Winery (where you can find some of the best wines in the state of New Mexico, including Jo Mamma's White.) She and her husband, Paul, and their son, Paul Michael, live in Bent, a small town halfway between Alamogordo and Ruidoso.